THE

NERVOUS

SYSTEM

THE

NERVOUS

SYSTEM

MICHAEL TAUSSIG

ROUTLEDGE
NEW YORK • LONDON

Published in 1992 by

Routledge
An imprint of Routledge, Chapman and Hall, Inc.
29 West 35 Street
New York, NY 10001

Published in Great Britain by

Routledge
11 New Fetter Lane
London EC4P 4EE

Copyright © 1992 by Routledge, Chapman and Hall, Inc.

Printed in the United States of America

Library of Congress and British Library cataloguing in publication data is available.

ISBN 0-415-90444-7 (HB)
ISBN 0-415-90445-5 (PB)

CONTENTS

ACKNOWLEDGMENTS

The author wishes to acknowledge the students in the Department of Performance Studies, New York University, for the stimulus they provided, the students in the Anthropology Departments of the Universidad de los Andes and the Universidad Nacional in Bogotá, Colombia, where the idea of the Nervous System was developed in 1987, Lorna Price for her careful and sympathetic copy editing, and the following journals for having first published seven of the pieces contained herein: *Social Text, Journal of Historical Sociology, History Workshop Journal, American Anthropologist, Social Science and Medicine, Cultural Anthropology,* and the *Stanford Humanities Review.*

The tradition of the oppressed teaches us that "the state of emergency" in which we live is not the exception but the rule.

Walter Benjamin, "Theses on the Philosophy of History."

WHY THE NERVOUS SYSTEM?

I know of investigators experienced in this art of diversion which is a return of ethical pleasure and of invention within the scientific institution. Realizing no profit (profit is work done for the factory), and often at a loss, they take something of the order of knowledge in order to inscribe "artistic achievements" on it and to carve on it the graffiti of their debts of honor. To deal with everyday tactics in this way would be to practice an "ordinary" art, to find oneself in the common situation and to make a kind of appropriation of writing itself.
—Michel de Certeau, *The Practice of Everyday Life*

I am working on the Nervous System, and it's turning out to be hard labor indeed. Sometimes I suspect it's working even harder on me than I am on it. This puts Hermeneutics and Reflexivity in a new light, since they're now exposed as a property of the NS itself and not of the individual subject— that curious entity from which many of us have grown to latterly distance ourselves. Thank God it's only a fiction. *Nervous System.* That's all it said, scrawled across a shed I passed on the ferry, gliding over the green waters of Sydney Harbor, whenever I went into the city, reading about the terror of the early 20th-century rubber boom in the lower Putumayo River in southwest Colombia. It was the early 1980s. The signs in the street were of unemployment, purple hair, and postmod anarchy. Apocalyptic omens. An underground doing time. And over there and far away, Colombia was in a state of siege. Torture by the State was commonplace. Paramilitary squads were on the make. Whenever I got up from my desk to cross the sunlit bay away from my other world over there and back then in those Putumayan forests, the Nervous System stared at me in the fullness of its scrawled, enigmatic, might. A portent? A voice from nowhere tugging at my distracted attention. For I could not believe let alone begin to explain the terrible material I was reading about over there and back then, and much less could I put words to it. Wrenched this way, then that, I believed it all, I believed nothing. On yes! I admit to falling foul of the whirlygigging of the Nervous System, first nervous, then a system; first system, then nervous—nerve center and hierarchy of control, escalating to the topmost echelon, the very nerve-center, we might say, as high as the soul is deep, of the individual self. The massive forebrain, protuberant and hanging over the landscape, like the mushroom-shaped cloud of civilized consciousness; then the mid-brain and stem with their more "primitive" (according to medical science) olfactory, memory, and autonomic nervous system functions, intrinsically central, older, and self-locating, and then, dribbling down somewhat like a kid's sandcastle, the spinal column with its branches, synapses, and ganglia. It's a complex picture. The tissue is irreplaceable. Its cells are unregenerative. Even while it inspires confidence in the physical centerfold of our worldly existence—at least that such a centerfold truly exists—and as such bespeaks *control, hierarchy,* and *intelligence*—it is also (and this is the damnedest thing) somewhat unsettling to be centered on something so fragile, so determinedly other, so nervous. And whenever I try to resolve this nervousness through a little ritual or a little science I realize this can make the NS even more nervous. Might not the whole point of the NS be it's always being a jump ahead, tempting us through its very nervousness towards the tranquil pastures of its fictive harmony, the glories of its system, thereby all the more securely energizing its nervousness?

"No passion so effectually robs the mind of all its powers of acting and reasoning as fear," wrote Burke in 1757 in his essay on the sublime. "To make any thing terrible," he noted, "obscurity seems in general to be neces-sary." And as if this were not enough, he followed with the disarming observation that in "reality a great clearness helps but little towards affecting the passions, as it is in some sort an enemy to all enthusiasms whatsoever."[1] But one thing was clear. What mattered for terror was how it was passed from mouth to mouth across a nation, from page to page, from image to body. There was truth enough. And here was I implicating myself into that very chain. Then it swung into view once again, *Nervous System,* now connect-ing, Yes! A System, all right, switchboard of the commanding heights, delicate in the power of its centrality. But there was no System. Just a Nervous System, far more dangerous, illusions of order congealed by fear—an updated version of what the poet Brecht had written in the 1930s, obsessed with ordered disorder, the exception *and* the rule. "Hard to explain, even if it is the custom, Hard to understand, even if it is the rule":[2]

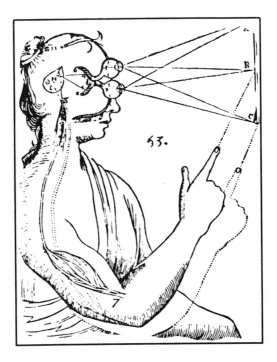

Fear rules not only those who are ruled, but
The rulers too[3]

Hence the sardonic wisdom of the Nervous System's scrawling incompleteness, its constant need for a fix. Which is what, if only there were time, gives me pause. How does one side-step the NS's side stepping? How does one intervene in the power of what Burke designated as its judicious obscurity wherein, without warning, the referent bursts through into the representation itself?

The following NS impulses are attempts at just such intervening; essays written for different audiences at different times from the late 1970s through to 1990. They span two books, the first written in the mid-1970s concerning the devil as a way of figuring the world historical encounter between what Marcel Mauss called *the gift* and what Karl Marx called *commodity fetishism,* the second written in the mid-1980s concerning terror and shamanism in the response to that world historical encounter.[4] Looking over these essays, I am struck by their distaste for the straight line, testimony to the unsteadiness characteristic of the Nervous System, which was surely ingrained in my character-armor from a tender age yet came only and fitfully to my awareness through grinding on Marx's strange concept of commodity fetishism, as filtered through the folklore of work and exchange in Colombian plantation towns and, later on, through a specific form of shamanic healing *and* terror, especially state and paramilitary terror.

In a langauge I find as tempting as it is undoubtedly precious, what I was sensitized to, in those early days in Western Colombia from 1969 onward amid the dirt-poor agribusiness slums and declining peasant plots, was a certain *poetics of the commodity;* as in one of the never-to-be completed sections of that name that Walter Benjamin proposed for his *Passagenwerk* study of the commodity in the social life of nineteenth-century Paris; as in so much of the work of the avant-garde, so many unsettling renditions of the form and allure of the object fatefully soaked in the spell of commodity-efflorescence, from the polyocularity of Cubist collage to Warhol's endless serializations, so much reified, commodity, soup. But what montage, what craziness is this? From Benjamin's Paris to the plantation town of Puerto Tejada on the garbage-infested banks of the Palo River in tropical Colombia! But then, after all, the plantation land invaded by malnourished squatters there in the 1980s wanting house sites adjacent to the town, was subsequently named by them—"The Heights of Paris."

It was to the curious doubleness in Marx's figure of the commodity that I was drawn, that quirky flickering unity formed by thingification and spectrality, which Georg Lukacs referred to as the *phantom objectivity* of capitalist culture, the sort of consciousness Marx highlighted in his notion that, thanks to the market and the revolution abstracting labor into homogeneous labor-power, things acquired the properties of persons, and persons became thing-like; hence the analogy he made with that curious notion drawn from Portuguese slavers and Auguste Comte of the African fetish as part of his way of dealing with the riddle of value.[5] The analogy at one points reads as follows:

> In order, therefore, to find an analogy, we must have recourse to the mist-enveloped regions of the religious world. In that world the productions of the human brain appear as independent beings endowed with life, and entering into relation both with one another and the human race. So it

is in the world of commodities with the products of men's hands. This I call the Fetishism which attaches itself to the products of labour, so soon as they are produced as commodities, and which is therefore inseparable from the production of commodities.[6]

The matter of factness of production becomes anything but matter-of-fact, and facticity itself is rendered marvelous, mist-enveloped regions of frozen movement, projections at a standstill, in which things that come from the hands of man change place with persons, the inside changes place with the outside as commodities erase the social nexus imploded within and become self-activating spirit, even Godlike, "things-in-themselves." Faced with this restless metamorphosing, how could one not despair at the mechanicians' attempting to feed the NS's desperate need for a fix by straightening out Marx's insight into the epistemic flip-flop back-tracking over the capitalist moonscape of subject and object? Quite apart from the Herculean labors of stout-hearted left positivists hammering away, how could one not despair, for instance, of Georg Lukacs' Weberian-inspired iron cage-form of straightening this out; Lukacs' emphasis on what he called *reification,* a type of death, the thingifying quality of commodity-inspired culture manifested in such disparate forms as bureaucratic planning and Warhol's all, all-alike, endless soup cans extending over the face of an ever more rationalized capitalist universe—what hits you as you wriggle out of the congestion of the city to leap westwards in the state-registered steel beast across the George Washington bridge onto Highway 101 starting with Exit 3 and numbered in order all the way to the Pacific coast where the pounding waves stop it short. A Cold War feat.

But what seems truer to this picture of a one-dimensional gridlocked Amerika as death-mask, and certainly more provocative, is the flip-flop from spirit to thing and back again—the decided undecidability that could so clearly, so mistily, be seen in Marx's statement regarding the fetish quality of commodities (let alone in the decided undecidability of the straighter than straight city streets from which the steel beast sprang, and in the globule-laden insides of those Campbell soup cans). The death-mask was only one side; the ascendant spirit it masked, the other. And where the action was, where the NS was put into high gear, was in between, zig-zagging back and forth in the death-space where phantom and object stared each other down.

Working out the gamut of possible reactions to this mobility of the NS meant, eventually, breaking free of the rosary-bead claims of cause-and-effect thinking in historical and social analysis, developing an entirely other mode not just of "thinking" but of working, applied thought, embodied thought, if you like, which in my line of business eventually boils down to putting marks on paper, writing, and the occasional use of visual images like the photograph. The focus of worry shifted from the object of scrutiny to the mode of its presentation, for it is there, in the medium of presentation, that social theory and cultural practice rub one against and inform the other such that there is the chance, small as it might well be, of what I will call "redeeming" the object—giving it another lease of life breaking through the shell of its conceptualizations so as to change life itself. There was no Theory outside of its being brought thus to life. Social analysis was no longer an analysis of the object of scrutiny, but of the mediation of that object in one context with its destination in quite another—for instance, Putumayan healers over there and back then, with you engaged with these stained-glass words here and now. Thus all social analysis is revealed as montage.

This became clearer to me as I tried to work my way free of various notions of "contradiction" and had to confront the power play at work on the musculature of a middle-aged woman patient in the ward of a university teaching hospital in the midwest of the USA in the late 1970s, a power-play in which anthropology's once long-standing preoccupation with magic, science, and religion was reborn in the encounter with modern medical reification and fetishization of the woman's body as social sign. Not for nothing was the title of that rumination, "Reification and the Consciousness of the Patient" (1980), a reference to the celebrated 1922 contribution to Marxist epistemology by Georg Lukacs, "Reification and the Consciousness of the Proletariat," the essay which Walter Benjamin credited as having a decisive influence on the Marxist direction his own work on allegory and modernism was taking at that time as he worked on "One Way Street" between 1924 and 1929.

It was from Benjamin's work that I was encouraged to think about the possibilities for NS writing as incantatory spells of mimetic-realism in which, by means of judicious "quoting" of the real, one is simultaneously intimate and shocked by it—wherein (to raise Marx's fetish-ghost yet again) the spirit of the matter meets the matter of spirit such that in the moving depiction of this moving reality to wound and heal, of what I now see as the NS, the rites of style are everything—words pressing into and impressed by the sensuousness of their referents, the power of arbitrariness of social conventions battling it out with the physical wallop of their effects, theory a never-to-be-sold-out implicitness in matter, sometimes conveniently storied. To categorize this as the project of doing or making theory, but implicitly in the synthetic density of its matter of factuality, is merely to grasp the first stirrings of a critical break from High Theory, while preserving its haughty suspicion of the obvious. Storied implicitness as a way of making theory make itself was something I several times aimed at, with variable success—as in "An Australian Hero" (1987), "Terror As Usual" (1989), Violence and Resistance in the Americas" (1990), and "Tactility and Distraction" (1990). What needed to be brought out was the curious activity wherein mine became but the latest, contiguous, link in a chain of narratives sensuously feeding back into the reality thus (dis)enchained.

I remember well the repeated shock of returning from the Putumayo to the university in the late 1970s, after the fragmented joke-riddled incompleteness of ways of talk, of active interpretation, so practical, so fabulous, in the all-night curing sessions there, coming back to face the demands for academic talk and writing—the demands for an explanation, the demands for coherence, the denial of rhetoric, the denial of performance, when what was crying out for a coherent explanation was the demand for such and the denial of such. What I was being invited to do in those hallucinatory curing sessions of magical practicality on the frontier where Indians cured colonists was to rethink the mode of work in which I was involved as work better approached from the tension involved in the disconcerting experiments in representation tried out by European and (as I later learnt to appreciate, early Soviet) Modernism—e.g. Joyce, Cubism, Woolf, Myerhold, Zurich, Dada, Berlin Dada, Constructivism, Brecht, Eisenstein, and Benjamin moving from allegory to the shock of montage and the liberating (messianic) mimetic snapshot of the "dialectial image."

For in those curing nights what I had to reckon with was the power of the mental image to alter the course of misfortune. Now surely I want to *historicize* this imagery with its play of angels and sacred gold, its wildness and montage, its possible locations in a giant and, strange to say, curing, narrative of colonial conquest, Christian redemption, and Statecraft—the point of this narrative being the way the Indian, the (phantom) object of scrutiny, is recruited as a healing object. But just as surely, and precisely on account of this content, I need to highlight its *physiognomic power,* its power to disturb the (collective) body. "Seeing this, you cure?" I remember a man asking the healer about his vision of angels and birds, shamans and soldiers, priests and books spewing gold, the soldiers dancing and singing like shamans themselves. "Yes, friend. Seeing that you cure," replied the healer, and at one point the man tried to get up out of his hammock, so real was this imagery, and join with the soldiers dancing and singing. And so it was explained to me that the healer passes on an image, the "painting" as it is called there, to the sick person who, seeing it, gets better—all this accompanied by waves of nausea gathering fires of sensory storm, vomit, and the cleansing pandemonium of purging. The man was climbing out of his hammock into his image, just as that queer thief, Jean Genêt, summed up the fix of the Nation-State, the erotic fetish-power of borders. "The crossing of borders and the excitement it arouses in me," he wrote, "were to enable me to apprehend directly the essence of the nation I was entering. I would penetrate less into a country than to the interior of an image."[7]

And so I got to thinking—passed on to me, and from me to you, how does this apply to my practice as a mediationist—and yours, as a reader—given the possibilities and even necessities for reconceptualizing the power of imageric and magical thinking in modernity? This was where Benjamin's arguments concerning the importance of mimesis and the power of image as bodily matter awakening memory, awakening collective dream-time in our era of mechanical reproduction, pressed upon me as both method and a program of practical inquiry—as I hope is obvious in some of the following essays, bearing in mind the unreliability of a left-handed method dependent on chance in dislodging habits deeply ingrained amid the corporality of the Nervous System's being. For precisely what calls the method into play, what gives it its chance no less than its necessity, are the fleeting instants of possibility which flash up in what Benjamin designated as "moments of danger"—which make it virtually impossible to succeed.

What was at stake, then, was not folk medicine in the trivialized sense with which a medical anthropology has now buried this object of scrutiny. What was at stake was the art of healing images lying at the cornerstone of power and representation, the space between art and life involved in the healing of misfortune. And nothing could be more off the mark in this regard than the application of a dominating Western dramatic tradition in social analysis, making sense by means of an adventure of the intellect struggling from darkness to light, from disorder to order, giving the Nervous System its daily fix.

If it was Putumayo healing that got me into this way of thinking about the magic of Enlightenment, the way its light weighed so heavily on the darkness of primitive tragedy, as represented, it was Benjamin's observation in his commentary on Brecht about an underground Western dramatic tradition resurfacing in Brecht's tragedies that provided me with an alternative stage. It came like a flash, I remember, in 1984, when I was battling with how to write Putumayo curing nights without pushing them into the Enlightenment soap opera, my wanting instead to preserve their hallucinatory montaged flowing and stopping and starting once again, the power of the mental image to hold a history of nations, of wildness as curative, of the continuous joking undermining of everything, testimony to Benjamin's highlighting Brecht's figure of water wearing away the granite. Here shock and montage came center-stage with impressive curing power—tumbling certainties into the imageric politics of reality-and-illusion, the curer's medium as much as terror's, too.

As I read the early 20th-century reports on terror in the rubber boom along the lower reaches of the Putumayo River, and simultaneously heard people around me in the early 1980s discussing the disfigured corpses found along the roads leading into Puerto Tejada in the canefields of western Colombia, far from the Putumayo, I came to feel that terror dissolved certainty every bit as much as it preyed on one's heartfelt desire to find its secret order. Yet the more one looked for the order, the more one was caught in its sticky web of evasions, bluffs, and halls of mirrors. And the more one tried to bluff back, fighting indeterminacy with indeterminacy, there waiting in the wings was Order with a giant rabbit-killer. Here, interpretation was no esoteric practice of the literary critic but a matter of survival.

Starkly relevant here was Benjamin's notion of history as state of siege. And of course it is the State which declares the state of siege and therewith ensures Leviathan's special effects, the fetish-power of the State-idea where the arbitrariness of power butts the legitimation of authority, where reason and violence do their little duet. "The tradition of the oppressed," he wrote at the end of the 1930s, "teaches us that the 'state of emergency' in which we live is not the exception but the rule." This was not only an attempt to designate a reality—one so common in Colombia and other Latin American countries and now, in 1991 so vivid in parts of the USA too. It was also designed to provoke a radically different way of seeing and reacting to history, because in a state of siege order is frozen, yet disorder boils beneath the surface. Like a giant spring slowly compressed and ready to burst at any moment, immense tension lies in strange repose. Time stands still, like the ticking of a time-bomb, and if we are to take the full measure of Benjamin's point, that the state of siege is not the exception but the rule, then we are required to rethink our notions of order, of center and base, and of certainty too—all of which now appear as state of sieged dream-images, hopelessly hopeful illusions of the intellect searching for peace in a world whose tensed mobility allows of no rest in the nervousness of the Nervous System's system. For our very forms and means of representation are under siege. How could it be otherwise?

To take social determination seriously means that one has to see oneself and one's shared modes of understanding and communication included in that determining. To claim otherwise, to claim the rhetoric of systematicity's determinisms and yet except oneself, is an authoritarian deceit, a magical wonder. Those of us who have had to abandon that sort of magic are left with a different wondering; namely how to write the Nervous System that passes through us and makes us what we are—the problem being, as I see it, that everytime you give it a fix, it hallucinates, or worse, counters your system with its nervousness, your nervousness with its system. As far as I'm concerned, and I admit to going slow with these NS matters, this puts writing on a completely different plane than hitherto conceived. It calls for an understanding of the representation as contiguous with that being represented and not as suspended above and distant from the represented— what Adorno referred to as Hegel's programmatic idea—that knowing is giving oneself over to a phenomenon rather than thinking about it from above.[8] And it calls for a mode of writing no less systematically nervous than the NS itself—of which, of course, it cannot but be the latest extension, the penultimate version, the one permanently before the last.

2

TERROR AS USUAL: WALTER BENJAMIN'S THEORY OF HISTORY AS STATE OF SIEGE

Terror as the Other

A question of distance—that's what I'd like to say about talking terror, a matter of finding the right distance, holding it at arm's length so it doesn't turn on you (after all it's just a matter of words), and yet not putting it so far away in a clinical reality that we end up having substituted one form of terror for another. But having said this I can see myself already lost, lost out to terror you might say, embarked on some futile exercise in Liberal Aesthetics struggling to establish a golden mean and utterly unable to absorb the fact that terror's talk always talks back—super-octaned dialogism in radical overdrive, its talk presupposing if not anticipating my response, undermining meaning while dependent on it, stringing out the nervous system one way toward hysteria, the other way toward numbing and apparent acceptance, both ways flip-sides of terror, the political Art of the Arbitrary, as usual.

Of course, that's elsewhere, always elsewhere, you'll want to say, not the rule but the exception, existing in An-Other Place like Northern Ireland, Beirut, Ethiopia, Kingston, Port au Prince, Peru, Mozambique, Afghanistan, Santiago, the Bronx, the West Bank, South Africa, San Salvador, Colombia, to name but some of the more publicized from the staggering number of spots troubling the course of the world's order. But perhaps such an elsewhere should make us suspicious about the deeply rooted sense of order here, as if their dark wildness exists so as to silhouette our light, the bottom line being, of course, the tight and necessary fit between order, law, justice, sense, economy, and history—all of which them elsewhere manifestly ain't got much of. Pushed by this suspicion I am first reminded of another sort of History of another sort of Other Within, a history of small-fry rather than of the Wealth of Nations, as for example in a letter in the *Village Voice* in 1984 from an ex-social worker in the state of Colorado, in the USA, commenting on an article on Jeanne Anne Wright who killed her own children. The social worker notes that it was axiomatic that the "deeper you dig, the dirtier it gets; the web of connections, the tangled family histories of failure, abuse, and neglect spread out in awesomely unmanageable proportions." When the social worker asked a young mother about the burn marks on her nine-year old daughter, she replied in a passive futile voice that her husband used a cattle prod on the girl when she was bad. Then she smiled, "as if it was the oddest thing," saying "It hurts too. I know 'cos he uses it on me sometimes." They lived "anonymous and transitory" in a refurbished chicken coop on a canal-lined road. One afternoon this social worker was taking the last of another woman's four children from her home when the woman leapt up and pulled down her pants to show him where her ex-husband had stabbed her in the buttocks. "Just as suddenly," he writes, the woman "realized what she had done and began to cry and to laugh, somehow at the same time, and somehow to mean both." And he concludes by saying "I am left with the impression of lives as massive, dense, and impenetrable as those nodes of collapsed matter out of which nothing escapes and whose only measure is what they absorb and conceal."

But what about the histories of the Big Fry, the Histories of Success? Are they so removed from this violent world whose only measure is what it absorbs and conceals? In talking terror's talk are we ourselves not tempted to absorb and conceal the violence in our own immediate life-worlds, in our universities, workplaces, streets, shopping malls, and even families, where, like business, it's terror as usual? In particular, as we zig-zag between wanting to conceal and wanting to reveal, might we not suddenly become conscious of our own conventions of coordinating power and sense-making and realize, as Walter Benjamin put it in his last writings written on the eve of World War II, that:

> The tradition of the oppressed teaches us that the "state of emergency" in which we live is not the exception but the rule. We must attain to a conception of history that is in keeping with this insight. Then we shall clearly recognize that it is our task to bring about a real state of emergency,

and this will improve our position in the struggle against Fascism. One reason why Fascism has a chance is that in the name of progress its opponents treat it as a historical norm. The current amazement that the things we are experiencing are "still" possible in the twentieth century is *not* philosophical. This amazement is not the beginning of knowledge— unless it is the knowledge that the view of history which gives rise to it is untenable ("Theses on the Philosophy of History").

In other words what does it take to understand our reality as a chronic state of emergency, as a Nervous System? Note the concept; please take care to note the issue before us. Not a knee-jerk application of postmodern anti-totalitarianism bent on disrupting an assumed complicity between terror and narrative order, but an opportunistic positionless position which recognizes that the terror in such disruption is no less than that of the order it is bent on eliminating.

Terror is what keeps these extremes in apposition, just as that apposition maintains the irregular rhythm of numbing and shock that constitutes the apparent normality of the abnormal created by the state of emergency. Between the order of that state and the arbitrariness of its emergency, what then of the center—and what of its talk?

Talking Terror 1

I had been invited by one of our more august institutions of the higher learning to talk on the terror associated with the Peruvian Amazon Company in the early twentieth-century rubber boom in the Putumayo area of Colombia. Before the talk I lunched with my host, a scholar, older than myself. With remarkable verve and flair for detail he compared different historical epochs for their amount of terror, concluding, over dessert, that our century was the worst. There was something weighty, even sinister, about this. We were drawing a balance sheet not just on history but on its harvest of terror, our intellect bending under the weight of fearful facts, and our epoch had come in first. We felt strangely privileged, in so far as we could equate our epoch with ourselves, which is, I suppose, what historical judgement turns upon. And in drawing our grim conclusion, were we not deliberately making ourselves afraid, in ever so sly a way enjoying our fear? But I myself find I am now a little frightened even suggesting this possibility. It seems plausible, yet over-sophisticated, mocking both fear and intelligence.

Tennis balls thwacked. The shadows thrown by the Gothic spires length-ened as the afternoon drew on. One could not but feel a little uneasy about the confidence with which terror was being mastered over linen napkins, a confidence shielding the unspoken fear the university community had of the ghetto it had disappeared several years back—"disappeared," a strange new word-usage in English as well as in Spanish, as in El Salvador or Colombia when someone just vanishes off the face of the map due to para-military death squads. The university in the USA is of course remote from that sort of thing. Death squads, I mean. But it is well known that some twenty-five years back this particular university, for instance, had applied relentless financial pressure on the surrounding ghetto-dwellers and that during that time there were many strange fires burning buildings down and black people out. There was hate. There was violence. Nobody forgot the dead white professor found strung up on the school fence. The university came to own the third largest police force in the state. Together with the city administra-tion it changed the traffic pattern, impeding entry to the area by means of a labyrinth of one-way streets. An invisible hand manipulated what it could of public culture and public space. It became unlawful to post certain sorts of flyers on university notice boards, thus preventing certain sorts of people from having any good reason for being in the vicinity. Thus, in time, while preserving the semblance of democratic openness, the university came to reconstruct the ghetto into a middle class, largely white, fortress within an invisible *cordon sanitaire*. Terror as usual, the middle class way, justified by the appeal to the higher education, to the preservation of Civilization itself, played out right there in the fear-ridden blocks of lofty spires, the fiery figures of the burning buildings, and the calm spotlights of policemen with their watchful dogs. We remember Walter Benjamin: "no document of civilization which is not at the same time a document of barbarism."

My thoughts drifted to a late nineteenth-century story written by Joseph Conrad's close friend, the larger than life eccentric Robert Bontine Cunning-hame Graham. In this story, "A Hegira," Cunninghame Graham relates how on a trip to Mexico City in 1880 he visited eight Apache Indians imprisoned in a cage and on public view in the castle of Chapultepec. As he left the city to return to his ranch in Texas, he heard they had escaped, and all the long way north he witnessed elation and pandemonium as in town after town drunken men galloped off, gun in hand, to track down and kill, one by one, these foot-weary Indians—half-human, half-beast, decidedly and mysteriously Other—slowly moving north through the terrain of Mexico, constituting it as a nation and as a people in the terror of the savagery imputed to the Apache. Yet when I'd finished telling the tale my host looked at me. "Do you know how many people the Apaches killed and how many head of cattle they stole between 1855 and 1885?" he asked. It was as much a challenge as a question, the sort of question you asked looking down the sights of a gun where reality equals a target. The implication was clear; there was "good reason" to fear and kill those Apaches. "But there were only eight of them, in the whole of Mexico, alone and on foot," I replied. "And a dog they'd picked up."

But later on, to my surprise, when the seminar got under way, my host, once so fiery and eloquent on the topic of terror, so in command of his vast history-machine, fell silent as the grave, slumped into the furthest recess of his padded chair. A young tenured professor chaired the occasion in a don't-mess-with-me manner, refusing to allow me to begin with the summary I'd prepared. "That won't be necessary!" he repeated archly, asking nearly all the questions which, like the host's reaction to the Apache story, were not only aimed at making sense of terror as somebody's profit, but in doing so furthered the terror he purported to be explaining. The sad greyness of the late afternoon spread through the room. Pale and forbiddingly silent, the graduate students sat as sentinels of truth for oncoming generations. Why were they so frightened? What did they feel? Maybe they felt nothing?

Reluctantly I met my host for a cup of coffee two days later at the university. He was insistent and invoked all sorts of nostalgia to smooth over unstated tensions. But what a climax! Where was the genteel comfort of his imagined past of heroic intellectuals in the sub-basement of what was said to be a perfect copy of an Oxford college where we now sat holding undrinkable coffee from a slot machine while four or five gangling young men from the ghetto horsed around menacing one another, and the clientele, teasing of course, as they played unbearably loud music from the jukebox? The host leaned forward against the noise. The arteries pulsed in his stout neck. "Have you read Bordovitch's work on the Stalin trials, published in Paris in the fifties?" he shouted.

"No," I had to confess.

He leaned forward again. "Do you know why the prisoners admitted to crimes they hadn't committed?" he demanded with a sharp edge to his voice. "Because they were deprived of sleep—for weeks at a time," he thundered. "In white cells with the light on all the time!"

He sat back, glowing like a white light himself, grimly satisfied, even a little exultant and happy now that he had pushed terror's dark murk well away from those politically staged performances where confusion and confession worked to each other's benefit. He insisted on driving me the five blocks to where I was staying. "Here your car is your tank," he said.

Talking Terror 2

In the Republic of Colombia in South America, an official State of Emergency has been in force, now on, now off, now on again, for as long as most people can remember. The timing and rhythm of the application and enforcement of this measure gives us some idea of the operation of states of what Bertolt Brecht surveying Germany in the thirties called "ordered disorder," and since decades Colombia has been defined as being in a state of chaos such that predictions of imminent revolution, a blood bath, or a military dictatorship have been made on an almost daily basis. Today, in a total population of some 27 million, being the third largest in Latin America, with widespread assassinations striking, so it is said, some thirty people a day, with 500 members of the only viable opposition party, the Uniòn Patriòtica, gunned down in the streets over the past two years, with an estimated 11,000 assassinations carried out by the more than 149 death squads recently named in the national Congress over roughly the same time period, and with over 1,000 named people disappeared (surely but a small fraction of the actual number)—there can be no doubt that a situation exists which is no less violent than it is sinister, and that its sinister quality depends on the strategic use of uncertainty and mystery around which stalks terror's talk and to which it always returns.

But is this situation widely understood, within or outside the country, as a State of Emergency in Benjamin's sense? Is it, in other words, seen as the exception or the rule, and what political and indeed bodily consequences might there be in constantly harping on the ideal of Order as in the prominent discourse of the State, the Armed Forces and the media with their incessant and almost ritualistic reference to the "state of public order," particularly when it seems pretty obvious that these very forces, especially the Armed Forces in an age as defined by Pentagon theorists as one of "low intensity warfare," have as much to gain from disorder as from order—and probably a good deal more? Indeed, in the case of the Armed Forces, disorder is surely intrinsic to its modus operandi wherein the arbitrariness of power is practiced as an exquisitely fine art of social control. Furthermore, what does it mean to define such a situation as exists in Colombia as *chaotic,* given that the chaos is everyday, not a deviation from the norm, and in a strategically important political sense is a disordered order no less than it is an ordered disorder? What does it mean, and what does it take to envisage a society as *breaking down* to the point of *dying*—as the headlines in the January 24, 1988, edition of *El Diario* of New York puts it for Colombia—when there is every reason to suggest that this state of emergency is most decidedly not the exception but the rule for this particular nation-state (if not for many others as well)? In the postmodern world, as the state, the market, and the transnational corporations enter into a new configuration of arbitrariness and planning, might not the very concept of the social, itself a relatively modern idea, be outdated in so far as it rests on assumptions of stability and structure? In which case what is all the talk about order about?

Looking at the social world in the tensed yet highly mobile way Benjamin encouraged us to do with his dictum about the constancy of the state of emergency, I think we can start to understand the flow of power connecting terror's talk with the use of disorder through assassination and disappearing people. This understanding requires knowing how to stand in an atmosphere whipping back and forth between clarity and opacity, seeing both ways at once. This is what I call the optics of The Nervous System, and while much of this is conveyed, in a typically oblique manner, in the notion of the normality of the abnormal, and particulary in the normality of the state of emergency, what needs pondering—and this is our advantage, today, in this venue, with *our* terror-talk which automatically imposes a framing and a distancing-effect—is the violent and unexpected ruptures in consciousness that such a situation carries. This is not so much a psychological as a social and cultural configuration and it goes to the heart of what is politically crucial in the notion of terror as usual.

I am referring to a state of doubleness of social being in which one moves in bursts between somehow accepting the situation as normal, only to be thrown into a panic or shocked into disorientation by an event, a rumor, a sight, something said, or not said—something that even while it requires the normal in order to make its impact, destroys it. You find this with the terrible poverty in a Third World society and now in the centers of U.S. cities too, such as Manhattan; people like you and me close their eyes to it, in a manner of speaking, but suddenly an unanticipated event occurs, perhaps a dramatic or poignant or ugly one, and the normality of the abnormal is shown for what it is. Then it passes away, terror as usual, in a staggering of position that lends itself to survival as well as despair and macabre humor. It is this doubleness of social being and its shock-changing that the Marxist playwright Bertolt Brecht used, but in reverse, so as to problematize the cast of normalcy sustaining the reality-effect of the public sphere. *Seismology,* a superior form of semiology, is what the critic Roland Barthes called this technique of Brecht's.

Terror's talk in such circumstances fluctuates between the firmly sensed and usually quite dogmatic certainties that there indeed exists a reason and a center, on the one hand, and the uncertainties of a diffuse, decentered randomness on the other. Take for instance the editorial of one of the country's main daily newspapers, *El Espectador,* 26th of February, 1986, entitled *El Desorden Publico.* First there is a breathless listing of the "successive acts of terror" that have "shaken the country" in the past week ... the mounting attacks on journalists, one being killed in Florencia, another in Cali, the confrontation of police with Indians in the remote desert peninsula of the Guajira where eight people were killed, the assassination of ten peasants in the municipality of La Paz in Santander, the blowing-up of oil pipe lines now amounting to 65 million pesos, the assassination of a young Unión Patriótica activist in Cauca, the attacking of a police post between Pereira and Armenia by a guerrilla unit of the EPL, which killed one policeman and wounded four others, massive peasant demonstrations in the frontier Department of Arauca, the escalation of drug trafficking and, on top of all this, according to the editorial, the double-game of the guerrilla, taking peace but making war.

"This, in broad strokes," continues the editorial, "is the internal situation of the country, convulsed and explosive" such that it seems as if there might be an intimate connection between the diverse factors that conspire against the maintenance of peace and public security. But although that may not exist, there are so many repeated outbursts from different battlefields that, wanting to or not, the forces that operate against public peace converge with equal and destructive impetus to the common task of destruction in which they find themselves engaged.

Terrible talk, indeed.

Forces become disembodied from social context as we enter a world in which things become animated, paralleling the impossibly contradictory need to both establish and disestablish a center, a motive force, or a reason explaining everything. Strangely this Nervous System acquires an animistic, even anthropomorphic, quality—factors conspiring, forces converging, forces finding themselves engaged in common destruction—and just as strangely, in the entire litany of terrifying *forces* recorded in the editorial, there is this terrifying absence of any mention of the *Armed* Forces of the State itself. Could these latter be the truly invisible dread that centers the Nervousness of the Nervous System whose semiosis involves not so much the *obvious* meaning but what Roland Barthes called the *obtuse* meaning of signs?

In the many written works by the foremost spokesman and guru of the Armed Forces, General Fernando Landazábal Reyes, terror's talk assumes the situation prevailing in Colombia is decidedly part of an order, a global order of cosmic confrontation between democracy and communism in which poor Third World countries are the first to be fractured and where the front line of combat is drawn. In his rendering of reality, in books such as *The Price of Peace* and *Social Conflict,* one senses quite acutely the comingling and fluctuation between the Positivist Style of the hard fact, the Abstract Empiricism (as Sartre would put it) of the diagrams depicting patterns of circular causation between poverty, morality, injustice, violence, and so forth, together with the spellbinding wonder of the metaphysics of patriotism, death, order, and hierarchy. As I see it these latter are the very things that create and control a sense of fixing together with a sense of slippage, especially obvious and important in the case of death, so finite a connection with the infinite, and even more obvious in the case of the new tactic of *disappearing* which, as Julio Cortazar pointed out in the early eighties, thinking not only of the 30,000 disappeared in Argentina, creates a new circle to

Dante's hell in that it combines the terrible fact of loss with the ever-present hope that the disappeared will tomorrow, the next day . . . re-emerge. Hence mothers are reported as saying that they wept tears of joy to find the dead body of their daughter or son, because at least then they were sure. But that is the exception. For most it's a dream world, which decidedly puts "magical realism" in a new light, as when they rush to a site where, in a dream, a friend has seen the disappeared. As Fabiola Lalinde, who last saw her son, a member of the Marxist-Leninist Communist Party, being put onto a truck by the Colombian Army, on the 3rd of October, 1984, puts it: "If the days are difficult, the nights are torture, especially when I dream of [the Spanish is *con,* thus meaning dreaming *with*] Luis Fernando."

> Because more than dreams they are real in that I see him return home with the smile that he always has, together with his tranquility and ease, and when I ask him where he's been and he's about to answer, that's when I always wake up, in that part of the dream. It's so real that at the very moment of awakening I have no idea what's happening or where I am, and to return to reality is sad and cruel after having had him in front of me. At other times I spend the night running through bush and ravines, searching amongst piles of cadavers, witnessing battles and Dantesque scenes. It makes you crazy. And this happens to the whole family, as well as to his friends. Even the neighbors have told me many times that they dream of him.

And our dreaming? For are we not neighbors too?

As for hard facts, General Landazábal is adamant, at least until September of 1986, that evidence indicating that the Armed Forces is behind many if not most of the assassinations and disappearances in Colombia is false. Questioned in *La Semana* by Antonio Caballero (whose name now appears on the Medellin Death List) regarding his statement that the only paramilitary groups in the country were the guerrillas, the general replied that while it was beginning to appear to him that there might perhaps be some sort of organization, even a nationally organized one, whose function was to assassinate members of the Unión Patriótica (by far the most popular left-wing party in Colombia), he really had no idea about this. Moreover, he went on, it was infamous to connect the Armed Forces with the assassins now supposedly so abundant in Colombia in the wake of the cocaine trade.

> That would be to enter into the most tremendous contradiction with the professional morality and honor of the Armed Forces. It is said that there

is a "dirty war" going on, but the Armed Forces do not participate in that. They combat subversion with all the means of the Constitution and the Law, but not by paying assassins on motorbikes or placing bombs. That would be infamous, and we cannot tolerate such infamy to be mouthed:

In Gabriel García Márquez' novel *Chronicle of a Death Foretold,* Santiago Nassar walks the hot Colombian town during the night's revelry unaware that he is being pursued by two men armed with knives passionately committed to killing him. A question of honor. It's a small enough town for its inhabitants to sense something strange. They see the armed men searching from place to place, yet they can't believe that they will really kill—or rather they believe and disbelieve at one and the same time, but proof comes sure enough with Santaigo Nasar's bloody disembowelment—all of which I take to be paradigmatic of what General Landazábal refers to as the "dirty war" which he says "is said to be going on." Of course the point of such a war, of the phrasing of such a war, which is also called by some national commentators a war of silencing, is that as the General says it is "said to be" going on which means, in political and operational terms, that it is and it isn't—in just the same way as the abnormal is normal and disorder is orderly and the whole meaning of the relatively modern term "society," let alone the meaning of the social bond, suddenly becomes deeply problematic. After all what does it mean to have a society at (undeclared) war with itself? "In Colombia," my twenty-year-old friend from one of the poor sugarcane towns of the Cauca Valley, Edgar, constantly assured me with smug finality, "You can't trust anyone."

We were in a bus in 1981 heading into the frontier province of the Putumayo, reading a *Chronicle of a Death Foretold,* and I commented how strange an air of reality the tale conveyed, everybody sensing yet not believing what was about to happen. "Ah *profesor,*" he replied, "but there's always one who knows."

In the murk, an eye watching, an eye knowing. Here you can't trust anyone. There's always one who knows. Paranoia as social theory. Paranoia as social practice. Note the critically important feature of the war of silencing is its geographical, epistemological, and military-strategic decenteredness— yet we cannot but feel that it is organized from some center no matter how much the general denies his knowing. The leaders of the Unión Patriótica say this (undeclared) war (which is said to be going on) is the outcome of the Pentagon's plan for Latin America, the infamous "doctrine of national security" which we can read about in the general's books where it is presented in a favorable, even redemptive, light.

Side by side with this doctrine, and the symmetrical paranoid circles of conspiracy traced around it, there is this new type of warfare that has come to be called "low intensity conflict" whose leading characteristic is to blur accustomed realities and boundaries and keep them blurred. That is another eye to contend with, grotesquely post-modern in its constitutive contingency.

Talking Terror 3

And now we start to feel this eye watching in other places as well. Hearing, too. The *tira* is what the students in the university of Bogotá called it, meaning spy, and it was, they intimated, right there in the classroom. Curiously this particular word for spy—the *tira*—also means throwing, and its opposite—pulling. And as if that isn't strange enough, *tira* is also used to mean fucking. All this makes for a curious network of associations, granting us some rare insight into the erotics not only of spying but of the terror-machine of the State as well, with its obscure medley of oppositions, seduction, and violence.

Sappo, frog, is the term used for the informer in the sugarcane towns in western Colombia, reminding me of the frog's role in sorcery and of its slimy habitat between earth, sky, and water, where it croaks songs of love and war yet, both like and unlike the informer, is suddenly muted when people pass by. When you walk through the cane fields at night—as only the peasants, cane-workers, and the occasional conspirator, revolutionary organizer, and anthropologist ever would—you become the auditory equivalent of a sensitive photographic plate, registering under the black canopy of the immense skies the deafening silence of suddenly stilled sound. And the frog? I guess it's all ears too.

But who knows from whence come these terms for spies and whence they go? Their awkwardly constellated meanings register a compound of slime and ominous quiet, no less obscure, and no less pointed, than the Death Squads themselves. In these suddenly muted fields of power the neatness of the symbol itself gives way to the rapidly pulsing underbelly, the pushing and pulling, of Nervous Systematicity.

And for the poor young men of Colombia, which is to say for the majority of young men, there is the eye of the *libretta militar* or miltiary pass, possession of which means that one has performed the eighteen or twenty-four months military service demanded by the state. If you don't have it, the authorities can pick you up as they please, and most employers will refuse to hire a man without one. At the dance-halls in Bogotá where the young unemployed and working class congregate on Saturday nights, it was not uncommon in 1986 for the police to drag off those without the *libretta*, often housing them down in the courtyard of the police station and leaving them there locked in the freezing night, especially if they couldn't come up with a satisfactory bribe. Every time a bus is stopped by the police or the army, the men are made to present their papers. Every time a *reten* or barrier is erected around what the forces of public order deem disorder, those who wish to pass have to present their papers, and to be without them may one day cost your life. This eye is merciless for the poor young men of the Republic who thereby become not only victim but victimizer, ensuring terror's normalcy.

Take the case of Jairo with whom I was speaking in one of the sugarcane plantation towns to which I have been returning every year since 1969 in the Cauca Valley in Western Colombia. Several months back he had finished his compulsory military service and now had his *libretta militar*. We started talking about the army and the guerrillas, about him being on patrol in the *cordillera central*. Did he ever get a chance to talk with the enemy? No! There was a young guy he once knew who lived down the street, though. And he waved his hand carelessly. "Why are they fighting?" I asked. He struggled for words. "It's to do with the government," he said eventually. "The guerrilla are against unemployment."

> "Well. What about that?"
> "It's bad because they are communists. They're against democracy."

He told me the same thing a few months later when, having searched for seven months he landed a construction job in Cali—a job that paid four dollars a day except that transport and lunch took close to half of that and the job would last only seven weeks so that the employer could avoid the social security costs that apply after eight weeks employment. That's the democracy he was defending. And it took him seven months to find that job—with his *libretta militar*. I've known him since he was a tiny boy and his mother is an even older friend of mine. He's exceptionally sweet and gentle. The other day he was washing my two and half year old boy's hair, all giggles and froth.

> "Do you get a chance to talk with the guerrilla?" I asked.
> "When we capture them."
> "Do they talk?"
> "We make them sing."
> "Do many sing?"
> "Most."
> "What about those who don't?"
> "We kill them. The *comandante* orders us to. We tie their hands behind their backs and stuff a wet towel over the mouth so that when they breathe they feel as if they're drowning. Most sing. Or else we put stakes up their fingernails. Those who lie, we kill, like when they tell us where the enemy is but they're not there. A lot depends on the *comandante*."

"And when the guerilla catches one of our officers," he added, "he's cut into pieces." All this transpired in the most matter-of-fact way, just like we'd been earlier talking of the tomatoes he was transplanting.

We got to talking about the "cleaning" or *limpieza* of Cali, that incredible process in which beggars, prostitutes, homosexuals, transvestites, and all manner of street people supposedly involved in crime and petty cocaine dealing were being wiped out by pistol and machine gun fire from pick-ups and motorbikes. That is what one heard every day. But obviously not just those sort of people were affected. Everyone was scared. Anyone could be a target. Students in Cali told me that merely with the sound of a motorbike they would hide themselves, and few people went out at night. While there is reason to distinguish this "cleaning" from the more conventionally defined political assassinations, there is also something they have in common—apart from the creation of terror through uncertain violence—and this has to do with the horrific semantic functions of cleansing, creating firm boundaries where only murk exists so that more murk can exist, purifying the public sphere of the polluting powers which the dominant voices of society attribute to the *hampa* or underworld whose salient political feature lies in its being strategically borderless—invisible yet infiltrating—but decidedly Other;

prostitutes, homosexuals, communists, left-wing *guerrilleros,* beggars, and what I guess we could call the dark threatening mass of the undeserving poor—which, when you think about it, doesn't leave too many people in the upperworld. In the fearsome logic of the political unconscious "the cleansing" or *limpieza* brings to mind supermarket shelves of endless cans of soap powders and car wax that daily scrub and polish this malnourished land. Now issuing forth a stream of cadavers, disfigured in bizarre ritualistic forms often derived from U.S. television imagery and commodities such as pesticides like Kan-Kill, this cleansing fervor is not without a certain genealogy and conscious manipulation.

As regards the genealogy, harken back to the representations of the *hampa* or criminal underworld of Havana in early twentieth century works of the celebrated Cuban anthropologist Fernando Ortiz in which crime is reduced to criminality and criminality is seen as the natural outcome of being black and practicing Santería. The underworld is the phantasmagoric paranoid construction of the ruling class, and with regard to the manipulation of this fertile imagery in Cali—like Havana, capital of sugar, slums of blacks— harken to Chris Birkbeck's study of the media and images of crime there in the seventies before the death squads had emerged in the mid-eighties. Comparing the newspaper accounts of crime with what he found by hanging out with police and prisoners while he was living in the slums, he found nothing to validate the ubiquitous assumption that an organized underworld existed outside of the imagination created by the press (or, I would add, created by the more important medium of the radio). Not only were the accounts in the newspapers extraordinarily exaggerated but, to my way of thinking, it was as if they were designed to create and reproduce a tropical version of the Hobbesian world, nasty, brutish, and short, in which (as my friend Edgar was almost ready to remind me) "you can't trust any one"— and thus create a city of the swamp shrouded in a nebulous atmosphere of insecurity, truly in a state of emergency.

Together with this Hobbesian fear in which it is precisely the individualization and freaky unexpectedness of violence that is strategic, there is a no less critically important countermove to claim an organized, structured, essentialist core to the dread—as with the notion of an organized underworld, a magically potent race apart, inhabiting both a metaphorical and an actual geographical zone within the city. This of course is the ultimate postmodern elusiveness, claiming both centeredness and decenteredness in a social struggle combining meaning and senselessness with torture and death, and Birkbeck could note in the press as early as 1977 the urgent call for a clean-up, for the *limpieza*—harbinger of our time now when the metaphor became blasting fact. "The city urgently needs aseptic treatment," said the daily newspaper, *El Occidente,* echoing previous demands for "eradicating foci of criminal activity," for "purification of the environment," and for "cleaning the center." What we have to understand, then, it is not merely some horrific process in which imagery and myth work out from a political unconscious to be actualized, but rather a socio-historical situation in which the image, of crime, for instance, is no less real than the reality it magnifies and distorts as terror's talk.

And now Jairo was talking, telling me about his having to resign, while in the army, from a special force he belonged to for three months in Palmira, the town across the river Cauca from Cali. As he put it, the mission of this force was to cruise around in taxis and on motorbikes—powerful motorbikes, he noted—so as to kill criminals, drug addicts, and *sicarios* or professional killers. The soldiers in his unit received booklets with photos of the people they had to kill, and they undertook target practice shooting at human forms from motorbikes and phony taxis. They never wore uniforms and their hair was grown longer than regulation. To kill they would get as closer as possible, with a colt .45 or a 9-mm pistol. There were eighteen of them, plus four sub-officials and one captain. They did most of their killing at night but worked through the city during the day getting to know their victims' habits. There were about fifty people on that death list.

It was straightforward. And only three weeks before, to the day, the general was quoted as vehemently denying any possible connection whatsoever between the army and death squads.

Taking Terror 4

Above all the Dirty War is a war of silencing. There is no officially declared war. No prisoners. No torture. No disappearing. Just silence consuming terror's talk for the main part, scaring people into saying nothing in public that could be construed as critical of the Armed Forces. This is more than the production of silence. It is silencing, which is quite different. For now the not said acquires significance and a specific confusion befogs the spaces of the public sphere, which is where the action is.

It is this presence of the unsaid which makes the simplest of public-space talk arresting in this age of terror—the naming by the Mothers of the Disappeared in public spaces of the name of disappeared, together with their photographs, in collective acts acquiring the form of ritual in which what is important is not so much the facts, since they are in their way well known, but the shift in social location in which those facts are placed, filling the public void with private memory.

The point about silencing and the fear behind silencing is not to erase memory. Far from it. The point is to drive the memory deep within the fastness of the individual so as to create more fear and uncertainty in which dream and reality commingle. Again and again one hears this from the mothers of the disappeared, like Fabiola Lalinde who dreams that her son, last seen being taken on a truck by the Colombian army, has returned to her. Just as he's about to answer her question, "Where have you been?" she wakes up and he's not there. "It's so real," she says, "that at the very moment of awakening I have no idea what's happening or where I am, and to return to reality is sad and cruel after having him in front of me."

"The true picture of the past flits by," as Benjamin expressed a cardinal principle of his philosophy of history, and "even the dead shall not be safe from the enemy if he wins. And this enemy has not ceased to be victorious." Other nights she races through bush and ravines hunting for her son in piles of cadavers.

Silencing serves not only to preserve memory as nightmare within the fastness of the individual, but to prevent the collective harnessing of the magical power of (what Robert Hertz, in his classic 1907 essay on the collective representation of death) called "the unquiet souls" of the space of death—the restless souls that return again and again to haunt the living, such as the souls of those who died violent deaths. This haunting contains a quotient of magical force that can be channeled by the individual, as you can witness in the Central Cemetery of Bogotá every Monday, the day of the *ánimas,* when masses of people, mainly poor, come to pray for the lost souls of purgatory, specific or in general, and by means of this achieve magical relief from the problems of unemployment, poverty, failed love, and sorcery. Summing this up is the image ubiquitous to Colombian folk religion

Anima Sola

(on sale outside the cemetery, for instance) of the *Anima Sola,* the Lonely Soul, a young woman, chained hands uplifted and about to be consumed by fire. Behind her are massive stone walls and a barred door, apparently closed.

What the Mother's of the Disappeared do is to collectively harness this magical power of the lost souls of purgatory and relocate memory in the contested public sphere, away from the fear-numbing and crazy-making fastness of the individual mind where paramilitary death squads and the State machinery of concealment would fix it. In so courageously naming the names and holding the photographic image of the dead and disappeared, the mothers create the specific image necessary to reverse public and State memory. As women, giving birth to life, they collectively hold the political and ritual lifeline to death and memory as well.

The place of the name in terror's talk is the place occupied by literal language, pre-lapsarian, the God-given world of names. But the name is also, as State-ordained *identification,* an essential requisite of bureaucratic procedure. This meeting of God and State in the Name, no less than the strange laws of reciprocity pertaining to the folk doctrine of Purgatory and sin, is also open to a certain appropriation in what I take to be a particularly male sphere of interaction between private and public spheres. I am referring to the history recounted (and thus collectivized) to a small public gathering in Bogotá by the Colombian Senator Iván Marulanda of how he had entered the Medellin offices of the F-2, one of the Colombian Army's many and ever-changing semi-secret units, to inquire into the whereabouts of a disappeared man. Iván was sure they were holding him, and just as surely the F-2 denied it. Forcing his way into the cells, Iván screamed out the man's name again and again, for this would be the last possible chance, and, like a miracle, the disappeared man's voice could be heard calling back. He was there. Meanwhile the police had diffused a notice to the press that the man's body had been found dead on a garbage heap in Medellin.

And in further connection with naming it should be pointed out that Iván Marulanda's name recently appeared on the Medellin Death List, along with the names of thirty-three others who have pitted their talk in public spaces against official talk. The world not only began with naming as with the original Adamic language, but may well end with it as well—perversely essentialist life and death names splicing the arbitrariness of the sign to the arbitrariness of the state's power.

But what about people like yourself caught up in such matters? What sort of talk have you got? What about myself, for that matter?

Talking Terror 5

> . . . and all the werewolves who exist in the darkness of history and keep alive that fear without which there can be no rule.
> Horkheimer & Adorno, *Dialectic of Enlightenment,* "The Importance of the Body."

It was at a friend's place in Bogotá in late 1986 that I first met Roberto. My friend is a journalist and had told me she was worried about him. Amnesty International had gotten him a ticket.out of the country, but he had not used it, and it was said that he was being shunned by his own political group as unstable. He was in his early thirties, an engineer, who in the very poor neighborhoods in the south of the city had, with a left-wing political group, been organizing meetings on silencing—on the repression of human rights. Together with another of the organizers he had been picked up from the meeting by the army at night, taken away, disappeared, and tortured—this in a country whose army totally denies its involvement in such activities. Thus, where the official voice can so strikingly contradict reality, and by means of such contradiction create fear, does Magical Realism move into its martial form. By a miracle he had not been killed when they put him in a bag, shot him through the head, and left him for dead in a public park. Like the disappeared that return alive in dreams, he had come back, if not to a dream, in the strict sense of the term, then certainly to an unreal life-state in which, being living testimony of what the army was doing, he was in constant fear of being killed and was forced into hiding while the army mounted a campaign saying he was nothing more than a "vulgar kidnapper." They had taken his papers, without which he couldn't acquire a passport, and his lawyer was adamant that if he went to the DAS (the Security Police) to renew his papers he would never leave their offices alive. After one brief and accurate notice in the country's leading dailies, nothing more had appeared in the media. And while he was desperately afraid of being found, it was the media that, in his opinion, could keep him alive. He had to keep his name alive in the same public sphere that could kill him.

A week or so later I bumped into him in the street carrying the morning's newspaper. He told me he was going to live in Europe, or Canada, in a week. "Don't you know?" he asked. "I was disappeared. The army tortured me for two days then shot me but the bullet passed along the back of my neck." His children were with their mother in a place where there were a lot of people for protection. On hearing I was leaving for a trip west for a week or more with my wife and three children he impressed upon me: "Always make sure that if anything happens to you there will be publicity. Make sure there are journalists who know where you are going. Don't associate with anyone on the Left. Just be a tourist." To my confusion he added: "Don't wear foreign clothes." He had a file on what he called "my case," and I said I would like to help.

Around five o'clock one afternoon he called without giving his name. "Do you know who is talking?" was his way of saying who he was. He wanted to meet at a busy supermarket and I went straight away. Approaching the meeting I began to feel nervous and scanned the cars for police spies. Everything started to look different, wrapped in the silent isolation of unknowable or ambiguous significance. He was pacing the pavement and I tried to make it look to anyone watching as if it was a delightful and unexpected encounter. He not quite so much. I said I had to buy bread. We entered the supermarket together with many women pushing one another in a ragged queue at the bread counter. I invited him to our place but he wanted to go to his so we walked there, in a roundabout way. There was a public phone on the corner and he asked if I wanted to call Rachel, which struck me as strange and I said I didn't.

He lived in a basement apartment which, to get into you had to pass through two doors, one after the other, each with two locks. He was clean and neat in a light brown sports coat and open shirt. The corridor leading to the apartment was dark and damp and he took a long time to open the second door. I struggled to find a topic of conversation. We entered into a vault-like space with a thick corrugated milky-green plastic roof over a tiny dining place. The apartment had been the courtyard of a three-storied house. Further inside there was a neatly made dark blue covered double bed with a white clothes cupboard forming one wall. There were three pairs of shoes neatly laid out. It was a friend's apartment and he said he had to leave in two days. More and more the place gave me the feeling of a cage or of a laboratory, with us both keepers and kept, experimenters and subjects of someone's experiment.

He sat me down at the tiny table littered with newspaper cuttings and magazines, a half-empty bottle of *Aguardiente Cristal,* and the remains of a giant bottle of Coca-Cola. There was one upright chair. "What would you like?" he asked. "Whatever you've got," I answered. He moved about awkwardly, groping for something to do, I suppose, and put a cutting in front of me. Very tidily blue-inked on the margin it read *El Espectador* 12.IV.86. There were photos of two young men. The one on the left was said to have been killed. The second was said to be Roberto, but he was unrecognizable to me without his beard, his mouth bashed wide, and two policemen watching him as he walked through a door. The article repeated what my journalist friend had told me about him being disappeared, and Roberto told me, in wonder, that the very park where the army disposed of him dead inside the bag was where ten years ago he had crash-landed in a plane in which all the passengers died except for him and one other.

As I read, trying to concentrate, I became aware not of being anxious— that would have been too direct, too honest a self-appraisal of what was going on—but of trying to repress wave after wave of foaming fear and thereby, somehow, merely through the awareness of the force of that repression, feeling in control instead of fearful. I remembered how only eleven days before, arriving at the airport at night after a year away from the country, we had been stopped abruptly out on the dark and isolated highway by men saying they were police. They went through our bags as if they were tearing them apart, saying they were looking for arms. Luckily there was a friend in a car behind with the lights on making it, I suppose, harder for them to screw us around and we were able, after showing them our papers from the local university, to resume our journey. "There are stories going around," a friend later told me, "of a certain general's bodyguard dressing up as airport police at night and hitting people up." Other people said it was because of a rumor that an important member of the M 19 guerrilla had flown in that day. Nobody could explain it, of course, but inexplicability is not the best thing to acknowledge in these situations of terror as usual as one fumbles with contradictory advice and rumors. In my notebook I had jotted down a short time later, having listened to many friends talking about "the situation"—"It all sounds so incredibly awful. And after two days I'm getting used to it." Roberto fussed around, poured a shot of *aguardiente* for me and fussed some more with copies of cuttings concerning his case. He couldn't find his keys, and I realized that you couldn't get out without them. Then we found them and he left without a word, the locks grating—all four of them—leaving me alone in the white cage whose door was reinforced on the inside by heavy gauge wire mesh, also painted white. I tried to read on, propelled by some dubious notion that this was being helpful, that this was what he clearly wanted me to do; to witness and to follow, in retrospect, the trajectory and ultimate disappearance of his case and hence his very being through the media trails of the public sphere while all the while there was a fluttering sensation which as soon as I was aware of it went away. It recurred, stronger. I felt I was being set up. I tried to read more but my eyes only flicked over the pages. Not a sound. A few minutes went by. I realized nobody knew where I was other than Roberto. Why hadn't I called Rachel? I looked up at the roof. It was only corrugated plastic. Almost transparent. Surely easy to break through? But then these places were built to be burglar-proof, and looking more closely it didn't seem that easy. But this was absurd. He'd be back soon. I was a miserable coward. I tried to read more of the cuttings. My eye was caught by random phrases, exacerbating the tension—as if all that horrific stuff scattered across the table in the feeble light of the Bogotá gloom filtered through the plastic was about what was about to happen to me. I had premonitions of how I would feel and to what desperate lengths I would go if I panicked. I didn't feel or allow myself to feel panicky at that stage. That was the most curious thing. I saw myself from afar, as it were, in another world, going crazy, not knowing what was happening, what was being plotted, what would happen next, unable to breathe. I looked again at the door with its tough wire. Immovable. It was raining hard. Every now and then a few drops fell through onto my head and neck. I turned back to the crumpled cuttings from the newspapers and the cheap Xerox copies of letters between institutions and government agencies and then, truly, waves of panic flooded over me absolutely unable to move waiting for the police to surge through the door. Any moment. Dark suits. Machine guns waving. Machismo ejaculated in the underground opera of the State. The handcuffs—*esposas,* in Spanish, also means wives—grinding into your wrists. Later, recounting what had happened to friends who lived all their life in Bogatá, I was made to realize that this fear was not without foundation since it is said to be not uncommon for victims of police or army brutality to become informers.

Then the door opened and in came Roberto with a small bottle of *aguardiente.* I was relieved but wanted to leave. The rain drummed down. Even the elements were against my leaving. He pulled up a stool by my side and poured a drink into two tiny olive-green plastic tumblers. "I'm not a drunk, Miguel," he said, and proceeded to tell me how he was tortured, how bad it was when they changed the handcuffs for rope, how he felt like drowning with the wet towel stuffed down his mouth, and what it was like being in the bag and shot but not killed. He leant his head forward almost onto my lap and guided my finger through the hair to the soft bulging wounds of irregularly dimpled flesh. "Like worshipers with Christ's wounds," murmured a friend days later to whom I was telling this.

"Surely the army knows you are here?" I asked. "No!" he replied, "I've learnt the skills of the urban guerrilla," and reaching for a blue writing pad he told me that he spent nearly all his time in the apartment and that he was writing about his case, trying, for instance, to win the attorney general over to his side and not believe in the campaign of defamation spread by the army. The attorney general had served as a judge in the small town in Antioquia where Roberto had been raised—malnourished from the start, he noted, in a large peasant family, and unable to walk until he was twenty-one months old after which, as a teenager, he had become a famous athlete. All this was in the letter to the attorney general.

He asked what I thought about his case and showed me more correspondence with Amnesty International. I mumbled about people I knew and ways of getting his story publicized, but I felt overwhelmed by the situation. Then he sprung it on me. "Could I stay in your apartment when you leave?" My heart sank. I so much wanted to help but to have him use the apartment would be to endanger a whole bunch of other people, beginning with Rachel and the three kids. I felt the most terrible coward, especially because my cowardice took the form of not being able to tell him that I thought his situation was too dangerous, for that would tear open the facade of normalcy that I at least felt we so badly needed in order to continue being and being together and that he needed to survive. In so many ways I too was an active agent in the war of silencing.

I feel terrible and less than human. I've become part of the process which makes him paranoid and a pariah. I am afraid of the powers real and imagined that have tortured and almost killed him. Even more I'm afraid and sickened by the inevitability of his paranoiac marginalization, people being suspicious of his miraculous escape, interpreting it as a sign of his possibly being a spy. And in the state of emergency which is not the exception but the rule, every possibility is a fact. Being victimized by the authorities doesn't stop with actual physical torture or the end to detention. In Roberto's "case" that's only the beginning. In a way he didn't come back to life at all. He's still disappeared, and only his case exists to haunt me in this endless night of terror's talk and terror's silence.

Talking Terror 6

An hour later I was with my kids at the Moscow Circus, which was playing in a sports arena by one of the freeways ringing the inner city. It was unreal enough, but coming on top of the episode at Roberto's it was devastatingly so. The rain was pelting down outside in the pitch-black night onto the heads of thin-faced hungry people clamoring for attention selling candies and peanuts while, in their rough-cut woolen uniforms the police—perhaps the very ones that had participated in Roberto's disappearance—maintained order with their sad sullen faces as we moved inside into another world where joy and expectancy shone from people's faces, so far from the fears and suspicions outside. Here we were immersed in quickly shifting scenes of clowns, trapeze artists, balance, strength, tension, as the performers spun in their glittering costumes. The pink mobile flesh, firm and muscled, of the acrobats in their gold and silver tights made me think of my finger on Roberto's wounds. Laughter and wonder rippled through the crowd. But what I remember most of all was the beginning. In the shifting tube of light formed by the spotlight in the immense darkness of the arena, two Colombian clowns were arguing with one another and in the process beating up a life-sized female mannequin. They began to tear the mannequin to pieces and beat it onto the ground with fury as the crowd laughed. Then the lights changed, music blared, and a disembodied voice came on:

"In 1986, this year of World Peace, we are proud to present. . . ."

This talk was given to the conference on "Talking Terrorism: Paradigms and Models in a Postmodern World," organized by the Institute of the Humanities of Stanford University, February, 1988.

VIOLENCE AND RESISTANCE IN THE AMERICAS: THE LEGACY OF CONQUEST

Keynote address for the Smithsonian Columbus Quincentenary Conference 'Violence and Resistance in the Americas: The Legacy of Conquest', May 4, 1989

For those of us who spend time wondering if not worrying about the social impact of ceremonial and the reproduction of dominant discourses, codes, and images by means of civic ritual, the Columbus Quincentenary provides much to think about—especially if you are part of the knowledge industry and even more especially if you are participating, as I am, in a Quincentennial rite. One of the first things such participation alerts us to, so I believe, is that the truth and knowledge produced by the immense apparatus of college teaching, research, scholarship, and funding thereof, is inevitably ritualistic and anchored in remembrance, no matter how scientific, in the Enlightenment sense of that term, such teaching and research may be. Therefore, far from being a special problem, my preoccupation with the way to represent the phenomenon called Columbus is merely a heightened version of the tension involved in this confusing yet ubiquitous mixture of truth with ritual, and ritual with remembrance.

A formative influence on the precise constitution of this mixture and its tension is paranoia, as if the make-up of knowledge, the Self, and the very principle of identity itself cannot exist without the fantasmic presence of a feared Other. Today, in this Columbus Quincentenary in the Smithsonian, one of the First World's great temples of Othering, the Other to be exorcised in this process of self-fashioning is that adulation of the Admiral as the Great Discoverer, an adulation that poetically sustains European Imperialism in the very notion of the newness of the New World.

As against this version of Columbus, our being here today perpetuates a different image of the New World's meaning for the Old, namely the well-known Black Legend, so dear to the Protestant Dutch and English critics of Spanish cruelty and devastation in the Indies. And while it is almost too easy to point out that this Black Legend conveniently served the economic interests of those burgeoning mercantile powers, Britain and Holland, serving to cover over the oppression their own overseas endeavors entailed, it is a necessary reminder because in focusing on violence and resistance in the Americas we do too easily project onto others unproblematized notions of violence and resistance that rightfully begin with us. Thus I want to ask what it means to turn the question away from Others, especially poor and powerless Others, and onto ourselves and our own quite violent practices whereby we figure ourselves through the creation of objects of study. Instead of making more knowledge industries about violence and about resistance, what about the politics of violence and resistance in the way we construct legacies and thereby generate power from the great gamut of stories, official and unofficial, of the violent American past?

The Heights of Machu Picchu

In 1983 I travelled for close to two months with an elderly Ingano medicine man named Santiago Mutumajoy from the forested lowlands of the Putumayo district of southwest Colombia through the highlands of Ecuador and Peru. With herbs and medicines, ready to take on patients, we hoped to compare notes with other healers in other localities so that we might better understand the ways by which the image of the shaman of the lowland forests served to further or abate misfortune. After many adventures and misadventures we found ourselves in the ancient Incan capital of Cuzco, and the day before we caught the train to visit the ruins of Machu Picchu, the papers were full of the news that archaeologists had at long last discovered the Incan secret by which the massive stones were so precisely fashioned and held together. But hadn't I seen exactly this story when I first visited Cuzco twelve years earlier, in 1971? I started to realize that this constant puzzling by the authoritative voices of society about purported secrets of monumental and large-scale Incan construction was itself a sort of ritual, an obsession, a way of defining a sense of mystery about the meaning of the pre-European, Indian, past so as to control the life of the present. What makes this defining mystery powerful is that it is part of a virtually unconscious way of constituting an alleged essence and originary point in the sacred time of the nation-state, and with that a particularly enduring notion of America, defined and perpetuated in the legacy of massive monumentalization of Indian ruins, nowhere more so than in the iconicity of Machu Picchu itself.

I was stunned by Machu Picchu, its sublime grandeur, the warm sunlight on the brooding quiet of the ruins. Of course I had seen it before, not only on a visit but in images adorning glossy magazines the world over. But they were only copies. This was the real thing. I leant over to my Indian companion from the woods of the Putumayo, like me, so far from home, and asked him what he thought of it all. "Only the rich," he said phlegmatically. "There weren't any poor people here. These houses were for the rich." He paused. "I've seen it before," he casually added. "These mountains. These stones. Exactly the same. Several times."

"What on earth do you mean?" I was not only incredulous but disappointed. Hadn't I gone to extraordinary lengths to bring him to this extraordinary place discovered if not by Columbus at least by Hiram Bingham and immortalized by the great poets such as Pablo Neruda with his epic poem, *Alturas de Macchu Picchu?* Of course 'discovered' is a rather self-serving concept here, recalling Edmundo O'Gorman's displacement of that term by the concept of the invention, not the discovery, of America. After all there were people tilling the fields of Machu Picchu when Bingham was guided there in 1911. What the 'discovery' of Machu Picchu amounted to was that local knowledge was exploited, providing the stepping stone to its erasure within a universalizing narrative constructing America, a narrative in which the ruins would achieve not merely significance but magnificence. One can hardly imagine poor Indians cultivating corn and potatoes on the terraces of Machu Picchu today! Yet as testimony to the precious and fleeting moment whereby invention becomes discovery, Bingham's book captures just that instant when real live Indians worked the soil of Machu Picchu, converting its terraces to their immediate needs. Among a dozen or so photographs depicting the discovery, Bingham has an arresting shot of two Indian women he met living there (p. 41). They have been posed standing barefoot on the spindly grass against great polygonal blocks of white granite of what he called the Memorial Temple of the Three Windows. In their rough woolen clothes with their respectful yet quizzical gaze back at us, these women seem no less rugged and timeless than the stones of memory themselves, but completely dwarfed by them.

"Yes, when I was healing with yagé," the old Indian man from the Putumayo was saying, "I saw it all before, all these cliffs, all these stones."

I was taken aback. Yagé is the most important medicine in the Putumayo. It comes from a vine in the forest and with its visions, the healer, as much as the sick person who also drinks it, can obtain insight into the cause of serious misfortune and power to overcome it. Such power, however, does not necessarily come from seeing the causes of misfortune but instead can come from having a particular image, a *pinta* or painting as it is referred to commonly, and one of the ways of becoming a healer is to buy such *pintas.* Thus when the old healer said that he had seen Machu Picchu in his yagé-induced visioning, you have to understand that this means something more than merely seeing something, because it is potentially an empowering and even a curing image.

How wonderful, I thought, in the very remoteness of his lowland forests the old man able to see this incredible place by means of mystical insights given to the guardians of ancient American shamanic lore. It made me curious. I wanted to better ascertain his connection to this Machu Picchu place high in the sun and the cold wind, so ponderously still in the muteness of its massive stones. Like a flash it occurred to me. "Look at the size of those stones," I said. "How was it ever possible to build like that?" I was echoing the newspaper, evoking national discursive formations much bigger than my own limited imaginings.

"That's easy to explain," he replied without so much as a blink. "The Spanish built all this." And he waved his arm in a peremptory gesture encompassing the great vista.

"What do you mean?" I feebly responded. I felt cheated.

"It was with whips," he said in a distinctly disinterested tone. "The Spanish threatened the Indians with the whip and that's how they carried those stones and set them in place."

As far as he was concerned this was a thoroughly unremarkable event, just as Machu Picchu itself was unremarkable. "That's exactly what the Spanish did to my father-in-law," he added. "An Indian went and told them that he was a sorcerer and so they punished him by making him carry stones to build their church. They said they'd whip him if he didn't do what they

ordered. His wife and children followed him along the path also carrying stones."

For my old Indian friend, at least, there was no mystical secret of ancient Indian technology. To the contrary, the mysticism lay with the need the wider world has to monumentalize the pre-European, Indian, past. For him these glorified ruins were monuments to racism and the colonial authority to wield the whip. And in so far as his yagé-inspired dream-image of the ruins was a curing image—as it most definitely is for the world at large— it is probably because of a deep-seated complicity on his part with that authority, using rather than simply resisting it. Here, at this point where meanings collide and thought is arrested, we should seize the opportunity to sort out our ideas about violence, resistance and the legacy of conquest.

Dream-Work

The old man's perception certainly caught me off balance, and I would assume it is unsettling for most of you, too. There is more than a touch of blasphemy here, so reverentially has the mightly Machu Picchu been impressed into our hearts.

> Come up with me, American love.
>
> Kiss these secret stones with me.
> The torrential silver of the Urubamba
> Makes the pollen fly to its golden cup.
> The hollow of the bindweed's maze,
> The petrified plant, the inflexible garland,
> Soar above the silence of these mountain coffers.

Thus, the poem of the esteemed Neruda, his finest work, according to his translator, Nathaniel Tarn, imaging the epic of all America in the stones of Machu Picchu, the city of the dead.

> Raised like a chalice
> In all those hands: live, dead, and stilled,
> Aloft with so much death, a wall, with so much life,
> Struck with flint petals: the everlasting rose, our home,
> This reef on the Andes, its glacial territories.

And it is with pain and remorse for the suffering occasioned by the construction of Machu Picchu that the poet shall bring his poem to an end.

> And leave me cry, hours, days, and years,
> Blind ages, stellar centuries.
> And give me silence, give me water, hope.
> Give me the struggle, the iron, the volcanoes.
> Let bodies cling like magnets to my body.
> Come quickly to my veins and to my mouth.
> Speak through my speech, and through my blood.

Yet the Indian healer from the Putumayo forests resist this mighty nostalgia that converts the tears occasioned by self-castigation into a life-stream of blood and words presumed to make common cause through the ruins with the travail of the Indian past, sentiments which had such an impact on the Peruvian government that it decorated Neruda in person. "My poem, *Alturas de Macchu Picchu,*" writes Neruda in his *Memoirs*, "had gone on to become part of Peruvian life; perhaps in those lines I had expressed sentiments that had lain dormant like the stones of that remarkable structure" (p. 324). But not only capitalist governments warmed to those sentiments. Che Guevara was also a great admirer of the poem. Neruda tells us that Che would read the *Canto General,* of which the *Alturas de Macchu Picchu* is a significant part, to his *guerrilleros* at night in the Sierra Maestra in eastern Cuba. Years later, after Che's death at the hands of the Bolivian government and the CIA, Neruda was told that in his campaign in Bolivia, Che carried but two books, a math book and the *Canto General* (p. 323).

The question arises, however, as to what sort of identity is being forged through such a representation of Machu Picchu—and on behalf of whom? For is not Neruda's a distinctly European, let us say a Columbus-derived, vision of the New World's rawness *vis-à-vis* civilization as a mixture of mathematics and epic verse? In which case one might want to ask what it then means to reawaken, as Neruda in his 1974 Nobel prize acceptance speech defined the poet's task, the old dreams which sleep in statues of stone in the ruined ancient monuments, in the wide-stretching silence in planetary plains, in dense primeval forests, in rivers which roar like thunder? For might it not turn out that these were all along the colonist's dreams? In which case the further question might be fairly put as to what other discourse is there, anyway, that is not hopelessly rigged by those dreams and the history such dreams underlay? Can the subaltern speak? Can we speak, let alone weep, for the subaltern? Or does our task lie elsewhere? Here indeed lies the issue of resistance.

This is why I think the old man's flash of memory and interpretation of the meaning of Machu Picchu is significant for us, gathered together to discuss violence and resistance in the legacy of the conquest of America. A mere fragment, whole in its partiality, unheroic yet capacious, coolly blood-less and tearless, drastically unmystical yet dependent on shamanic flights of vision and dreaming, his is quintessentially the marginal discourse that eludes essentialization in the outrageously carefree way it snakes through the semantic mills of colonial subject-positioning—at the cost, of course, of the ambiguities of indeterminacy, the charge of ignorance as to true history, and the political isolation that absorbs marginal discourse. As the object of colonial knowledge-making and representation, which in fact gives him, just like Machu Picchu itself, much of his shamanic power, this particular Indian stands deafer than any stone to these heartfelt appeals to the Indian past for a contemporary national if not continental identity on the part of states or revolutionary projects. He turns our expectations upside down, no matter how sophisticated or cynical we might be, and what is more he seems to do this in a relaxed and even unthinking sort of way, not trying to shock or consciously resist the frames into which history and our expectations would hold him as fast as the stones of Machu Picchu itself. And in this unintention-ality of his, I take his cryptic style of montage to be of paramount importance for its pointed effect on us.

The Meaning of Context: Mediation and Montage

As such the old man's style cannot be separated from its context, a context that merely begins with the magnificent heights of the Machu Picchu and extends, through me, the conveyer of this story, to this other, quite different magnificence, of the Smithsonian with which it is today, by virtue of this Quincentenary, indissolubly, instrumentally and symbolically, connected. Thus I want to stress context not as a secure epistemic nest in which our knowledge-eggs are to be safely hatched, but context as this other sort of connectedness incongruously spanning times and juxtaposing spaces so far apart and so different to each other. I want to stress this because I believe that for a long time now the notion of contextualization has been mystified, turned into some sort of talisman such that by 'contextualizing' social relationships and history, as the common appeal would have it, significant mastery over society and history is guaranteed—as if our understandings of social relations and history, understandings which constitute the fabric of such context, were not themselves fragile intellectual constructs posing as robust realities obvious to our contextualizing gaze. Thus the very fabric of the context into which things are to be inserted, and hence explained, turns out to be that which most needs understanding! This seems to me the first mistake necessary for faith in contextualization. The second one is that the notion of context is so narrow. It turns out in Anthropology and History that what is invariably meant by appeals to contextualize is that it is the social relationships and history of the Other that are to form this talisman called the context that shall open up as much as it pins down truth and meaning.

I say, to the contrary, that this is a deeply mystifying political practice in the guise of Objectivism, and that first and foremost the procedure of contextualization should be one that very consciously admits of our presence, our scrutinizing gaze, our social relationships and our enormously confused understandings of history and what is meant by history.

This is not autobiography. This is not narcissistic self-indulgence. It is neither of these things because first it opens up to a science of mediations— neither Self nor Other but their mutual co-implicatedness—and second because it opens up the colonial nature of the intellectual relationship to which the contextualized other has for so long been subjected.

It is also montage—the juxtaposition of dissimilars such that old habits of mind can be jolted into new perceptions of the obvious. In fact we have been surreptitiously practising montage all along in our historical and anthropological practices, but so deeply immersed have we been in tying one link in a chain to the next, creating as with rosary beads a religion of cause and effect bound to a narrative ordering of reality, that we never saw what we were doing, so spellbound were we by our narrativizing—and thus we repressed one of the very weapons which could resist, if not destroy, intellectual colonization and violence.

Therefore, if it is the institution of Anthropology in the context of this Columbus Quincentenary ritual that allows me to act as the conveyor of an old man's perception of monumentalized ruins, and thus jump-cut and splice space and time, abutting context with context, Machu Picchu with the Smithsonian, then this has now to be seen as its own style of neo-colonial montage—a non-Euclidean ordering of space and time that we took so for granted that we didn't even see it. All ethnographic practice is blindly dependent on this cutting and splicing, abutting context to context, them to us. The task now is to bring this to conscious awareness, which I choose to do by thinking about the old man's style of montage—part of my point being that I think you will not easily accept it.

For surely it has struck you as interesting, if not bewildering and paradoxical, how wrong he is as regards space and time, yet how unsettling he is with regards to the truth-effect of his statements? He must be mightily wrong when he says he has seen Machu Picchu in his yagé-stimulated dreams and visions. Although we can accompany the poet, and my ethnographic textual representation, for some reason we cannot accompany the healer from the forest on such vast southbound flights of the eye in an instant of time across hundreds of miles of Andean cloud forest. And as regards time, he is decidedly anachronistic in his notion of the Spanish and the timing and nature of what we call, as in this Columbus Quincentenary, "the conquest." For the Spaniards he is referring to are the Capuchin Fathers from Igualada, close to Barcelona, Spain, serving as missionaries in the Putumayo from 1900 onward and whom the Indians referred to as *los Españoles*. Thus, owing to particularities and coincidences of a local history, the old man has collapsed three centuries of what figures as American history into a flashing instant of time, a monad, in which the ruins are emblematic of recurrent neo-colonial violence practiced on Indian labor, Indian land, and on the very concept and image of what it means to be designated as Indian. What, I feel compelled to ask, might this sort of historiography—for it is certainly history in the graphic mode—teach us?

Monuments create public dream-space in which, through informal and often private rituals, the particularities of one's life makes patterns of meaning. These patterns are neither terribly conscious nor totalizing but instead contain oddly empty spaces capable of obtuse and contradictory meanings swirling side by side with meaning reified in objects such as the famous stones of Machu Picchu set into the sublime landscape of the Andes. What we daydream about in places like these may well contain images and strands of images that are a good deal more ideologically potent than what we get directly in school or from the Church and political doctrine, but at the same time this very capacity of the monumentalizing day-dream to deepen and strengthen ideology rests upon the existence of strategic vacuities and switch-points that can radically subvert ideology and the authority sustained. A site like Machu Picchu is a sacred site in a civic religion in which day-dreaming naturalizes history and historicizes nature. Think back for a moment to the first photographs of Machu Picchu as frame-frozen images of this dual process, the photograph, for instance, of the Indian women dwarfed by the great granite block, rugged yet precisely worked and thus poised between nature and culture, on the threshold of history where invention becomes discovery itself. The compelling narrations that make nations, no less than worlds like the New World, utilize this day-dreaming capacity to naturalize history as in stones and Indians, and, conversely, to historicize nature as in reading a history into those stones and those Indians. Hence the heartfelt rhetoric to make the stones of history and the Indian speak, and in lieu of that, speak for them and channel the day-dream into waking consciousness. In this regard Machu Picchu is one of the New World's great sites, perhaps its greatest, for rendering the collective dream-work that naturalizes America and holds the American project in creative tension with the Primitivism it requires and daily reproduces.

And this is why the old Indian healer's yagé dream-vision perception of the ruins of history is important. Not only because it so easily shrugs aside that Primitivism and hence the Great American Project. Nor because in so doing it creates a discourse counter to the official voices and authorized versions and representations of the past. Surely all of that. But more important still is that his dream-vision so disturbingly engages with our day-dreaming precisely where we have been mobilized as Subjects—indeed professional Anthropologizing Subjects—for the American Project. For in my very attempt to use him as a true Indian voice, he disarmingly dislodges that essentialization. That is the crucial point. His dreaming catches and tugs precisely where the strategic vacuities and switch-points exist in the understructure of our dominant discourses, and in doing so has the effect of all good montage, which is to shock patterns of connections into quite different patterning, capturing what Stanley Mitchell calls in this regard the infinite, sudden or subterranean connections of dissimilars, catching our breath, so to speak. All of which is to ask, what then? Where will this breath go? What song will we go on to sing if not the *Canto General?*

The Mothers of the Disappeared: Dialectic at a Standstill

It is here where I want to move from the all too eloquent silence to which the dead of the ruins of Machu Picchu have been subjected, to consider the role of the mothers of the disappeared *vis-à-vis* the violent silencing enacted by State terror in much of Latin America over the past decade.

First I want to point out that what I think is extremely important in their activity is that they contest the State's attempt to channel the tremendous moral, and indeed magical, power that the dead hold over the living, especially those who die (or disappear) due to violent or mysterious circumstances—those whom Robert Hertz in 1907 called the souls of the "unquiet dead" forever impinging on the land of the living. As I see it, in assassinating and disappearing people, and then denying and enshrouding the disappearance in a cloud of confusion, the State (or rather its armed and policing forces) does not aim at destroying memory. Far from it. What is aimed at is the *relocation and refunctioning of collective memory*. It is of fundamental importance to grasp this point. The State's interest is in keeping memory of public political protest, and memory of the sadistic and cruel violence unleashed against it, alive! (Foucault's notion of control through norm, through normalization, could not be more irrelevant. Combining violence with law, the State in Latin America rules through the strategic art of abnormalizing. It is Kafka and Bataille who are relevant here.) The memory of protest, and the violence enacted against it by the State, best serves the official forces of repression when the collective nature of that memory is broken, when it is fragmented and located not in the public sphere but in the private fastness of the individual self or of the family. There it feeds fear. There it feeds nightmares crippling the capacity for public protest and spirited intelligent opposition. And that is why the actions of the mothers of the disappeared strike me as so important. For they create a new public ritual whose aim is to allow the tremendous moral and magical power of the unquiet dead to flow into the public sphere, empower individuals, and challenge the would-be guardians of the Nation-State, guardians of its dead as well as its living, of its meaning and of its destiny. And it is this that lies behind Walter Benjamin's injunction (in his "Theses on the Philosophy of History") that "even the dead will not be safe from the enemy if he wins. And this enemy has not ceased to be victorious."

I think that Benjamin would have conceived this resurrection of the dead from the privatized interior of the Self into the public sphere as a movement creating a shock, the dialectic at a standstill. At other times he referred to this dialectic as a messianic cessation of time, equivalent to what he called "a revolutionary chance in the fight for the oppressed past." You can sense the awesome potential of this shock in the dialectic of reality and illusion occurring within the isolated fastness of the dreaming self as you listen to Fabiola Lalinde, for instance, speaking of her son last seen being boarded by the Colombian army onto a truck in October, 1984. Now he returns to her in her dreams. Just as he's about to answer her question, "Where have you been?" she wakes up. "It's so real," she says, "that at the very moment of awakening I have no idea what's happening or where I am, and to return to reality is sad and cruel after having him in front of me." The true picture of the past flits by. Gone. Other nights she dreams of running through bush and ravines, searching piles of cadavers. What is more, her son returns in dreams to her friends and neighbors too.

As I scan this thread connecting the purgatorial space of the disappeared with the recuperation of collective memory by the mothers of the disappeared in various Latin American countries, I see the way by which an essentialist view of woman has been radically refunctioned by women in relation to the State, parallel to the way the old Indian healer from the Putumayo refunctioned Machu Picchuism. Such refunctioning of assumed essences is part of the struggle for the definition of the past, as it flashes forth involuntarily in an image at a moment of danger. As I understand this refunctioning with reference to the mothers of the disappeared and current State terror in Latin America, these women are wresting from the State its use of woman to not only embody the nation and the people in a moment of intense political crisis, but the embodiment of memory itself at that precise moment when it is the aim of the State to bury collective memory in the frightened fastness of the individual soul. This can be seen by juxtaposing in the form of a dialectical image two uncannily similar yet radically different photographs, the one presented by Hiram Bingham in his book on the discovery of Machu

49

Picchu, portraying two Indian women posed in front of an immense granite slab said to belong to the temple of memory (p. 41) and, for comparison, the photograph from Hernán Vidal's book, *Dar la vida por la vida,* depicting two women who, on the 18th of April, 1979, together with fifty-seven other people, mainly women, chained themselves to a national monument, namely the Chilean Congress.

In the former photograph Indian women have been posed to register, so it seems to me, not merely the discovery of the ruins by the *mister* from the First World, but a powerful sense of almost natural connectedness of the present to antiquity. In the Chilean image, however, the constellation of women, memory, and the eternalization of the present in the past has been radically broken apart and reconstellated through a courageous and inventive ritualization of monumentalized public space—the space which Vidal defines as the most heavily charged with Chilean constitutional history. Bearing photographs of the disappeared, these women (and a few men) have placed their very bodies as symbols of a people enchained against that which would try its utmost to use the symbols of woman and family to sustain the Patriarchal State and Capitalism and therewith justify State terror. The interweaving of individual and collective memory created by this counter-ritualization of public monuments can unleash feelings of self-confidence which in turn inspire visions and joy—as we hear in the words of one of the participants.

With all the nervousness of the night before, I dreamt of my disappeared husband. I dreamt that there was knocking at the door and then he entered. I felt indescribable joy and knelt in thanks at seeing him. He looked just the same as when he was arrested on the 29th of April, with his blue clothes, just as he was, with his grey hair going bald, with his smile, his small teeth. I felt him in the bed. I felt him in my arms. And when I awoke, with my arm like this, embracing my loved one, I saw that there was nothing by my side. I quickly said to myself, "He's gone to the bathroom." But then reality brusquely returned and I realized that everything I had experienced that night was just a dream. I arose early and happy. In all the actions, not only this one, I have a vision. That the day following, in a quarter of the city, a married couple will wake to see in the newspaper a photo of us in a hunger strike or chained, and they will feel good, they will be joyful because someone is showing the face of the people, someone is keeping the fight going (Vidal p. 132).

Our Move

At which point I feel it fair to ask about us. What do we do from this point on? Carry out more studies of other people's resistance? Surely not. For while it is crucial that the whole world be informed of injustice when it occurs, and makes that injustice its concern, surely part of that concern should now be with the whole Western project of self-fashioning through constructing the Third World Other as an object of study? Surely it is this project that has to be radically rethought and refunctioned? To deny the authority once invested in the memory of Columbus in favor of a project to consider violence—always elsewhere—and resistance—always by the poor and powerless, strikes me as running the risk of continuing the early colonial project but under a liberal guise made all the more deceitful by the rhetoric of Enlightenment science, as in the appeals for an ethnographic practice which strives to grasp the natives' world and point of view—for their own good, of course!

In place of such grasping I think this great occasion of the Columbus Quincentenary can serve as the time to begin the long overdue task of refunctioning Anthropology as a First World pursuit—just as the old healer refunctioned the meaning of the past monumentalized by its ruins, just as the mothers release the power of the spirits of the disappeared so as to wrest tradition away from a conformism that is about to overpower it.

Such a refunctioning of Anthropology would have to turn its resolute gaze away from the poor and the powerless to the rich and the powerful—

to current military strategies of "low intensity warfare" as much as to the role of memory in the cultural constitution of the authority of the modern State. After all, who benefits from studies of the poor, especially from their resistance? The objects of study or the CIA? And surely there is more than an uncomfortable grain of truth in the assertion that in studying other people's resistance, heroic or Brechtian, one is substituting for one's own sense of inadequacy? For all the talk of giving voice to the forgotten of history, to the oppressed, and the marginal, it is of course painfully obvious that the screen onto which these voices are projected is already fixed—and that it is this screen, not the voices, where the greatest resistance lies, which is why something more is required than the injunction to study up instead of down, or to study the political economy of the world system rather than local meanings. For what such simplistic injunctions overlook is precisely our profound entanglement and indeed self-constituting implication in that screen of interpretation which in itself is the great arena where world history, in its violence as in its easy harmonies, in its sexualities and National-State formations, folds into rules of customary sense.

Yet I do not think, just as Hegel in his parable of the Master and the Slave did not think, that such scrutiny can be undertaken alone. To assume it could, would be to fly in the face of what I take to be axiomatic as to the dependence of being on other. What is more, there are too many ghosts to be settled, too much violent history to be reworked, which is why I have tonight felt impelled to invoke two powerful images of constructed Others whose place in fashioning universal history has been profound beyond words—namely, the woman as mother, embodiment of memory and the people, and the Indian as healer of the American project. In invoking their presence I have not tried to speak for them, whatever that might mean. Nor have I made it my goal to carry out what in Anthropology and History is called contextualization and thereby "explain" them, whatever that might mean. What I have tried to allow is for their voices to create in the context of our hearing contradictory images, dialectical images I will call them, in which their attempts to redress the use of themselves as mnemonics for the vast projects of building other selves, white male selves. Nation-States, and America itself, bring our own expectations and understandings to a momentary standstill— and thereby present us with the opportunity, if not the necessity, to commence the long overdue discovering of the New World in place of its invention.

4

AN AUSTRALIAN HERO

This is a type of fairy tale, a very modern one to be sure, which engages with a point of view laid out by Walter Benjamin fifty years ago concerning the function of the fairy tale in combating the forces of mythology. In his essay on "The Storyteller," Benjamin says that the fairy tale tells us of the earliest arrangements that mankind made to shake off the nightmare which myth had placed upon its chest. In the figure of the fool, the tale shows us how mankind can act dumb before the myth, and the wisest thing it teaches is to meet the forces of the mythical world with courage, high spirits, and cunning—the characteristics, by and large, that Benjamin singled out as making up the hero of a Brecht play.[1] Think of Mother Courage and of Galy Gay, let alone of the Good Soldier Schweik of whom Brecht was so fond. Of course, these are hardly heroes in either the classical or the modern sense, but then maybe our sense of "tragedy" with which the hero is so intertwined gives us too mythic a sense of evil which it is nowadays the task of the ordinary person—the Brechtian "hero"—to suffer as an everyday occurrence.

The hero I want to tell you about is an Australian man, old, rather deaf and with poor eyesight, who came from the bush and served as a horseman and then in the trenches with the Australian and New Zealand Army Corps, the ANZACS, in WWI. The tale he tells is worth retelling. I think, because of what it may teach us about ways to deflate the heroism that is used by the state to invigorate if not invent traditions that make for a culture of nationalism—a culture, of course, that once set, becomes a powerful tool in the arsenal of social control, used not only by the state but also one which we non-heroes practice daily over ourselves too.

And here it needs emphasizing how Australian nationalism is fatefully invested in the mythology of war, notably the sacrifice and defeat of the Gallipoli campaign in the Middle East in WWI. In this society where there exists little by the way of God, virtually no enlivening of private or public life by ritual, no spirits of fairies or hobgoblins, no Day of the Dead or Halloween or Saints Days, phantoms or bugaboos, and no founding myth of origin nor purgative revolutionary break from its colonial master, it is singularly the task of the war memorial to give society's official voice its transcendant tone. (Indeed, the quintessentially Australian hero of D'Arcy Niland's 1955 Australian novel, *Shiralee,* is a drifter described as "a man of thirty-five, built like a cenotaph, squat and solid").

How deeply nationalism is part of us, how deeply it invests our being as social being, is a crucially important and vexing question. Much of anthropology concerned with symbol, ritual, and narrative, from Victor Turner to Michel Foucault, for example, claims something like an organic unity between the seal of the symbol and the wax of the recipient, between the discourse and the citizen. The Romantic aesthetics of symbol, from Hegel and Goethe onwards, and the structuralism of de Saussure converge on this point, and it is the task of the soldier's tale to take the weight of the myth off our chest by reminding us that nevertheless there exists some space between meaning and its object, and that indeed the sign is arbitrary in a decidedly political sense and because of politics. Yet, it is important to note, I feel, that if the soldier's tale serves in some way to de-mythologize and hence de-narrativize history, it also serves to re-enchant the world, to invest the notion of heroism, for instance, with new meanings that crack open the reified exterior with which its usage by the state has wrapped it in medals and decorations.

And this, I believe, brings us back to the notion not just of the fairy tale but to what Walter Benjamin called the dialectical fairy tale, both demythifying and re-enchanting, de-fetishizing and de-reifying, using the cunning of reason as in the fairy tale, to trick mythic powers. In her exegesis of Benjamin's Arcade Project, Susan Buck-Morss describes his conception of such a tale in oppositional cultural practice as one in which

> The dreaming collective of the recent past appeared as a sleeping giant ready to be awakened by the present generation, and the mythic powers of both [the recent past and the present generations'] dream states were affirmed, the world re-enchanted, but only in order to break out of history's mythic spell, in fact by reappropriating the power bestowed on the objects of mass culture as utopian dream symbols.[2]

And such a proposal assumed that in our age of commodity culture that collective symbolic meaning is transferred to new generations not through stories, myths, or fairytales but through things, namely the commodities we buy, sometimes sell, and in a very limited way, can be said to produce.

Which brings us to how I met the old soldier—through the market mechanism of my answering an advertisement in a Sydney daily paper in 1981 concerning a Holden car *For Sale.* There are many ways, now I think back, of conceptualizing that encounter of buyer, seller, and commodity, but one at least deserves mention; the old Australian ANZAC, the new Australian, myself, not only in a junior generation to the soldier but also the child of what in Australia came to be called 'New Australians' as my parents were Austrian refugees from WWII; and thirdly a different sort of Australian, the *commodity in question itself,* namely the Holden automobile—nothing less than Australia's first *own car,* as the advertisements put out by General Motors of the USA proudly proclaimed in the late 1940s when I was eight years old and barely able to read such things. In the market, fashion sustains the notion of history as progress, but the child reverses this so that the new is located in mythic time and adds to the treasure house of ur-symbols. "At first, granted, the technologically-new gives the effect of being just that," wrote Benjamin in the notes to his never-completed Arcades Project,

> But already in the next childhood memory it changes its characteristics. Every child accomplishes something great, something irreplaceable for humanity. Every childhood, through its interests in technological phenomena, its curiosity for all sorts of inventions and machinery, binds technological achievement onto the old world of symbols.[3]

From the outset the old soldier, whose name was Sid, called me Kev, short for Kevin. Nothing I said would budge him in this, and with the passage of time, as our conversation knitted its way through our negotiating, I came to settle with my new identity as some sort of quintessential Australian pastoral-proletarian name, as Sid explained why he had to sell the Holden to which he was so attached.

Despite his failing eyesight and venerable age it had been possible for him, through friends, to fiddle a renewal of his driver's license every year by going to the state of Queensland, just across the border from where he had spent much of his life with cattle and horses. Queensland, it might be mentioned, has a reputation amongst the liberal intelligentsia for being "the deep north" on account of the corruption and racism which appear to have continued unabated from the times when "blackbirding" or kidnapping of Pacific Islanders was done to procure cheap labor and when Queensland threatened to assume imperial status by annexing parts of New Guinea. It was, I believe, with the 2nd Australian Light Horse Regiment, drawn largely from Queensland, that Sid had served in the Australian Imperial Force, the AIF, an army, it may be noted, under the command of Lord Kitchener, Secretary of War of His Majesty's Government of Great Britain. Perhaps it was through old soldier friends that Sid had managed to trick the law; but now, law aside, he had to admit as he gingerly took me for a test drive along the quiet streets of a well-manicured South Sydney lower middle class suburb, that he was unsafe at just about any speed.

It was truly a fine car, that Holden, six cylinders of throbbing power, fully automated, and in the sort of immaculacy that you find only among people who have never owned a car before and treasure it as an extension of themselves. Advertised as "Australia's Own," it had in fact come from the "States" (as the USA is called) in the late 1940s, to a people without a TV or private swimming pools, let alone much by the way of cars. Why! In the suburb where I lived in Sydney there wasn't even a sewage system, and a couple of men came by each week in a truck to carry away the night-soil. Still, all things considered, we all knew we lived in the best possible country with the best of everything, including scenery and toilet facilities. When people took their once-upon-a-lifetime trip "overseas" (to Europe, obligatorily England, occasionally the USA) the first thing they'd tell you about was the shocking state of the bathrooms in Italy or France. As for the States! It reeked of artifice to the extent that it assumed a threat to masculinity, what with all that air-conditioning, show of emotion, and that baroque chrome dripping off their automobiles! It reminded one of the distinctions we schoolkids used to hear and repeat about "our" troops and the "Yanks" (as the US soldiers were called) up on the infamous-sounding Kokoda trail in New Guinea in WWII where the Aussies did all the fighting and had little more than their wits and bare hands while the flabby Yanks trailed behind saturated with coca-cola and ice-cream.

Yet here we were with the economic boom of the fifties about to burst forth and no less than what was to be our own Aussie car fabricated on our shores but displaying those same curaveous American lines we so heartily despised. There was a sort of colonial semiotic of car design constituting our traffic with the trim little boxy British bodies up till then ruling the roost (p. 58). Perhaps the contradiction was made sweet for us by the planners at General Motors who, in creating the Holden, australianized the design, making it less flashy and more toughly austere and prim at the same time, hence more in keeping with the older colonial relationship of the Aussie bushman and the British Empire. But, of course, it needed the changes in the design of international capitalism to make this a living and aesthetically effective contrast—a contrast that amounted to an archaeology of colonial relationships writ into automobile bodies with the older British layer now serving as an aesthetic modification to the new and developing American infrastructure.

It was truly remarkable, looking back, how easily the Holden was accepted as "Australia's Own." "It has become recognized," writes Sir Larry Hartnett, managing director of General Motors Holden during the crucial planning stages, as "the car for Australia, made in Australia by Australians."[4] In the USA it was Democracy, as put by Lincoln. In Australia it was something even better—the automobile as national symbol representing independence, freedom, equality (since the one type of car was meant for everyone!) and, so superbly in the case of Sid's later model, finger-tip automated control. From being a country that, as we kids were told, rode on the sheep's back. Australia was now set to be taken for a ride in the Holden, with all the connotations of progress, mechanization, and national independence it represented. Why! As Sir Larry Hartnett points out, in his book *Big Wheels and Little Wheels,* it was by building the Holden that we were able to obtain TV (with overseas funds made available by not importing cars)![5] But perhaps the most truly Australian thing about the car was not as widely recognized as it might have been: namely the three million Australian pounds put up by the Australian Labour Party Government, then headed by Ben Chifley, so that GM could proceed not only to make the Holden but also fabulous

"Trim Little Boxy British Bodies."

sums of money without investing a cent.[6] The most widely circulated picture of the first Holden shows Prime Minister Chifley in a reverential pose by the right fender with his hat in hand as if in church. Subsequent modifications of this further develop the idea of an icon until something quite holy emerges. The only other picture of the first Holden in the brochure put out by General Motors Holden (*The Holden Story*) has two young women no less curvaceous than that very same fender (p. 60). But Sir Larry Hartnett's views of the car's importance were more prosaic, although he was well aware of nationalist aesthetics.[7] His major concern was to provide Australia with an industry that could absorb the vast amounts of manpower, industrial capital, and technical skill made possible by WWII and its cessation. Otherwise, he argued, "we would be risking a national economic disaster," and he pointed out that "from the employment point of view, the making of motor cars provides endless jobs. A car is like shoe leather: both begin to wear out from the day they first hit the road."[8] So much for the holy icon. So much for the beautiful women.

Fishermens Bend, November 29, 1948. The Prime Minister of Australia, Right Hon. J. B. Chifley, beside the first Australian mass produced car which he named 'Holden.' A total of 120,402 132.5 cubic inch six cylinder 48/215 Holden sedans were built. The original price was £733 ($1,466) including tax.

Twenty-five years after the first Holdens came out they were subject to nationwide nostalgia as in the film *FJ Holden,* together with a variety of artworks, thereby joining other recently celebrated icons of Australian identity: the kangaroo, the koala bear, and the aborigine. In their blending nature with culture so as to "naturalize" the latter and establish a sense of deeply rooted and even primeval identity, these icons can be seen, perhaps, as forming a series in which the Holden, as the latest, signifies not merely the transition from the bush to the modern urban and mechanical age but also and therewith indicates the profound connection between invented images of the archaic and of the modern—a point Benjamin made repeatedly about commodities.

I had plenty of time, if not exactly leisure, to admire the Holden as Sid, with the patience of Job, drove at a snail's pace from stop sign to stop sign, feeling rather than seeing his way. He drew my attention to the elaborate tape-deck he'd had installed in Queensland and to the fact that the car was not only "fully automated" but was the first Holden model to be so. It had a lot of power: power brakes, power steering, and with the flick of the driver's finger any window in the car could be raised or lowered. Sid's enthusiasm was infectious. Only much later, swinging down the steep curves onto the Roseville bridge, did it occur to me what a death-trap was constituted by this heedless flight into automation because what could you do to save yourself at high speed on these curves if the engine cut out—making it virtually impossible to steer?

To all intents and purposes—and here we may well ask whose—Sid personified what the Australian historian Russel Ward in 1958 termed "The Australian legend" or national mystique of the typical Australian as a person whose roots lie in the vast outback, an improvising, tough, taciturn, hard-drinking and gambling man with an intense hatred for authority, deference, and class distinctions, a man who will stick to his mates through thick and thin.[9] By 'mates' is meant male companions and the typical Australian according to legend is thus very much a he.

I felt a little unbalanced looking at Sid, larger than the legend itself yet obviously so happy in the splendor of all this automated modernity he was selling me. It seemed not just incongruous but a betrayal of Australian self-reliance, that intrinsic toughness of being as encrusted in the leathery and potentially cancerous pores of sunburnt drovers and their skinny cattle dogs, all ribs and balls as the saying was, in a sparse and thoroughly minimalist image. Yet there was a strange, marginal detail to absorb, and that was the cardboard clipped with clothes-lines pegs to the sun visors. Sid had put it there because the makers of the car, General Motors, had not sufficiently taken into account the fierce sun of these southern skies.

This was reassuring. It seemed to indicate that the seduction of man by the machine, let alone by the multinational corporation, was far from decided and that there was still active some elemental bond between man and the frontier, not so much with nature as in it and using it against itself, in likeness of some Aussie confidence trick.

"The true picture of the past flits by," wrote Walter Benjamin in his last writings, the *Theses on the Philosophy of History*. "The past can be seized only as an image which flashes up at an instant when it can be recognized and never seen again."[10]

And here was this image flashing up, provoked by Sid's àrtful improvisation, a memory of my teachers at school with labored intensity passing on the tradition of the ingenuity with which the Australian soldiers at Gallipoli fooled "Jacko" Turk and how that ingenuity was the cultural if not genetic heritage of Australian outback life itself. To cover their retreat from Gallipoli (surely cause for national humiliation) the soldiers fixed empty cans to the triggers of their .303 rifles so that they would receive, drop by drop, water from above the rifle until, when the weight was sufficient, they would fire on their own and conceal the retreat from what was the largest amphibious

operation in the whole history of warfare till that time, engaging during its 259 days of fighting almost half a million allied soldiers from India, Senegal, France, Nepal, England, New Zealand, and Australia, of whom slightly more than half became casualties, and about which a British Royal Commission declared two years later "from the outset the risks of failure attending the enterprise outweighed its chances of success."[11] (Needless to say we kids at school never heard of the soldiers from India, Senegal, France, Nepal, nor, perish the thought, from England.)

But it was not the immensity of the death and struggle which flashed forth in my mind so much as this absurd detail of the water gun and the triumphal sagacity of the *gestus* with which my teachers made the drama of tradition. Looking back I can now see that the art of oppositional practice evoked in this and similar stories was not merely ascribed to the mythical Australian character, forged in the outback. It was also, as this memorizing indicates, a practice that could be neatly co-opted by the Nation-State, through the medium of the Army in WW1, for instance, and then in the system of public schooling where the tradition was passed on by the authority of the State itself.

The talent for mechanical improvisation as mythologized by the legend of the water gun is something one finds highly developed amongst people throughout the Third World. It cannot be said to be the specialty of a particular society or ethnic group. Surely Mr. Ward is correct in intimating that the traits that constitute the Australian legend stem from a special social class relationship, that of the pastoral proletariat of the nineteenth century, often nomadic drovers and shearers. It is this class character that ensures a merger between mechanical ingenuity and oppositional practice, yet that in itself in no ways explains why that particular class was rendered in the way it was so as to represent the nation as a whole, and, by and large, still does, generations after that small class of men has virtually disappeared. Even the aboriginal stockmen now ride motorbikes instead of horses. But of course it is difficult to see how they could have provided much of a model for the Australian legend because, apart from their blackness, they themselves became far more attracted to the image of the American cowboy than to the fateful love affair with the hateful British.

And it is here that in good measure we find an answer as to why the way of life of the shearer and the drover—or, rather, *the way of life as it came to be represented*—was taken up as the image of the whole society—or at least of its masculine half. The meaning of all this lies in the fact of difference, namely difference with the colonial Other. As Mr. Ward remarks in the foreward to the second edition of his book, *The Australian Legend,* the cluster of traits making up the typical Australian were seen as typical "*not* because most Australians ever possessed these traits but because the minority of bush-dwellers that did differed most graphically from the average Briton and so were seen as indentifiably Australian."[12] But where does Mr. Ward, or anyone else, find that privileged position outside of the stream of tradition, whereby an essence can be attributed to a class of people as the real stuff from which ephemera of a national mystique sprang forth?

The sources of tradition flow to one's heart's content, wrote Benjamin.[13] They converge to form the stream of tradition, and it is the tradition which forms our view of the source. But we must try not to be diverted by this spectacle. We must neither seek the reflection of the clouds in the stream nor run away from it so as to drink from the source and "pursue the matter itself" behind peoples' backs. He wants us to ask "Whose mills does this stream activate? Who is utilizing its power? Who dammed it?" And in identifying the forces operative, so the picture of the landscape changes through which this stream, let alone Bold Jack Donaghue, The Wild Colonial Boy, runs:

> It was for the sake of five hundred
>   pounds I was sent across the main
> For seven long years in South Wales
>   to wear a convict's chain.
> *Chorus*
>   Then come, my hearties, we'll roam the mountains high!
>   Together we will plunder, together we will die!
>   We'll wander over mountains and we'll gallop over plains—
>   For we scorn to live in slavery, bound down in iron chains.

Trapped by the police, the Wild Colonial Boy responds:

> "Resign to you—you cowardly dogs! A thing I ne'er will do,
> For I'll fight this night with all my might," cried bold Jack
>   Donahoo.
> "I'd rather roam these hills and dales, like wolf or kangaroo,
> Than work one hour for Government!" cried bold Jack Donahoo.[14]

And like the multitude of Australians who later at Gallipoli as wild colonial boys fought all night with all their might like wolf or kangaroo, Bold Jack Donahoo met his death, the difference being that while he fought against the government the ANZACS fought for it—and the British crown as well.[15]

In his memoir, *Goodbye to All That,* the English writer Robert Graves cites his countrymen's wide-eyed view of its white colonial troops in WWI. They were barbarians, anarchic and bloodthirsty, preferring to bayonet than to shoot, and the recent Australian revival of the case of Breaker Morant in the brilliant film of that name (directed by Bruce Beresford) illustrates one of the political uses of that image, namely the deployment of Australians as barbaric counter-guerrilla troops by the British high command in the Boer War, fighting fire with fire, in a manner of speaking.

Encouraged by the high command to reproduce the British view of their colonial selves, atavistic and wild, these colonially constituted Australians could nevertheless be court martialled by the British and executed by firing squad, as was the Breaker, for being too colonial, in this wild sense, when their deeds, or rather misdeeds, became an excuse for Germany to threaten joining in the war on the side of the Boers.

From the film (which was photographed in South Australia) one would hardly know that there were any Black people in South Africa, and this surely accentuates the fact that the white Australian troops stood in a similar mythic relation to the British officers and crown as did the Blacks of South Africa (just as the Blacks of Australia, the Aborigines, subject to genocide in the years prior to the Boer War, stood to the White Australians). It should also be appreciated that Breaker Morant—named 'Breaker' on account of his horse-breaking prowess—was not an Australian by birth or upbringing. Instead his Australianness lay in his being an outcast Englishman, one banished from the blessed isle to the sunburnt country on account of some unmentionable affront to English middle-class manners. Thus his character combined both the attraction and repulsion with which Australians tend to view Britain, and the heroic image bestowed on him by this recent and sophisticated film is stirring testimony to this. His aristocratic, English style is in fact the source of his attractiveness to an Australian audience; his being outcast by England makes such appreciation licit.

But when I asked Sid about the Breaker he replied, "Yes, Harry Morant you mean," and paused. "He was a bad one that fella." But he couldn't or wouldn't say any more. He looked a little uncomfortable and I was somewhat taken aback at what amounted to a curt denial of the story made by the film out of the Breaker's death as a heroic victim of colonial manipulation. What more might Sid have known, I asked myself.

But here obtrudes another and more pointed question as to whether the story the storyteller of war might want to tell is freely available, anyway. Might it not be a fragmented experience or one beyond communication that is perforce altered as soon as it is moulded by the narrative form ready at hand—in this Australian case the narrative not just of sacrifice whose blood nourishes the idea of the nation, but also of the battler who, in the tragedy of always losing, gains heroic status because he has stuck to the rules of the egalitarian game and refused the enticements of rank and power? Such a man might be hard to push around. That is true. But he is also a man who may not merely accept defeat but feel ennobled by it. Under appropriate conditions it may in fact be very easy to push such a man around. How the storyteller might evade this fate of narrativization instead of fueling it is one of great questions posed for the politics of cultural opposition in our time, and this question might be answered by posing another. Now that the very last survivors of Gallipoli are dying, who will tell their story and how will it be told? Perhaps the release in 1980 of the film *Gallipoli* provides an answer. For not only is its timing so precise but, in continuing the tale about if not of the dead, the film lifts it from the realm of the storyteller through whom history spoke and becomes the spectacle of history itself.

A lavish and successful commercial film, scripted and directed by young Australians, *Gallipoli* has been widely interpreted as a strong anti-war film, let alone one which "stuck it to the poms"—i.e., the British—as responsible for taking advantage of the flower of Australia's manhood. Those of us who grew up in the same era as the film's director, Peter Weir, and the script-writer, David Williamson, know full well that a serious, even momentous, ideological issue is involved in this film which in no way can pretend to be simply the story of Gallipoli because that story does not exist outside of its myth and that myth expresses great complexity of feeling, as can be witnessed, for example, on ANZAC Day, the annual Australian remembrance of the war dead on what Russel Ward has called 'the Australian national day above all others.'[16] I remember as a child the enormous crowds, the quiet, then the cheering as row after row of veterans marched the streets hour after reverent hour. But later on, as a university student, one became aware of an almost blind fury of student protest directed at this annual ritual of what seemed like the sanctifying of war. Given the strength and complexities of the ANZAC mythology, such cultural opposition remained forever inchoate. The mythology resisted critique because of the way it had come to embody patriotism and did so by making not only sacrifice but failure into heroic virtues. Out of this came the film.

In contrast to the film *Breaker Morant*, *Gallipoli*, has as its hero a blonde angel, an archetypally innocent country boy from Western Australia who volunteers with enthusiasm and whose death on the slopes of Gallipoli is shown as deeply intertwined with British exploitation of its ANZAC forces. But although this hero is blonde against the Breaker's darkness, he is also part of the wild colonial boy image which, as with the myth of the Wild Man in the European Middle Ages, is both demonic and godly at the same time. The godly quality is evoked by the British Commander-in-Chief, Lord Kitchener's right-hand man, Sir Ian Hamilton, who in describing the life-invigorating spirit emerging from the valley of death that was Gallipoli, asks the readers to raise their eyes twenty-five degrees

View from Anzac, looking across the country towards Suva Bay and showing the broken ground over which the Australian troops later advanced during the battle of Sari Bair. (Admiralty Official Photograph.)

> to the top of the cliff which closes in the tail end of the valley and you can see Turkish hand-grenades bursting along the crest, just where an occasional bayonet flashes and figures hardly distinguishable from Mother Earth crouch in an irregular line. Or else they rise to fire and are silhouetted against the sky and then you recognize the naked athletes from the Antipodes and your heart goes into your mouth as a whole bunch of them dart forward suddenly, and as suddenly disappear.[17]

Then comes the never-ending trickle of the wounded and dead in a stream of bandages and blood. Some poets and writers, noted General Hamilton, see only carrion and savagery in war and refuse war the credit

> of being the only exercise in devotion on the large scale existing in this world. . . . To me this is no valley of death—it is a valley brim full of life at its highest power. Men live through more in five minutes on that crest than they do in five years of [the Australian country towns of] Bendigo or Ballarat.[18]

The blonde angel of Weir's film is not only a British image of *Australian* wildness. Such an angel hails also from a tradition of consuming importance to the British ruling class, the classical appreciation of ancient Greece. "You will hardly fade away," wrote Sir Ian Hamilton in a preface addressed to the soldiers of Gallipoli,

> until the sun fades out of the sky and the earth sinks into the universal blackness. For already you form part of that great tradition of the Dardanelles which began with Hector and Achilles. In another few thousand years the two stories will have blended into one, and whether when "the iron roaring went up to the vault of heaven through the unharvested sky," as Homer tells us, it was the spear of Achilles or whether it was a 100-lb shell from Asiatic Annie won't make much odds to the Almighty.[19]

And in Peter Liddle's book, *Gallipoli 1915,* there is a stunning photograph of a vast group of slouch-hatted soldiers backed by the sharp silhouettes of the Sphinx and a soaring Egyptian pyramid. The caption reads: "Outside Mena Camp. Australians before making their own history!"[20] A similarly situated photograph of Australian women nurses on camels in front of the Sphinx disclaims such history-making prowess. Its caption reads simply, "Nursing Sisters Sightseeing." Not even their nationality is deemed worthy of mention.[21]

The British novelist Compton Mackenzie was an officer in the Gallipoli campaign and has left us this sensual, indeed erotic, image of the Australian soldiers there, an image which fuses their wildness, nudity, beauty, and heroism into the figure not only of the ancient Greek gods but also (as did General Hamilton) with the earth, in this case stained an attractive warm apricot color with their blood.

> Much has been written about the splendid appearance of those Australian troops; but a splendid appearance seems to introduce somehow an atmosphere of the parade ground. Such litheness and powerful grace did not want the parade ground; that was to take it from the jungle to the circus. Their beauty, for it really was heroic, should have been celebrated in hexameters not headlines. As a child I used to pore for hours over those illustrations of Flaxman for Homer and Virgil which simulated the effect of ancient pottery. There was not one of those glorious young men I saw that day who might not himself have been Ajax or Diomed, Hector or Achilles. Their almost complete nudity, their tallness and majestic simplicity of line, their rose-browned flesh burned by the sun and purged of all grossness by the ordeal through which they were passing, all these united

to create something as near to absolute beauty as I shall hope ever to see in this world. The dark glossy green of the arbutus leaves made an incomparable background for these shapes of heroes, and the very soil here had taken on the same tawny rose as that living flesh; one might have fancied that the dead had stained it to this rich warmth of apricot.[22]

The blonde angel of Peter Weir's ostensibly anti-British film, *Gallipoli,* is prefigured in this extraordinary effort of the British imperial imagination.

Bean's diaries and notebooks (almost 300 volumes) laid out for work on the *Official History*. In the background his staff. A. W. Bazeley (left) and J. Balfour. (Australian War Memorial)

And like Compton Mackenzie, Weir also contrives to give his gods a comical side—as befits strong men under duress, especially those in the subordinate ranks of a colonial army. Except for the blonde angel. His innocence puts him above all that. Only then can beauty and death fuse in a naked yet majestic simplicity of line.

But to C.E.W. Bean, the writer of the official history of the ANZACS and in many ways the shaper of their tradition, the ANZACS were not Greek gods but decidedly Australian. Born in Australia (in 1879), but educated in England, (Clifton College, then Oxford), he had spent time as a lawyer in the outback of New South Wales and was convinced that the special conditions of Australia gave to its soldiers equally special qualities of initiative and bravery. Even if not actually from the outback (and only the minority were), Bean's Australians were profoundly shaped by outback tradition, as that tradition was specified by the ideal of a one-class society without distinction by birth or wealth in which the only social restraint a man recognized was self-imposed. "This characteristic," Bean noted in the opening pages of *The Official History of Australia in the War*, "gave him a reputation for indiscipline, but it endowed him with a power of swift, individual decision and, in critical moments, of self-control, which became conspicuous during the war. A doubt had sometimes risen," he concluded, "as to whether the discipline necessary in an effective army or navy could ever be tolerated by young Australians."[23]

As someone else said, they were not soldiers but fighters.[24]

And as fighters they were not of society but of nature. In fact they were children of nature, not of class conflict in the sheep and cattle industry of the outback. Of course it is what nature means as a social category and as an imaginative stimulus that is here decisive, and that meaning could not but be testimony to the persuasiveness of imperialist poetics—as in the following comment by Bean regarding the innate tendency of other nations' soldiers to be led by the innately leaderless Australian ones:

> The British 'Tommies' among whom he [The Australian Soldier] afterwards mixed, best-natured of men, extraordinarly guileless, humble-minded to a degree . . . looked up to the Australian private as a leader. If he was a good Australian he led them into good things, and if he was a bad Australian he led them into evil, but he always led. He was more a child of nature even than the New Zealanders. When the Americans forgathered with him at the end of the war, he led them also.[25]

Bean strove to depict the Australian as a new breed of man developed by a new type of society—a man whose special features were brought out by the War as much as the War was needed to create out of those self-same features the culture of nationalism. In addition to emphasizing this new man's love of freedom and his peculiar independence of character, Bean dwelt on the fact that although basically irreligious, this new man was nevertheless bound by the moral law of mateship. This law the good Australian could never break. And while it was inherited, in Bean's estimate, from the gold-miner and the bushman, it could be projected onto the polity of nations in the strife of their warring and need. Even Britain, so it appears, could be seen as a mate, and behind Britain the Empire itself. So much for Bold Jack Donahoo! Were it not for what Bean termed the feminine sensitivity with which this new man hid his feelings, such jingoism would be obvious. In Bean's words,

> if a breath stirred which seemed to pretend harm to any member of the family of nations to which he belonged, at that moment an emotion ran deep through the heart of the Australian people. The men who did not wave flags, who hated to show sentiment, who spent their day jogging round the paddock fences on horseback in dungaree trousers, with eyes inscrutable in the shade of old felt hats, men who gave dry answers and wrote terse letters—these became alert as a wild bull raises his head, nostrils wide, at the first scent of danger. Any sympathetic human being living in the "naval crisis" of 1909 could not but detect, far below the superficial political squabble, the swift stirring of emotion which passed through the heart of that silent sensitive body of working men and women which makes the real nation. . . .[26]

Which makes "the real nation" . . . Hence there seem to be two nations in one. Behind or beneath the Nation-State conscious and aware of itself as a result of War there is this other nation, the real nation and this, so it would seem, is bound by racism and by mateship. Only in one point was the Australian people palpably united prior to the War, according to Bean, and that was "in determination to keep its continent a white man's land," and the Australian historian Bill Gammage introduces his 1974 account of Australian soldiers in the Great War by noting the fear of Asian invasion as a chief motive for Australian affection for the British Empire; i.e. in the red, white, and blue wall provided by the Royal Navy, stemming the yellow tide.[27]

The culture of nationalism activates and indeed thrives upon sentiments active in what we could call "civil society" (in contradistinction to the State), and here mateship—the moral law replacing religion according to Bean— is of strategic importance. As with Stanley Diamond's analysis of the way the developing State of Dahomey took advantage of the best friend relationship,[28] so we can discern the way that the State in Australia built from mateship not only the discourse of imperial relations but also the practice of war.

This latter aspect caught Bean's eye. "Mateship is the one law which the good Australian must never break," he wrote, and the legal inflection— law—already signifies the State appropriation. "It is bred in the child and stays with him through life," he continued.

> In the last few moments before the bloody attack upon Lone Pine in Gallipoli, when the 3rd Australian Infantry Battalion was crowded on the

"... in whose depths they wage their victorious combat."

fire-steps of each bay of its front-line trend waiting for the final signal to scramble over the sandbags above, a man with rifle in hand, bayonet fixed, came peering along the trench below. 'Jim here' he asked. A voice on the fire-step answered "Right, Bill; here." "Do you chaps mind shiftin' upon a piece?" said the man in the trench. "Him and me are mates and we're goin' over together."[29]

Bean adds that the same thing must have happened many thousands of times in the Australian divisions, "The strongest bond in the Australian Imperial Force," he reiterates, "was that between a man and his mate."[30] Fifty years later the historian Bill Gammage found no reason to modify this opinion. He claims that men actually deserted from base camps to go into the combat line with their mates. From the letters and diaries of soldiers he culls exemplary acts of self-sacrifice, such as that of the man who laid down his life by giving his gas mask to a friend. It was on this tenacious loyalty that the towering edifice of war rested. The mutuality knew no bounds. Mates were immune from general custom, writes Gammage. "They could abuse a man, use his possessions, spend his money, and impose where others could not." And, finally, we are left with this image of love among the dead scattered in No Man's Land. Gammage tells us of the Australian soldier, shot through the arm, staying for seven days with his wounded mate in No Man's Land at Fromelles, scavenging food and water from the dead at night while slowly dragging him to safety.[31] But mateship did more than bind the common soldiers to one another. It also bound the common man to the strategies of control exercised by the officer class. Gammage notes that what he calls "a kind of mateship" practised by the officers vis a vis their troops "was a chief cause for the effectiveness of the Australians in battle."[32]

So far from home mates were all most Australians had. Gammage concludes, "and they became the AIF's greatest cohesive influence, discouraging shirking, and lifting men above and beyond the call of duty."[33]

As might be expected, then, mateship was central to the film *Gallipoli* and I asked Sid if he had seen the film as it had just been released and was attracting a lot of comment. But he hadn't and seemed totally disinterested. It turned out that he had volunteered and been sent to the Middle East en route to Gallipoli but had remained in Egypt to care for the horses. He was a country boy from Queensland and a skilled horseman. Perhaps he was a figure in the mind's eye of Australia's celebrated bush-poet. A. B. Patterson, of "The Man from Snowy River" fame who also cared for the army's horses in Egypt and wrote a ballad for *Kia Ora Coo-ee,* a monthly magazine of the Anzacs in the Middle East in 1918, about the 'rankless, thankless man/ who hustles the Army's mules.'

> You'll see a vision among the dust like a man and mule combined—
> Its the kind of thing you must take on trust for its outlines aren't defined,
> A thing that whirls like a spinning top and props like a three-legged stool,
> And you find its a long-legged Queensland boy convincing an army mule . . .

with the stanza ending,

> It's a rough-house game and thankless game, and it isn't a game for a fool.
> For an army's fate and a nation's fame may turn on an army mule.[34]

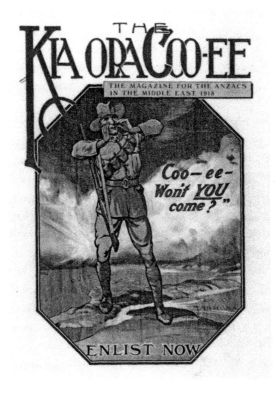

I asked Sid what he did after that and he told me he went to France as an infantryman. A big battle was about to begin, an immense push forward by the allies in which huge numbers of men would die and be wounded. In his book on Gallipoli, the Australian Alan Moorehead describes the rhythm of combat and mood there as one of depression and irritability when combat was at a low ebb, and the men fighting with one another or even paying money in order to be in the thick of combat, the bayonet charges or whatever, when such was at hand.[35] But Sid's tale was somewhat different.

Amid the bursting shells he and his mate replaced the lead in their .303 cartridges with German shrapnel. Waiting until some stretcher bearers were close by, Sid fired at point-blank range into his mate's thigh. Their plan was that then his mate would fire into his and then the stretcher bearers would come running and take them to hospital and hence out of the war—hardly the type of mateship or use of it that the official voice of the burgeoning nationalism rested upon. But what happened was that Sid's bullet hit the major artery in his mate's thigh and blood fountained out in such quantities and speed that he lost consciousness and was unable to fire back at Sid.

"What could I do? Me mate was lying there dead and I had to go and fight and probably get killed too?"

"What happened?"

"Well, he got carried away and I went to see him months later in hospital in England and he was havin' a fine time sittin' up in bed with the nurses. His leg was withered, but . . . he told me things was bonza and he was goin' home to Australia and was gonna marry one of them nurses."

Years later Sid met up with his mate dressed up in his uniform and medals and plumes in his slouch hat. It was ANZAC Day and they marched together with their medals, Australian heroes.

I asked him about his contact with British soldiers. He remembered meeting up with five and later seeing only two of them. The other three had been wiped out by a shell. One of the survivors, a young kid really, told him about it and went on to say that he'd heard his mother was in prison in England for stealing firewood from the landed estate near her home. With the submarine blockage the British people suffered many hardships and she could not buy fuel.

"I looked at the young fella," Sid told me, "and I said to him, 'Look it's a funny thing yer know, mate, but it wouldn't matter much who won this flamin' war. Yer three cobbers are dead and yer ol' mum's in prison . . . No! It wouldn't matter who won this war!"

The U-boat blockade had a momentous impact on the fortunes of a small firm in Australia too. Its name was Holden and it had been started in 1854 by an Englishman of that name who created a leather and saddlery business. Moving into carriage-making in the early 20th century, the Holden company was able to take advantage, in 1917, of the market opened up for the manufacture of car bodies on account of the Government ban on the importation of complete vehicles, consequent to the threat to shipping lanes posed by the U-boats. By 1923 Holden Motor Body Builders had become one of the largest industrial enterprises in Australia and signed an agreement with General Motors Export Company to manufacture car bodies, in return for which GM agreed to supply designs, data, and technical "know how."

On November 29th, 1948, General Motors Holden unveiled the 48-125, the first "Australian" motor car.

We had got to the end of our test drive and when we opened the glove-box to get the car's papers there fell out a postcard. It was from Russia and Sid asked me to read it. An old Australian friend of his had sent it as a memento of a tourist trip and was lauding the virtues of the Soviet Union, its full employment and so forth. It turned out that Sid was not only sympathetic with communism but an ardent Stalinist. I kept thinking back to the way he loved the centralized automatic control of Australia's Own, the Holden; how you could raise and lower everyone's window from the driver's panel, and so forth. Like everything else about Sid, here at least the control mechanism was clear and up front. But with a democratic state apparatus and its associated civil culture a different type of control exists, one that uses mateship and oppositional practice, for example, in a way such that people feel they are doing something natural, not imposed. C.E.W. Bean had said, for instance, that the British Empire at the time of WWI was an organization of semi-autonomous parts—in keeping with liberalism. "The British policy," he wrote in the official history of the War, "left it to whatever virtue and good sense existed in each portion of the race to see the need ... and this was precisely the opposite," he went on to say,

> to that of the rigid and calculating organization upon which the German Empire was built. It was of the essence of liberalism: it avoided all imposed control and placed its trust in the good sense and feeling inherent in men left free.[36]

But there is no freedom outside of culture, and for many of these men the culture of nationalism their colonially created image as bushmen and as ANZACS helped weave together became their shroud, as it will for others to come—especially if Sid, the old bushman, has his way. Asked how he could justify Stalin's slaughter of millions of Russian peasants in the 1930s he instantly responded, "Why! The same thing has to happen here. They're just a lot of Cocky Farmers, you know!"

I drove off newly possessed by Australia's Own.

CANE TOADS: AN
UNNATURAL HISTORY

In this Baudrillardian age of the hyperreal, nowhere more intense than in the great antipodean fiction called Australia, so sensitive to First World fashion, the crucial question both for politics and aesthetics is whether the signifier is empty or, simply, open. Baudrillard's acute proposal was that we are now experiencing a world in which experience relies predominantly on image, that the image is the latest form taken by the commodity, and that such imagery confounds the "normal" or hitherto normal notion of the sign in that the signifier does not stand for a thing or a more substantial reality, but is in some profoundly real sense complete in itself. Hence the power of the advertising image and the news media, especially the visual image on TV. Hence Ronald Reagan. Hence empty. Or is this an emptiness capable of being filled by innumerable meaning-makers, as Michel de Certeau would have it, invoking a world of anarchist semioticians striking back at the emptiness of postmodern life?

This latest version of free will versus necessity is marvelously highlighted by the 46-minute color film *Cane Toads: An Unnatural History*, a film which creates almost unnatural delight whenever it is shown. A hit if ever there was one, it focuses on what people, in the multiplicity of their different social classes, genders, and statuses, have to say about a loathsome and rapidly multiplying animal, the cane toad, introduced in the 1930s from Hawaii by science, the state, and big business to combat a pest destroying the sugarcane industry. The people are Australians, seen live in their natural habitat of the "deep north," meaning the state of Queensland, renowned in the sophisticated south for its racism, police corruption, and rednecks.

Indeed their leader for many a decade, a certain right-wing populist, Mr. Bjelke Petersen, is said to have been nicknamed the cane toad. Now whether this was on account of his looks (iconicity) or what he stood for (indexicality and arbitrariness), whether this was because in being likened to an animal he was made more endearing, or more frightful—that is the insolubly ambiguous empowering stuff of which this brilliant film is made, deploying what is to my mind a quite extraordinarily effective method of sociological inquiry—namely the reading of societal meanings into the animal kingdom.

Thus ordinary Queenslanders, lonely housewives, scraggy old farmers, sweet little children, murderous motorists, rotund Rotarians, and many officials, ecologists, and scientists are able to freely vent and invent their media-mediated, populist, and official feelings in answer to a simple question: What do you think about the toad? Every now and again interspersed amongst this great Balzacian gallery of Queensland human types, we get a close up of the toad's gleaming eye, the bags of loose flesh (if it can be called flesh) pulsating around its quivering throat, or the highly poisonous sacks its shoulder hides. My teenage son (from Sydney) especially loves the sequence where an old timer (whose voice is not all that unlike the croaking of the toads) reaches lyric heights in describing how he likes at nights to listen to the croaking of the toads mating in his lush backyard.

This is the world of Kafka with the ape reporting to the academy, of the investigation of the dog, of Josephine the mouse-singer, of Gregor Samsa metamorphosing into a gigantic insect. Delineated in a shifting multiplicity of forms, the modern social world is here delineated through the intermediary of the toad in such a way that the humans become somewhat like animals, and the the toad becomes somewhat human. This is a striking alienation-effect, and the shock is not merely of the stranger in our midst, but of an interchanging structure which allows fantasy to flourish, where modern secular mythology is grounded in the Queensland social soul.

Here, to my mind, is where mimesis and instrumental rationality are repositioned. In *Dialectic of Enlightenment,* Max Horkheimer and T.W. Adorno argued that far from being erased by modern social forms, mimesis was instead refunctioned. The Jew in Central Europe became the Nazi's signifier of the animal world and of animality. Likewise, the organic splendor of the structured human body in the Nuremburg rallies was the passionate consequence of animality orchestrated into public spectacle of the state. So, in less striking form, perhaps, mimesis is similarly utilized in liberal democracies, as with Blacks in the USA, or in Queensland itself, land of the toad.

But Mark Lewis' film reverses this. By taking us into fantasies about the toad and, more importantly, by getting people on film to show us themselves doing this, as they go along, so to speak—inventing *in situ* in response to the filmmaker's challenge—he not only displays the mimetic fusion between toad and society, but simultaneously radically deranges the ways by which mimesis is used in our century for the return of the repressed so as to kill and control people. He makes us laugh and wonder at the way the mimetic works in social forms, especially now when nature, the mimetic faculty, as with the toad, is striking back at the attempt to dominate it. For the toad is unstoppable, breeding like crazy, spreading out from Queensland across Australia Felix.

This is a particularly Australian tale to tell here, of course, the tale of White Australia's deep committement to keeping Others out and the way that this committment has long been mimeticized—animalized, biologized, as with the stocky gentlemen in long socks up to their ruddy knees who, arms aloft as if carrying the holy flame itself, pass through the aisles of the airliners landing on Australian soil so as to spray the passengers free of plague. Sir James George Frazer could not have done better in those pages of *The Golden Bough* where he vividly evokes primordial rites aimed at stemming the magical power of the stranger. This film of the toad adds to that White story, telling us of the way that the scientists, the state, and the Colonial Sugar Refining Company can, when money's at stake, ignore the fierce taboos of the Great Cleanliness of popular as much as official culture and indeed allow the monstrous Other, the toad, to enter the life-blood of the nation's imaginary.

This film, needless to say, is a shot in the arm for the flagging discussions waging about "ethnographic representation." For it not only represents *intersecting* points of view—popular, populist, and statist—and it not only presents society's metaview of itself through its on-the-spot mimetic discursivity concerning things toad, but true to best of reflexive hermeneusis even attempts to give the toad's point of view of Australia as well. It is a constrained view, as one might expect. Australia swings into sight through the cracks in a box, then extends into a broad stream of rumbling as the goods-train rumbles north. With this cramped thin ribbon of vision, the film shows us the animal eye-world, inviting us to all the more effectively explore our own lifeworld.

REIFICATION AND THE CONSCIOUSNESS OF THE PATIENT

The Marxist Problem: Reification

By means of a cultural analysis of an illness and its treatment in the USA in 1978, I wish to direct attention to the importance of two problems raised by Marxism and by anthropology concerning the moral and social significance of biological and physical "things." I am going to argue that things such as the signs and symptoms of disease, as much as the technology of healing, are not "things-in-themselves," are *not only* biological and physical, but *are also* signs of social relations disguised as natural things, concealing their roots in human reciprocity.

The problem raised by Marxism comes from the famous essay of Georg Lukács published in 1922 entitled "Reification and the Consciousness of the Proletariat," an essay which had explosive impact on the European Communist movement, in good part due to its critique of "historical materialism" as developed by Engels, Lenin, and the theoreticians of the German Social Democrat Party. In essence, Lukács charged that the concept of objectivity held by capitalist culture was an illusion fostered by capitalist relations of production and that this concept of objectivity had been thoughtlessly assimilated by Marxist critics who were, therefore, upholding basic categories of the social form they thought they were impugning. Lukács attempted to construct a critical sociology of bourgeois knowledge which assailed the very theory of knowledge or epistemology which he felt was basic to capitalist culture. The Kantian and neo-Kantian antinomies between "fact" and "value," as much as the empiricist copy-book theory of knowledge sharply dividing "objectivity" from "subjectivity," were, in Lukács opinion, tools of thought which reproduced capitalist ideology (even if they were deployed within a so-called "historical materialist" framework of analysis). The roots of the thought-form which took the capitalist categories of reality for granted were to be found, he argued, in what he called the "commodity-structure," and a chief aim of his essay was to draw attention to the central importance of the analysis of commodities in Marx' portrayal and critique of capitalism. There was no problem in this stage of history, claimed Lukács, that did not lead back to the question of the commodity structure, the central, structural problem of capitalist society in all its aspects. Intrinsic to this problem lay the phenomenon of reification—the thingification of the world, persons, and experience, as all of these are organized and reconstituted by market exchange and commodity production. The basis of commodity-structure, wrote Lukács, "is that a relation between people takes on the character of a thing and thus acquires a 'phantom objectivity,' an autonomy that seems so strictly rational and all-embracing as to conceal every trace of its fundamental nature: the relation between people."[1]

It is with the phantom-objectivity of disease and its treatment in our society that I am concerned, because by denying the human relations embodied in symptoms, signs, and therapy, we not only mystify them but we also reproduce a political ideology in the guise of a science of (apparently) "real things"—biological and physical thinghood. In this way our objectivity as presented in medicine represents basic cultural axioms and modulates the contradictions inherent to our culture and view of objectivity. Rather than expound further, I now wish to exemplify these all too abstract orienting premises by means of a concrete ethnographic analysis of a sickness. But before doing so, I have to draw attention to a problem raised by anthropology, namely by Evans-Pritchard's classic analysis of Azande witchcraft published in 1937.[2]

The Anthropological Problem: The Biological Body and the Social Body

It is surely a truism that the sense of self and of the body change over time and vary among different cultures. In modern capitalist culture the body acquires a dualistic phenomenology as both a thing and my being, body and "soul." Witness Sartre's chapters on the body in *Being and Nothingness*.[3]

Of course the physicians who have taken care of me, the surgeons who have operated on me, have been able to have direct experience with the body which I myself do not know. I do not disagree with them. I do not claim that I lack a brain, a heart, or a stomach. But it is most important to choose the order of our bits of knowledge. So far as the physicians have had any experience with my body, it was with my body in the midst of the world as it is for others. My body as it is for me does not appear to me in the midst of the world. Of course during a radioscopy I was able to see the picture of my vertebrae on a screen, but I was outside in the midst of the world. I was apprehending a wholly constituted object as a this amongst other thises, and it was only a reasoning process that I referred it back to being mine: it was much more my property than my being.

As it oscillates between being my property and my being, especially when diseased, my body asks me "Why me? Why now?" As Evans-Pritchard observed, these are the questions foremost in the Azande attribution of serious sickness or misfortune to witchcraft or sorcery—i.e., to the malevolent disposition of critically relevant social relationships. Science, as we understand it in our day and age, cannot explain the human significance of physical effects. To cite the common phraseology, science, like medical science, can explain the "how" but not the "why" of disease; it can point to chains of physical cause and effect, but as to why I am struck down now rather than at some other time, or as to why it is me rather than someone else, medical science can only respond with some variety of probability theory which is unsatisfactory to the mind searching for certainty and for significance. In Azande practice, the issues of "how" and "why" are folded into one another; etiology is simultaneously physical, social, and moral. A cause of my physically obvious distress is to be located in my nexus of social relations involving someone else's unjustly called-for malevolence. This property of my social nexus expresses itself in physical symptoms and signs. My disease is a social relation, and therapy has to address that synthesis of moral, social, and physical presentation.

There are two problems raised by this account. First, do patients in our society also ask themselves the questions that the Azande do, despite the disenchantment of our age, and its incredulity regarding witchcraft and sorcery? Second, have we not falsified Azande epistemology, following Evans-Pritchard, in distinguishing the "how" from the "why," "fact" from "value," and immediate from ultimate causes? Unless we firmly grasp at the outset that these are not the salient native distinctions but that they are ours which we necessarily deploy in order to make some sense out of a foreign epistemology, we will fail to appreciate what is at issue. The salient distinction to note is that in Azande epistemology there is a vastly different conception of facts and things. Facts are not separated from values, physical manifestations are not torn from their social contexts, and it requires therefore no great effort of mind to read social relations into material events. It is a specifically modern problem wherein things like my bodily organs are at one instant mere things, and at another instant question me insistently with all too human a voice regarding the social significance of their dis-ease.

Paul Radin in his discussion of the concept of the self in "primitive" societies makes the same point. He suggests that the objective form of the ego in such societies is generally only intelligible in terms of the external world and other egos. Instead of the ego as a thing-in-itself, it is seen as indissolubly integrated with other persons and with nature. "A purely mechanistic conception of life," he concludes, "is impossible. The parts of the body, the physiological functions of the organs, like the material objects taken by objects in nature, are mere symbols, *simulacra*, for the essential psychical-spiritual entity that lies behind them."[4]

As it oscillates between being a thing and my being, as it undergoes and yet disengages itself from reification, my body responds with a language that is as commonplace as it is startling. For the body is not only this organic mosaic of biological entities. It is also a cornucopia of highly charged symbols—fluids, scents, tissues, different surfaces, movements, feelings, cycles of changes constituting birth, growing old, sleeping and waking. Above all, it is with disease with its terrifying phantoms of despair and hope that my body becomes ripe as little else for encoding that which society holds to be real—only to impugn that reality. And if the body becomes this important repository for generating social meaning, then it is in therapy that we find the finely gauged tuning whereby the ratification of socially engendered categories and the fabulation of reality reaches its acme.

In any society, the relationship between doctor and patient is more than a technical one. It is very much a social interaction which can reinforce the culture's basic premises in a most powerful manner. The sick person is a dependent and anxious person, malleable in the hands of the doctor and the health system, and open to their manipulation and moralism. The sick person is one who is plunged into a vortex of the most fundamental questions concerning life and death. The everyday routine of more or less uncritical acceptance of the meaning of life is sharply interrupted by serious illness, which has its own pointed way of turning all of us into metaphysicians and philosophers, (not to mention critics of a society which leaves its sick and their families to fend for themselves). This gives the doctor a powerful point of entry into the patient's psyche, and also amounts to a destructuration of the patient's conventional understandings and social personality. It is the function of the relationship between the doctor and the patient to restructure those understandings and that personality; to bring them back into the fold of society and plant them firmly within the epistemological and ontological groundwork from which the society's basic ideological premises arise. In modern clinical practice and medical culture, this function is camouflaged. The issue of control and manipulation is concealed by the aura of benevolence. The social character of the medical encounter is not immediately obvious in the way that it is in the communal healing rites of "primitive" societies. With us, consultation and healing occurs in privatized and individualistic settings, and the moral and metaphysical components of disease and healing are concealed by the use of the natural science model.

As Susan Sontag has recently emphasized,[5] while the symptoms and signs of disease usually have a decidedly and all too material quality, they are something else besides. We might say that they are social *as well as* physical and biological facts. We glimpse this if we reflect but for a moment on the vastly different meanings conveyed by signs and symptoms at different points in history and in different cultures. Fatness, thinness, blood in one's urine, let alone blood *per se*, headache, nightmares, lassitude, coughing, blurred vision, dizziness, and so forth, acquire vastly different meanings and significance at different times in history, in different classes of society, and so on. Two points are raised here. The manifestations of disease are like symbols, and the diagnostician sees them and interprets them with an eye trained by the social determinants of perception. Yet this is denied by an ideology or epistemology which regards its creations as really lying "out-there"—solid, substantial things-in-themselves. Our minds like cameras or carbon paper do nothing more than faithfully register the facts of life. This illusion is ubiquitous in our culture, is what Lukács means by reification stemming from the commodity-structure, and medical practice is a singularly important way of maintaining the denial as to the social facticity of facts. Things thereby take on a life of their own, sundered from the social nexus that really gives them life, and remain locked in their own self-constitution.

> Today in various nooks and crannies called consultation rooms, diagnosticians listen for the same elements and when they find them they do not say, I can put these things together and call them hysteria if I like (much as a little boy can sort his marbles now by size, now by colour, now by age); rather, the diagnostician, when he has completed his sort says: This patient is a hysteric! Here, then, is the creator denying authorship of his creation. Why? Because in turn he receives a greater prize; the reassurance that out there is a stable world; it is not all in his head.[6]

What is revealed to us here is the denial of authorship, the denial of relationship, and the denial of the reciprocity of process to the point where the manifold armory of assumptions, leaps of faith and *a priori* categories are ratified as real and natural. In another idiom, the arbitrariness of the sign is disconfirmed and no longer seen as arbitrary because it is affixed in the patient, therewith securing the semiotic of the disease *langue*. And if the diagnostician is thereby reassured as to the reality of the world as thinghood writ large, and by this dispenses with the discomfort of being at too close quarters with the reality of what is but the social construction of reality, it is not that it is "all in his head" but that it is all in the relationship of physicians and patients which is at stake. The relationship is worked over and sundered. Reciprocity lies victim to the assault performed on it. Likewise, the patient and the concept of disease have been recruited in the service of building a reality whose stability, which cannot be denied so long as professional expertise bears down, is nevertheless prone to violent altercations as the pressure of denied authorship and reciprocity makes its presence felt. This presence of denial is itself masked by the illusion of reciprocity of a different sort; the niceties of style in the bedside manner and the culture of caring. Foucault directs our attention to this in his discussion of changes in psychiatry, in terms that apply to all of modern clinical science:

> Madness no longer exists except as *seen*. The proximity instituted by the asylum, an intimacy neither chains nor bars would violate again, does not allow reciprocity; only the nearness of observation that watches, that spies, that comes closer in order to see better, but moves ever further away, since it accepts and acknowledges only the values of the Stranger. The science of mental disease . . . would not be a dialogue . . . .[7]

Because it does this, medical practice inevitably produces grotesque mystifications in which we all flounder, grasping ever more pitifully for security in a man-made world which we see not as social, not as human, not as historical, but as a world of *a priori* objects beholden only to their own force and laws, dutifully illuminated for us by professional experts such as doctors. There are many political messages subtly encouraged by all of this for those who become patients, and we all become patients at some time, and we are all patients in a metaphorical sense of the social "doctors" who minister our needs. Don't trust your senses. Don't trust the feeling of uncertainty and ambiguity inevitably occurring as the socially conditioned senses try to orchestrate the multitude of meanings given to otherwise mute things. Don't contemplate rebellion against the facts of life for these are not in some important manner partially man-made, but are irretrievably locked in the realm of physical matter. To the degree that matter can be manipulated, leave that to "science" and your doctor.

The Patient

By way of illustration (rigorously preserving the anonymity of the people and organizations involved) I want to discuss the situation of a forty-nine year-old white working class woman with a history of multiple hospital admissions over the past eight years with a diagnosis of polymyositis— inflammation of many muscles. According to medical authority, this is a fatal chronic disease consisting in the progressive deterioration of muscle. Classified as a rheumatoid disease of unknown cause, treatment consists largely in the administration of heavy doses of steroids at the times when the disease waxes in order to decelerate the inflammation. I met her in the wards of a prestigious teaching hospital in 1978, where we talked for some four hours on five occasions. I introduced myself as a physician and anthropologist, interested in patients' views of sickness.

She described her condition as disease of the muscles. They deteriorate, and it's terminal. It is a terrible tiredness, she says, which comes and goes in relation to stress. What worries her is being without control during the acute phases. As she puts it, the switch to her body, between her mind and body, becomes switched off. The attic is cut off from the basement. When she gives examples, it is always in situations where she is working for others;

washing the dishes for example. When asked what she thought might be the cause of her disease, it turned out that she constantly asked herself why she had it, never stopped asking herself "Why? Why me, Oh Lord, why me?"

Her search for explanation and meaning remains dissatisfied with what the medical profession offers. As we shall see, she demands a totalizing synthesis which she herself provides by reading contradictory cultural themes into her symptoms, signs, and progress. These contradictions are exhibited by her reactions to the *obiter dicta* of medical professionals, to the patterns of discipline enforced by the hospital, and to the conflicts systematically coursing through society in general. Moreover, her mode of understanding and explanation runs counter to the master paradigms in our culture which dichotomize mind from matter, morality from physical determinism, and "things" from the social context and human meaning in which they inhere. In being foreign to accepted cultural consciousness, in these crucial ways, her attempts to provide a synthetic understanding of physical things cannot but be tensed and prone to instability.

Her first response was to say that the cause of her condition is "an unhappy reason." At the age of fifteen and contrary to her mother's desire, she married a factory worker who, due to his alcoholism, soon became unable to support her and the five children born in the following five years. She had a tubal ligation followed shortly thereafter by a restagement, and then six more pregnancies all resulting in miscarriages. She took in washing, ironed, and gleaned garbage for bottles which she sold. There was rarely money sufficient for food and she was constantly exhausted and hungry. She would go without food in order to give it to the children who were frequently sick. In turn, she caught many of their sicknesses, because she was so weak and tired. Life was this endless round of poverty, exertion, exhaustion, and sickness. "Surely that could cause polymyositis," she says. "You can take a perfect piece of cloth and if you rub it on the scrub board long enough, you're going to wear holes in it. It's going to be in shreds. You can take a healthy person and take away the things that they need that are essential, and they become thin and sickly. So I mean . . . it all just comes together." She has never approached her doctors with this idea because "They would laugh at my ignorance. But it does seem right; that tiredness and work all the time. Take the children of India without enough food, dragging their swollen bellies around, tired and hungry. Surely they could have this disease too. Only because they haven't got hospitals, nobody knows it."

In making these connections, the patient elaborates on the connection she has in mind between polymyositis as muscle degeneration and her life-experience of oppression, of muscular exertion, and of bodily sacrifice. What seems especially significant here is that the causes she imputes as well as her understanding of the disease stand as iconic metaphors and metonyms of one another, all mapped into the disease as the arch-metaphor standing for that oppression. This could well form the highly charged imagery leading to a serious critique of basic social institutions. But, as we shall see, other aspects of the situation mitigate this potentiality.

She then went on to develop the idea that there also exists an hereditary or quasi-hereditary causal factor. In her opinion, one of her daughters is possibly afflicted with the disease, and two of that daughter's daughters also. She feels extremely close to this daughter, to the point where she maintains that there is a mystical attachment between them, of Extra-Sensory Perception, as she says. Even when they are far apart physically, each one knows what is happening to the other, especially at a time of crisis, when they come to each other's aid. She elaborates on the concept that the disease is present in this matriline, manifesting itself in four distinct stages correlated to the four ages of the four females involved. In passing, it is worth noting that the males in the family history come in for little mention with the exception of her first husband who is seen as a destructive and even evil figure. Her immediate social world is seen by her as centered on the history of four generations of women, beginning with her mother who raised the family in dire poverty. This characteristic matriline of reciprocating women in the networks of working class families is in this case vividly expressed by the mystical closeness she feels for her daughter, and by the mapping of these social relations into the disease as a metaphor of those relations.

The fact that the youngest granddaughter involved was seriously ill when a few months of age, and that the doctors found an "orgasm" in her blood, suggests to the patient the possibility that a foreign agent or bacterial etiology plays a part too; the foreign agent disappearing into the body to slowly develop the fullblown presentation of the disease at a later date. The attribution of disease to a foreign agent would seem as old as humankind. But only with modern Western medicine and the late nineteenth century "germ theory of disease" did this idea largely shed itself of the notion that the foreign agent was an expression of specific social relations. In this patient's case, however, the foreign agent etiology is systematically woven into the fabric of her closest relationships and metaphorically expresses them.

Finally, the patient develops the idea that God stands at a crucial point in the causal complex. She mentions that God gave her this disease in order to teach doctors how to cure it—a typical resolution of the oppositions redolent in her account of passivity and activity, receiving and giving, crime and sacrifice. She notes that in the Bible it is said to seek first and then go to the Lord, meaning, she says, go first to the medical profession and then try out religion. It is this long march that she has indeed put into practice as much as in her working through a theory of etiology. At this stage of our discussion, she summarized a good deal of her position thus.

"You see, protein builds muscle and yet my children were lucky if they got protein once a month, and I was lucky. Now I have polymyositis, plus the arthritis, and my daughter has arthritis of the spine, and her little daughter is affected by it, has inherited it, plus her younger daughter yet. Now there seems to be a pattern there. You see I was deprived of it and my children were deprived of it and we've both come down with a chronic disease. We're not too sure that she doesn't have polymyositis. The breakdown of the muscles and the tissues due to strain and work were weakened by the fact that you didn't have enough protein and so on, so that when the bug comes along, you are a prime target for it! . . . God gives us a free will. I went very much against God's will . . . when I went out and got married at fifteen, stomped my feet and told my mother I'd go out and get pregnant if she didn't let me marry the boy. I don't believe that God gave me the disease, but he *allowed* . . . me to get the disease. He suffered me over many mountains. And on the same hand, I was in the perfect situation for contracting the disease or for the development of the disease whether it's hereditary or catching . . . nobody knows yet . . . Does that make sense? When I'm laying quietly thinking . . . the train of thought goes along and you wonder why? You know; Oh why me Lord? Why all the ups and downs? But it's not God's fault that I got sick; it's the fault of the environment I lived in! Now, with God's help which I hadn't asked for at that time, I could have overcome many of my hardships but I was too proud! And we have to be humble before God . . . So you see our environment has very much to do with our health and with our mental outlook on life . . . it has everything to do . . . our morals and clean living, a proper diet . . . all these things they all go together . . . they all fit into a neat little puzzle if you sit long enough and look at them right. You have a neat little puzzle that all fits very neatly together. . . ."

This moving passage calls for far larger commentary than I can make here. Her concern with the meaning and especially with the moral meaning of her illness stands out, reinforcing the argument that behind every reified disease theory in our society lurks an organizing realm of moral concerns. In her case, God is by no means seen as the prime or even ultimate cause of her disease. Rather, it is the moral quality of her actions, in going against her mother and so on, and the moral actions of her husband, which offended the moral code embodied in God's directives, that determined which way the potentialities inherent to her material situation or environment would develop. The elegant simplicity of Evans-Pritchard's exegesis and solution of Azande epistemology into "mystical," "scientific," and "empirical" categories, as a way of bridging their belief system with ours, becomes of dubious value. It is hard here to see a simple chain of causes stretching from ultimate to immediate, along the lines suggested by Evans-Pritchard for the Azande. Instead, we are presented with a system of internal relationships, a series of encysting and encysted contingencies permeating each other's potentials drawn into one grand pattern—or, rather, into "one neat little puzzle that all fits very neatly together."

In so far as modern medical practice ostensibly focuses exclusively on the "how" of disease, and reifies pathology in doing so, it might appear to be performing a rather helpful and healthy maneuver in expunging guilt. But as the situation so movingly reveals, nothing could be further from the truth. Through a series of exceedingly complex operations, reification serves to adhere guilt to disease. The real task of therapy calls for an archaeology of the implicit in such a way that the processes by which social relations are mapped into diseases are brought to light, de-reified, and in doing so liberate the potential for dealing with antagonistic contradictions and breaking the chains of oppression.

In talking about her relationships with other sick people in the ward, the patient noted that "I couldn't have survived without the help of the other patients these eight weeks." She dwelt on the fact that hospitalization drew patients to one another in very personal and usually sympathetic ways. "I really do think you have a better understanding of people and their likes, dislikes, and their personalities here. Being sick gives you a tolerance for other people's faults. You really have a better bond because that person already knows your faults. You know. You don't have to put on a false face. These are things that, uh, a doctor naturally doesn't have time to sit down and think about. . . . They don't feel the pain. They give an order what to do but they don't feel the pain. So they really don't know what type of hazard you're going through."

She has made firm friendships with patients whom she now visits when out of hospital, but with the staff "it's different because naturally your doctor and your nurse have your medical part to think of. Where we lay here and we talk about our families and the things we like to do or the things we like to eat, you become on a more intimate basis. It's . . . the professional part is gone. But your doctor is still . . . even though he's becoming more lenient in his ways, I believe he's still got to keep the upper hand professionally."

Following her statement that she couldn't have survived the past eight weeks if it hadn't been for the other patients, she goes on to discuss her physical therapy. "You see I can't walk. I'm just now learning all over again from my illness. You have to learn. You have to relearn to take one step at a time . . . like a child. I've been confined solely to this bed. If my tray had been left over there by the nurse . . . her mind is on another medical problem that she's got to face next. But Becky who's lying in the bed next to me can get up and move over and get my stuff where I can reach it. Or . . . if I can't reach my light, she'll turn her light on for me and then tell them who needs service. Now I'm able to stand if you give me the proper instructions, and, and . . . but you see I'm re-educating all the muscles and Becky couldn't help me there. Where see the professional, your young professional girl is trained to teach. . . . On the other hand the professional couldn't give me the personal attention that Becky has given me. Something just as simple as pulling the curtains back so that I can see more than just a curtain and the white ceiling. I can't get up to do it myself, but Becky can. Your friendship and your mutual understandings, you know, you really get to know a person whether they're kind or really interested in you. Such as I spoke every morning very kindly to this elderly lady (in the opposite bed). I know she can hear me but she wants absolutely nothing to do with me. She's far above me. I take it she has money. Her daughter is a doctor. She wants nothing to do with me and yet I haven't hurt her. . . . I don't have any small children, but Becky does and I've gone through the things she is now going through so we have mutual interests. I'm the grandmother of nineteen."

I ask her why another patient couldn't help her walking. She replies. "Because she would teach you *wrong*, when a professional already knows and has evaluated your muscle strength. And there, uh, you know automatically that you can trust the nurse. But Becky hasn't been taught how to grab me or stabilize me . . . or to tell me which muscle to use to keep myself from collapsing. So, see, she can't help me professionally. So our whole friendship has to be on a . . . on a I like you and you like me basis. That technician still has her mind working on far beyond mine. Mine is strictly in trying to accomplish what she has already learned and knows."

I ask, "But say the professional teaches you to walk backwards and forwards between a couple of things several times a day. Couldn't someone like Becky who isn't bedridden help you to exercise?"

"No! Because she doesn't know the extent of your energies."

"But the professional does?"

"The professional has to figure this out before she starts the exercises."

"You yourself wouldn't know the capacity of your own energy so you could tell?"

"No! No!"

Here the loss of autonomy to which Ivan Illich refers in his book *Medical Nemesis* is strikingly expressed.[8] The potential within the patient as much as that which exists between patients for developing a therapeutic milieu is agonizingly cut short. The relationship with other patients becomes almost purely "expressive," while the relationship with the professionals becomes purely "instrumental." As each type of relationship is driven to its extreme in pure subjectivity and pure objectivity, so each is threatened with self-destruction as it teeters on expressiveness without substance, and instrumentation without expression or participation. The replication of our cultural epistemology into subjecthood and objecthood is here presented in its most naked form. The same epistemology is also replicated in the patient's understanding, reinforced by the professionals, of the workings of her body; namely the structure and function of musculature. As opposed to an organic conception of the inner dialectical interplay of muscles with one another and with thought and will, here muscle function is conceived of atomistically, separate from mind and will, and each muscle is objectified as something separate from the synergistic interplay of musculo-skeletal holism. And in her regarding the professional as knowing better than she as to the extent of her energies, we may well regard the alienation of her own senses as complete, handed over to the professional who has become the guardian or banker of her mind.

This splitting of subjectivity from objectivity as represented by patienthood and professionalism, respectively, resulting in the capturing of her subjectivity by the professional, is as much a result of the patients' inability to develop the mutual aid potential still present in the patient subculture as it is due to the relationship between professional and patient. The former derives from the latter, and both contrast strikingly with the social relations and culture described by Joshua Horn for the Chinese hospitals in which he worked from 1954 to 1969.

> The patients often select representatives to convey their opinions and suggestions to teams of doctors, nurses and orderlies who have day-to-day responsibility in relation to specific groups of patients. These teams meet daily to plan the day's work. Ambulant patients play an active part in ward affairs. They take their meals in the ward diningroom and many of them help patients who are confined to bed, reading newspapers to them, keeping them company and becoming familiar with their medical and social problems. I conduct a ward round in a different ward each day and as I do so, I usually collect a retinue of patients who go with me, look and listen and often volunteer information.[9]

The alienation of the patient's self-understanding and capacity is all the more striking when we learn that she has extensive practical experience with physical therapy and that out of the hospital context and away from the aura of professionals, she does in fact regard herself as skilled and powerful in this regard. Speaking about her sprained knee suffered some years back she says, "And then I had to learn to walk again. I'm always learning to walk! I really ought to be well-trained. I could be a therapist. ... I trained my daughter after she had polio. And they refused to take her at the polio center. I taught her to walk. Her left side was paralyzed (the same side that the patient always refers to as her weak and occasionally almost paralyzed side). . . . I learnt from a friend. I used to have to get up and I'd sit on top of her and stretch her hamstrings and stretch her arm muscles and things and it was three months before I got any response at all. And then one night when I was stretching her hamstrings she screamed because she said that it hurt too much. Well I sat down and had a good cry. Mother couldn't even continue therapy that night. And from then on, the more it hurt, the more therapy I gave her. And the year from the day that they told me she'd never walk again, I walked back in to the doctor and I showed her what one person could do with God's help. You have to be gentle. And this comes from love, compassion, and the desire to help another human being. And you'd be surprised how really strong my hands are I never lose the strength of my hands. I don't know why. But through all of this I have never completely lost my . . . my hands."

So, we are faced with a contradiction. And this contradiction is just as much present in the hospital situation and in the professional-patient relationship so that the loss of autonomy and the cultural lobotomization is never complete. For a few days later the patient refused what was considered an important part of her treatment, just as during an earlier stay in hospital she created a wild scene by throwing her coffee on the floor when the staff refused to give her more medication for pain.

On this earlier occasion she insisted that her pain was increasing. The staff regarded this as "secondary gain." The nurses' plan was to "give support and reassurance; allow the patient to express her feelings. Monitor emotion regarding status and shift." It is, of course, this mode of perception— "monitor emotion . . ."—which so tellingly contrasts with the type of observation that passes between patients, and which should be referred to my earlier citation from Foucault, the perception which

> does not allow of reciprocity: only the nearness of an observation that watches, that spies, that comes closer in order to see better, but moves ever further away, since it accepts and acknowledges only the value of the Stranger.

Following the innovation and supposedly more human "problem-oriented approach," which is now also taught to medical students, the nurses' progress notes are written up in the form of the different problems the patient has.

Each problem is then analysed into four parts in accord with the S.O.A.P. formula: Subjective (the patient's perception), Objective (the nurse's observation), Analysis (interpretation of data), and Plan. Soap—the guarantee of cleanliness and the barrier to pollution! Subjectivity, objectivity, analysis, and plan! What better guarantee and symbolic expression could be dreamt of to portray, as if by farce, the reification of living processes and the alienation of subject from object? And, as one might suspect, this formulation is congruent with the need for computerizing records and more rationally preparing safeguards against malpractice suits. The Plan? "Give support and reassurance. Relate feelings of trust." How much does this packaging of "care," "trust," and "feelings," this instrumentation of what we used to think of a spontaneous human transitiveness and mutuality, cost, according to Blue Cross?

A few days later, the patient complained of more pain, and of her inability to urinate (although according to the nursing staff she could urinate). The night following she became angry and threw her coffee at a nurse who then called a doctor. He reported; "Patient had a significant episode of acting out. Accused nursing personnel and myself of lying and disrespect. Extremely anxious and agitated. Crying. Had thrown a cup of coffee at the R.N. (Registered Nurse). Patient refused to acknowledge any other precipitating event or underlying emotion. Husband arrived and calmed patient down. Psychiatric recommendation with Dr Y and began initiating dose of Haloperidol. Will also add 75 mg/day amitriptiline for apparent on-going depressive state with anxiety." (Haloperidol is described by Goodman and Gillman[10] as a drug which calms and induces sleep in excited patients. Because it produces a high incidence of extrapyramidal reactions it should be initiated with caution.) This is the first time that the doctor's notes mention that the patient is distressed, although the nurses' notes chart her increasing dissatisfaction going back over several days. The nurse's report of the same incident leaves out, for the first time, the S (subjective category) and goes straight to Objectivity: "Patient was so upset when she was told that somebody said that she can get out of bed and use the bedside commode. She said that nurse is . . . and for her anger threw her cup of coffee on the floor. Crying and wants her husband to be called because she's very upset. Saying dirty words." Analysis: "Patient is very upset." Plan: "Dr X notified and patient was told to calm down since she's not the only patient on the floor, that others are very sick and upset from her noise. Patient claims that she is not sick. Patient quiets down when her husband came and friendly to the nurses." The next day the doctor's notes say that the patient is quite angry and that her anger takes the form of sobbing and threatening to leave hospital and warn friends about care here. The day after that, the nurses report that the chaplain talked to the patient for half an hour so she'll be able to release all her tensions, anxiety, and conflict. The chaplain said that she's angry of something. The Plan notes that the chaplain will come every day and that she's a bit nicer to the staff and courteous when she needs something. The doctor's notes describe the patient as "stable" and thereafter never mention her scene. The nurse's report says that she is still complaining of pain, Subjective category, and requesting pain medication, Objective category. As for her "anxiety problem" the Objective entry says "she is talking about how people don't believe she can do nothing for herself." And the next day she went home.

It is surely of some importance that the patient was examined (sic) by a psychiatrist the morning of the same day when she later threw her coffee (on the floor, according to the nurses; at a nurse, according to the doctor). The nurses' report noted that she was crying and trembling following the visit of the psychiatrist, whose own report says that the "evidence is strongly suggestive of an organic brain syndrome." She said it was January when it was December. The psychiatrist had just wakened her. She "demonstrated some looseness of associations," "at times was difficult to follow as she jumped from topic to topic," and on serial subtractions from 50 she made three errors. Having stated that the evidence was strongly *suggestive* of an organic brain syndrome (i.e., a physical disease of the brain) the psychiatrist in his Recommendations wrote: "Regarding the patient's organic brain syndrome . . ." In other words, what was initially put forward as a suggestion (and what a suggestion!) now becomes a real thing. The denial of authorship could not be more patent.

The significance of this episode is that apart from illustrating yet another horror story of hospitalization it reveals how the clinical situation becomes a combat zone of disputes over power and over definitions of illness and degrees of incapacity. The critical issue centers on the evaluation of incapacity and of feelings, such as pain, and following that on the treatment necessary. Here is where the professionals deprive the patients of their sense of certainty and security concerning their own self-judgement.

By necessity, self-awareness and self-judgement require other persons' presence and reflection. In the clinical situation, this dialectic of self and other must always favor the defining power of the other written into the aura of the healer, who must therefore treat this power with great sensitivity lest it slip away into a totally one-sided assertion of reality, remaining a relationship in name only. The healer attempts to modulate and mold the patient's self-awareness without dominating it to the point of destruction, for if that happens then the healer loses an ally in the struggle with dis-ease. Yet, as illustrated in this case study, a quite vicious procedure precludes this alliance and the patient is converted into an enemy. It is not, as Illich maintains, for example, that patients lose their autonomy. Far from it. Instead, what happens is that the modern clinical situation engenders a contradictory situation in which the patient swings like a pendulum between alienated passivity and alienated self-assertion.

Paradoxically, this follows from an ever-increasing self-consciousness on the part of health professionals to be more humane and to self-consciously allow the patient's definition of the problem a privileged place in the medical dialogue, only to co-opt that definition in a practice which becomes more rationalized as it becomes less humanized. This rationalization amounts to an attempt to wrest control from the patient and define their status for them by first compartmentalizing the person into the status of patienthood, then into the status of thinghood as opposed to that of a mutually interacting partner in an exchange, and then into the categories of Objective and Subjective, working through these reifications by an Analysis and a Plan. The analogy with the rationality of commodity production is complete. As with automobiles on the assembly-line, so with patients and with health itself, the difference, the pathos, and the occasional problem bearing mute testimony to the fact that unlike automobiles, patients do think and feel, and that sickness is as much an interactive human relationship as a thing-in-itself.

My intention here is not only to direct attention to the callousness that results. In addition, we have to deal with the complicated mystification present in healing in any culture, but which in our own modern clinical setting perniciously cannibalizes the potential source of strength for curing which reposes in the inter-subjectivity of patient and healer. In the name of the noble cause of healing, the professionals have been able to appropriate this mutuality and in a very real sense exploit a social relationship in such a way that its power to heal is converted into the power to control. The problems that ensue, at least as illustrated in this case study, lie in the very nature of the clinical setting and therefore are especially opaque to the therapists. As the chaplain so forlornly noted, "She's angry of something," and this anger stems from the contradictions which assail the patient. On the one hand she sees the capacity for "mere" patients to form a therapeutic community. But on the other hand, she denies the flowering of this potential because of her being forced to allow the professionals to appropriate her discretionary powers, while at another instant she rebels against this appropriation. The circuit of reification and re-subjectification is inherently unstable. Health professionalization of this all too common type does not guarantee the smooth control that the staff demand, let alone what patients need. All of which will assuredly be met by yet further rationalization and more professionalization.

On her later admission to hospital and shortly after first talking to me about patients supporting one another, only to claim that it required a professional therapist to help her walk, the patient suddenly refused the ministrations of the Occupational Therapists. She complained that all her day was taken up with therapy, that the Occupational Therapist took an hour a day, and that she had time neither to use the bedpan, to comb her hair, nor to listen to her religious music. "When I'm sick," she declared, "I can't work eight hours a day! And yet the whole theory of my disease and getting better is rest. And so I broke down this morning and I told the Occupational Therapist I had to cut her hour out. I've got to make an hour sometime during the day when I can just relax and not be getting in and out of a chair which hurts me severely. There's no time for anything of a personal nature . . . so the stress and the emotional conflict is there. And there's never any time to solve it by myself. And there was no place . . . because there are only eight hours. I can't put twelve hours into eight!"

Again we see that the passive alienation embodied in her relation with the professionals, which at first sight appears to be a *fait accompli*, registers an abrupt rupture, a "scene," which ripples panic amongst the staff.

The Occupational Therapists, the Physical Therapists and the Social

Workers were all deeply upset by this gesture which they saw as a denial of their efficacy and of their jobs. When I asked them why they couldn't leave her alone for a week, their leader replied, "It's my Blue Cross, Blue Shield payments as much as hers!" So, they drew up a contract with the patient, nowadays a typical procedure in the hospital as it is in many American schools.

The staff and the patient both sign a written contract stating, for example, "What you *do* have choices about," "What you do *not* have choices about," "Objectives," "What *we* will do," "What *you* will do." In this patient's case the contract stated as "objective," walk 30 feet three times a day. "What *we* will do," protect two 45 minute rest periods. "What *you* will do," try and walk. The underlying motive, as described by some theorists of medical contracting, is that the staff will reward the patient for complying with their desires (positive reinforcement), rather than falling into what is seen as the trap of the old style of doing things which, supposedly, was to reinforce noncompliance by paying more attention to such behavior than to compliance. It is, in short, Behaviorism consciously deployed on the lines of market contracts in order to achieve social control. It is the medication of business applied to the business of medicine. Rewards cited in the academic and professional journals dealing with this subject are lottery tickets, money, books, magazines, assistance in filling out insurance forms, information, and time with the "health care provider."[11] It has been found that patients often choose more time with the "health provider" and help in untangling bureaucratic snarls so as to obtain insurance benefits and medical referrals.

The very concept of the "health care provider," so disarmingly straightforward, functional, and matter-of-fact, is precisely the type of ideological labeling that drives patients into so-called noncompliance. The "health care provider," in antediluvian times known as the nurse, doctor, etc., does not provide health! Health is part of the human condition, as is disease, and the incidence and manifestations of both are heavily determined by the specificities of social organization. Health care depends for its outcome on a two-way relationship between the sick and the healer. In so far as health care is provided, *both* patient and healer are providing it, and, indeed, the concern with so-called noncompliance is testimony to that, in a back-handed way. By preestablishing the professional as the "health care provider," the inherited social legacy that constitutes medical wisdom and power is *a priori* declared to be the legitimate monopoly of those who can convince the rest of us that this wisdom comes from society and nature in a prepackaged commodity form which they and only they can dispense. And in choosing as rewards for noncompliant patients help in overcoming the snarls which the "health care providers" provided, is to heap absurdity on deception. But the real pathos in this is neither the absurdity nor the deception. It is that it appears in our day and age, to be so perfectly straightforward and reasonable. This is the mark of ideology; its naturalness. And if its nature is to be found in the realm and language of marketing, so that medical culture and healing too succumb to the idiom of business, then we must not be all that surprised. For ours is the culture of business which puts business as the goal of culture.

In the same way that freedom and a specific type of individualism came long ago to be asserted with the rise of the free market economy, so the introduction of contracting in healing today is seen by its proponents to be a bold blow for the assertion of human rights, shattering the mystification of the feudal past when patients complied with doctors' commands out of blind trust. The proponents of contracting in clinical settings also tell us that the doctrine on which it is based, Behaviorism and the "laws" of reinforcement and extinction, have led to "the treatment of maladaptive human behaviors, including psychoses, retardation, alcoholism, low work productivity, and criminality."[12]

Maladaptation is of course not a thing, but a purely normative concept traveling under the disguise of scientific jargon. More often than not it serves in contexts such as these to smuggle in a particular intention or value by making it appears to be a fact like a fact of nature. The assimilation of low work productivity, criminality, and psychosis to one another as parts of the same fact, maladaptation, and now to patients who disobey doctors' "orders," serves to remind us just how colossal a distortion is involved by reifying social relations so that pointed political values smuggled under the guise of technical constructs remain immune to criticism, stamped with the authority of the hard and impenetrable scientific fact. Once again, the nature of truth is seen to lie in the truth of nature, and not in some critical way as dependent upon the social organization of facts and nature.

In the case of the patient described in this case study we might note the following. She had every good reason for not complying with the staff's orders. This reason was not appreciated by the staff. It was seen as a threat to their power and to the coffers of Blue Cross. It was not the case, as the aforementioned authorities on contracting say, that because she was noncompliant she was getting more attention from the staff. It was totally the opposite. When she was complying she was getting too much attention, and all she wanted was free time. The immediate cause of her frustration was intimately related to the bureaucratic pressure of her daily routine. The contracting strategy chosen by the staff was thus ingeniously selected to meet this by further bureaucratizing an agreement, the contract, so as to formally deformalize her time into therapy time and "free time," time which any freedom lover would have naively thought was hers in the first place, anyway, and not something to be owned and dispensed by the staff. The idea that she was free to choose and contract, and the idea that contracting *per se* is both sign and cause of freedom, is as pernicious an illusion that the free time the staff were granting her was not rightfully hers in the first place.

The argument in favor of contracting, that it clears away the mystifications in the murky set of understandings existing between doctor and patient, that it increases the power, understanding, and autonomy of the patient, is a fraud. Moreover, it is a fraud which highlights the false consciousness as to freedom and individualism upon which our society rests. Can autonomy and freedom be really said to be increased when it is the staff which has the power to set the options and the terms of the contract? If anything, autonomy and freedom are decreased because the illusion of freedom serves to obscure its absence. Furthermore, the type of freedom at stake in the contracting amounts to a convenient justification for denying responsibility and interpersonal obligations, just as in the name of contract and free enterprise the working class at the birth of modern capitalism was told that it was as free and as equal as the capitalists with whom they had to freely contract for the sale of their labor-power. There is little difference between that situation, the capitalist labor market, and the one which concerns us wherein the clinical setting becomes a health market and one contracts as a supposedly free agent with the "health care providers" so as to grant the latter the right to appropriate the use-value power embodied in the healing process.

Far from increasing patient autonomy (as its proponents argue), the design of contracting is unabashedly manipulative.

> Requests for 15 min of uninterrupted conversation with a team member, games of checkers, cards and chess, Bible reading, discussion of current events and visits from various team members are examples of rewards chosen by patients. Such examples as these imply that patients place considerable value on our interactions with them. It also indicates that because patients value our relationships with them, we are in a powerful position for influencing the choice of behavior the patient ultimately makes; e.g., compliance versus non-compliance.[13]

Just as we were wont to believe that medical care differed from business, as in Talcott Parsons' analysis whereby the "collectivity orientation" of the medical profession was opposed to the business ethic of self-interest, only to become increasingly disillusioned, so now we find that even friendship is something to be bargained for and contracted by fifteen minute slots. After all, if health becomes a commodity to be bought and sold, is it any wonder that friendship should likewise become a commodity? And if social relations and friendship become things, like this, it is equally unsurprising that the subject becomes object to him or herself so that

> ... the patients find it very rewarding to improve their own baseline. This perhaps is the most meaningful reward of all. Improving one's baseline indicates to the patient that he is essentially competing against himself. He views himself as the one controlling his own behavior. This eliminates the need for increased interaction when the behavior is unacceptable. In other words, the patient graphically knows his behavior is unacceptable and we as professionals are free to "ignore" the unacceptable behavior.[14]

Anthropology: The Native's Point of View

If contracting represents the intrusion of one dimension of the social sciences, Behaviorism, into medical practice so as to improve and humanize medical care, then Anthropology too has something to add; namely a concern with the native's point of view. The idea here, as put forward by Kleinman et al.[15] in a recent article in the *Annals of Internal Medicine*, is that disease and illness represent two different realities and that illness is shaped by culture. *Disease* represents organ dysfunction which can be measured by the pathologist and measured in the laboratory, while *illness* is what that dysfunction means to the person suffering it. Cirrhosis of the liver, for instance, can be represented in "disease" terms: by the micropathologist in terms of the architectural distortion of tissue and cellular morphology, by the biochemist in terms of changes in enzyme levels, and so on. But to the person afflicted with the "disease," it means something else and this something else is the "illness" dimension: the cultural significance of the term "cirrhosis," the meanings read into the discomforts, symptoms, signs, and treatment of the "disease," and so on. This is the native's point of view, and it will of necessity differ from the doctor's "disease" viewpoint. Stemming from their reading of Anthropology and from their own experience with folk medicine in Third World cultures, Kleinman *et al.* hold this difference between "disease" and "illness" to be of great importance. They advocate an addition to the training of medical personnel so that they too will become aware of this difference and act on it. This they call "clinical social science" and its focus shall be with the "cultural construction of clinical reality." Learning and applying this shall improve doctor-patient relationships and the efficacy of therapy, overcoming the communication gap between the "doctor's model of disease" and the "patient's model of illness." As with contracting, noncompliance and the management of human beings is of prime concern.

> Training modern health professionals to treat both disease and illness routinely and to uncover discrepant views of clinical reality will result in measurable improvement in management and compliance, patient satisfaction, and treatment outcomes.[16]

Elucidation of the patient's model of illness will aid the clinician in dealing with conflict between their respective beliefs and values. The clinician's task is to educate the patient if the latter's model interferes with appropriate care. Education by the clinician is seen as a process of "negotiating" the different cognitive and value orientations and such negotiation "may well be the single most important step in engaging the patient's trust."[17] Like so much of the humanistic reform-mongering propounded in recent times, in which a concern with the native's point of view comes to the fore, there lurks the danger that the experts will avail themselves of that knowledge only to make the science of human management all the more powerful and coercive. For indeed there will be irreconcilable conflicts of interest and these will be "negotiated" by those who hold the upper hand, albeit in terms of a language and a practice which denies such manipulation and the existence of unequal control. The old language and practice which left important assumptions unsaid and relied on an implicit set of understandings conveyed in a relationship of trust is to be transformed. The relationship is now seen in terms of a "provider" and a "client," both "allies" in a situation of mutual concern. Kleinman *et al.* demonstrate this democratic universe in which far from cleaning up the old-fashioned mystifications as embodied in trust relationships, new mystifications are put in their place which are equally if not more disturbing. With their scheme the clinician

> . . . mediates between different cognitive and value orientations. He actively negotiates with the patient as a therapeutic ally. . . . For example, if the patient accepts the use of antibiotics but believes that the burning of incense or the wearing of an amulet or a consultation with a fortune-teller is also needed, the physician must understand this belief but need not attempt to change it. If, however, the patient regards penicillin as a "hot" remedy inappropriate for a "hot" disease and is therefore unwilling to take it, one can negotiate ways to "neutralize" penicillin or one must attempt to persuade the patient of the incorrectness of his belief, a most difficult task.[18]

It is a strange "alliance" in which one party avails itself of the other's private understandings in order to manipulate them all the more successfully. What possibility is there in this sort of alliance for the patient to explore the *doctor's* private model of both disease *and* illness, and negotiate that? Restricted by the necessity to perpetuate professionalism and the ironclad distinction between clinician and patient, while at the same time exhorting the need and advantage of taking cultural awareness into account, these authors fail to see that it is not the "cultural construction of clinical reality" that needs dragging into the light of day, but instead it is the clinical construction of reality that is at issue.

The Cultural Construction of Clinical Reality, or the Clinical Construction of Culture?

This is where sensitive anthropological understanding truly sheds light. The doctors and the "health care providers" are no less immune to the social construction of reality than the patients they minister, and the reality of concern is as much defined by power and control as by colorful symbols of culture, incense, amulets, fortune-telling, hot-and-cold, and so forth.

What is significant is that at this stage of medicine and the crises afflicting it, such a project should emerge. What is happening is that for the first time in the modern clinical situation, an attempt is underway to make explicit what was previously implicit, but that this archaeology of the implicit cannot escape the demands for professional control. The patient's so-called model of illness differs most significantly from the clinician's not in terms of exotic symbolization but in terms of the anxiety to locate the social and moral meaning of the disease. The clinician cannot allow this anxiety to gain either legitimacy or to include ever-widening spheres of social relationships, including that of the hospital and the clinician, for more often than not once this process of thought is given its head it may well condemn as much as accept the contemporary constitution of social relationships and society itself.

Attempts such as those advocated by Kleinman *et al.* to make explicit what was previously implicit, merely seize on the implicit with the instruments of modern social science so to all the better control it. Yet in doing so they unwittingly reveal all the more clearly the bare bones of what really goes on in an apparently technical clinical encounter by way of manipulation and mediation of contradictions in society.

The immediate impulse for this archaeology of the implicit, this dragging into consciousness what was previously left unsaid or unconscious in medical practice, comes at a time when the issue of the so-called noncompliant patient (like the illiterate schoolchild) is alarming the medical establishment, now concerned as never before with the rationalization of the health assembly-line and with rising costs. In this regard, it is a scandal and also self-defeating to appeal to Anthropology for evidence as to the power of concepts like the "patient's model" and the difference between the "how" and the "why" of "disease" and "illness." For the medical anthropology of so-called "primitive" societies also teaches us that medicine is preeminently an instrument of social control. It teaches us that the "why" or "illness" dimension of sickness bears precisely on what makes life meaningful and worthwhile, compelling one to examine the social and moral causes of sickness, and that those causes lie in communal and reciprocal inter-human considerations which are antithetical to the bases of modern social organization patterned on the necessities of capitalist and bureaucratic prerogatives. As Victor Turner concludes in his discussion of the Ndembu doctor in rural Zambia:

It seems that the Ndembu "doctor" sees his task less as curing an individual patient than as remedying the ills of a corporate group. The sickness of the patient is mainly a sign that "something is rotten" in the corporate body. The patient will not get better until all the tensions and aggressions in the groups interrelations have been brought to light and exposed to ritual treatment ... The doctor's task is to tap the various streams of affect associated with these conflicts and with the social and interpersonal disputes in which they are manifested, and to channel them in a socially positive direction. The raw energies of conflict are thus domesticated in the service of the traditional social order.[19]

And Lévi-Strauss reminds us in his essay, "The Sorcerer and His Magic," that the rites of healing readapt society to predefined problems through the medium of the patient; that this process rejuvenates and even elaborates the society's essential axioms.[20] Charged with the emotional load of suffering and of abnormality, sickness sets forth a challenge to the complacent and everyday acceptance of conventional structures of meaning. The doctor and the patient come together in the clinic. No longer can the community watch them and share in this work. Nevertheless, whether the patient wants to accept penicillin or not, whether the rest of us are physically present in the clinic or not, the doctor and the patient are curing the threat posed to convention and to society, tranquilizing the disturbance that sickness unleashes against normal thought which is not a static system but a system waxing, consolidating and dissolving on the reefs of its contradictions. It is not the cultural construction of clinical reality that is here at issue, but the clinical construction and reconstruction of a commoditized reality that is at stake. Until that is recognized, and acted upon, humanistic medicine is a contradiction of terms.

MALEFICIUM:
STATE FETISHISM

We spent our time fleeing from the objective into the subjective and from the
subjective into objectivity. This game of hide-and-seek will end only when we
have the courage to go to the limits of ourselves in both directions at once. At
the present time, we must bring to light the subject, the guilty one, that monstrous
and wretched bug which we are likely to become at any moment. Genêt holds
the mirror up to us: we must look at it and see ourselves.

—Sartre, *Saint Genêt*

I: THE STATE AS FETISH

My concern lies with this endless flight in modern times back and forth
from the hard-edged thing to its ephemeral ghost and back again, which, in
what must surely seem a wild gesture, I see as a spin-off of what I plan to
call *State fetishism*, so studiously, so dangerously, ignored by the great theorists
of the poetics of the commodity-fetish such as Walter Benjamin and T. W.
Adorno, with the crucial exception of the implications of the latter's early
work with Max Horkheimer on German fascism in *Dialectic of Enlightenment*.[1]
It is to the peculiar sacred and erotic attraction, even thralldom, combined
with disgust, which the State holds for its subjects, that I wish to draw
attention in my drawing the figure of State fetishism, and here we would do
well to recall that for Nietzsche, good and evil, intertwined in the double
helix of attraction and repulsion, are so much aesthetic-moralistic renderings
of the social structure of might. Given the considerable, indeed massive,
might of the modern State, it would seem obvious enough that here we
encounter the most fabulous machination for such rendering: "I know
nothing sublime," wrote the young Edmund Burke in his enquiry into our
ideas of the beautiful, "which is not some modification of power."[2] But how
is it possible to emote an abstraction, and what do I mean by State fetishism?

I mean a certain aura of might as figured by the Leviathan in Hobbes'
rendering as that "mortal god," or, in a quite different mode, by Hegel's

intricately argued vision of the State as not merely the embodiment of reason, of the Idea, but also as an impressively organic unity, something much greater than the sum of its parts.[3] We are dealing with an obvious yet neglected topic, clumsily if precisely put as the cultural constitution of the modern State—with a big S—the fetish quality of whose holism can be nicely brought to our self-awareness by pointing not only to the habitual way we so casually entify "the State" as a being unto itself, animated with a will and mind of its own, but also by pointing to the not infrequent signs of exasperation provoked by the aura of the big S—as with Shlomo Avineri, for instance, writing in the Introduction to his *Hegel's Theory of the Modern State*:

> Once one writes 'State' rather than 'state,' Leviathan and Behemoth are already casting their enormous and oppressive shadows,

while the celebrated anthropologist, A.R. Radcliffe (in his student days nicknamed "Anarchy") Brown, in the preface to the classic *African Political Systems* (first published in 1940) also puts his finger on the palpable unreality of State fetishism when he denounces it as *fictional*.[4] Yet he writes as if mere words, very much including his own, were weapons; being such they can whisk away the spell of their own mischief.

> In writings on political institutions there is a good deal of discussion about the nature and origin of the State, which is usually represented as being an entity over and above the human individuals who make up a society, having as one of its attributes something called 'sovereignty,' and some-times spoken of as having a will (law being often defined as the will of the State) or as issuing commands. *The State in this sense does not exist in the phenomenal world; it is a fiction of the philosophers.*[5]

"What does exist," he goes on to declaim, "is an organization, i.e. a collection of individual human beings connected to a complex set of relations." He insists that "there is no such thing as the power of the State; there are only, in reality, powers of individuals—kings, prime ministers, magistrates, policemen, party bosses and voters." Please note here the repeated emphasis on Being—on "what does exist," and powers contained therein. It's all so plausible at first and so desirable too, this seduction by real policemen, real kings, and real voters. And don't think I'm pulling your leg here. Jean Genêt might pull at the policemen's penis in search of the really real. But we who might learn some lessons about Stately reality from Anarchy Brown and the genealogy of Anthropology figured by his stately presence should pause and think about why he is so hostile to what he describes as the fiction of the State—the big S. For what the notion of State fetishism directs us to is precisely the existence and reality of the *political power* of this *fiction*, its powerful insubstantiality.

The State as Mask

Some thirty years after Radcliffe-Brown's dismissive *pronunciamiento* on the unreality of the big S, Philip Abrams in a truly path-breaking analysis, referred to this fiction in a way at once more clear and complicating:

> The state is not the reality which stands behind the mask of political practice. It is itself the mask which prevents our seeing political practice as it is [and] it starts its life as an implicit construct; it is then reified— as the *res publica*, the public reification, no less—and acquires an overt symbolic identity progressively divorced from practice as an illusory account of practice.[6]

And he calls on sociologists to attend to the senses in which the state does *not* exist. Like Avineri he sees the big S as misrepresentation—Radcliffe-Brown's "fiction"—yet credits it, as does Avineri, with mighty force, not merely in the maw of Leviathan but more to the point in work-a-day "democracies" such as Great Britain's, where "armies and prisons, the Special patrol and the deportation orders as well as the whole process of fiscal extraction" depend critically on State fetishism.[7] For, he argues, it is the association of these repressive instruments "with the idea of the state and the invocation of that idea that silences protest, excuses force and convinces the rest of us that the fate of the victims is just and necessary."[8]

Now the question has to be raised as to what can be done to this misrepresentation by means of which reification acquires alarming fetish-power? Abrams' striking figure of mask and reality—of the State as not the reality behind the mask of political reality, but *as the mask* which prevents us seeing political reality—is a dazzling and disturbing representation. For it not only implicates the State in the cultural construction of reality, but delineates that reality as masked and inherently deceptive, real and unreal at one and the same time—in short, a thoroughly nervous Nervous System.

Therefore how strikingly fitting, how (unintentionally) magical, is Abrams's response to the power of the reality-effect of the mask. "My suggestion," he writes,

> is that we should recognize that cogency of the *idea* of the state as an ideological power and treat that as a compelling object of analysis. But the very reasons that require us to do that also require us not to *believe* in the idea of the state, not to concede, even as an abstract formal-object, the existence of the state.[9]

And as an inspired dada-like shock tactic exercise in how to pull this off, he recommends that we should, as an experiment, try substituting the word *God* for the word *state*—which is exactly what I intend to do, since State fetishism begs just such an excursus, provided one is up to dealing with the profound ambiguity which, according to one track of influential Western analysis, the sacred is said to contain.

The Impure Sacred

What I want to consider is the everlastingly curious notion, bound to raise hackles, that not only God but evil is part of the notion of sacredness—that bad is not just bad but holy to boot. Emile Durkheim labeled this holy evil in 1912 as "impure sacred" and scantly illustrated it in but seven pages in his major work on primitive religion, by reference to the fresh human corpse, to the forces conjured by the sorcerer, and the blood issuing from the genital organs of women—all of which, he insisted, from his ethnographic evidence from central Australia as much as from W. Robertson Smith's *The Religion of the Semites*, inspired men with fear, into which horror generally entered, yet could, through a simple modification of external circumstance, become holy and propitious powers endowing life. While according to this formulation there is the most radical anatagonism between the pure and the impure sacred, there is, nevertheless, close kinship between them as exhibited in the fact that the respect accorded the pure sacred is not without a measure of horror, and the fear accorded the impure sacred is not without reverence. Hence not just Genêt the homosexual in a homophobic society, not just Genêt the thief, in a State built on the right to property, but Saint Genêt.

Reason & Violence

Before you use a military force, you should use the force of reason.
—Governor Mario Cuomo[10]

Where this confluence of the pure with the impure sacred is most relevant to the modern State is where the crucial issue of "legitimacy" of the institution abuts what Max Weber regarded as a crucial part of the definition of the State—namely, its monopoly of the legitimate use of violence within a given territory. The other part of that definition, of course, as with Hegel's, was the State's embodiment of Reason, as in the bureaucratic forms.

What needs emphasis here is how this conjuncture of violence and reason is so obvious, and yet is at the same time denied, and therefore how important it is for acute understanding of the cultural practice of Statecraft to appreciate the very obtuseness of this obviousness, as when we scratch our heads about the concept of "war crimes"—it being legal for the US State to incessantly bomb the Iraqi enemy, but a crime for the Iraqi State to beat up the pilots dropping the bombs. Such legal niceties testify to the self-contradictory yet ever more necessary attempts to rationalize violence.

That is why there is something frightening, I think, merely in saying that this conjunction of reason and violence exists, not only because it makes violence scary, imbued with the greatest legitimating force there can be, reason itself, and not only because it makes reason scary by indicating how it's snuggled deep into the armpit of terror, but also because we so desperately need to cling to reason—as instituted—as the bulwark against the terrifying anomie and chaos pressing in on all sides. There has to be a reason, and we have to use reason. Yet another part of us welcomes the fact that reason—as instituted—has violence at its disposal, because we feel that that very anomie and chaos will respond to naught else. And consider how we slip in and out of recognizing and disavowal. Consider this as Stately cultural practice. Nothing could be more obvious than that the State, with its big S rearing, uses the sweet talk of reason and reasonable rules as its velvet glove around the fist of steel. This is folklore. This is an instinctual way of reacting to the big S. But on the other hand this conjunction of reason-and-violence rapidly becomes confusing when we slow down a little and try to figure it out: so much reason versus so many units of violence? the mere threat of violence hovering way in the background of Kafka's cave? different types of people affected in different places and different times get a different mix? And so forth. Weber himself registers this latent yet vital presence of violence where he notes in his famous essay, "Politics As A Vocation," delivered at Munich University in 1918, that even with the legitimacy of domination based on rationally created rules, which he portrays as "the domination exercised by the modern 'servant of the state' and by all bearers of power who in this respect resemble him," that "it is to be understood that, in reality, obedience is determined by highly robust motives of fear and hope."[11]

And in noting Weber's inclusion if not emphasis on violence as what defined the modern State, we cannot forget how decidedly flat, how instrumental, his notion of violence generally seems to be; how decidedly reified it is, as if violence were a substance, so many ergs of spermatic effluvial power that the father exerts in the private fastness of the family, with permission of the State, and that the State exerts over civil society and, at times, over other States. What is missing here, and I mean this to be a decisive critique, is the intrinsically mysterious, mystifying, convoluting, plain scary, mythical, and arcane cultural properties and power of violence to the point where violence is very much an end in itself—a sign, as Benjamin put it, of the existence of the gods.[12]

So, what I wish to suggest with considerable urgency is that what is politically important in my notion of State fetishism is that this necessary institutional interpenetration of reason by violence not only diminishes the claims of reason, casting it into ideology, mask, and effect of power, but also that *it is precisely the coming together of reason-and-violence in the State that creates, in a secular and modern world, the bigness of the big S*—not merely its apparent unity and the fictions of will and mind thus inspired, but the auratic and quasisacred quality of that very inspiration, a quality we quite willingly impute to the ancient States of China, Egypt, and Peru, for example, or to European Absolutism, but not to the rational-legal State that now stands as ground to our being as citizens of the world.

1886, A Surreal Moment, The Reemergence of the Sacred: Torture Should Give Way to Totemism

W. Robertson Smith (author of *The Religion of the Semites*), wrote a letter in 1886 to the publisher of the *Encyclopaedia Britannica*, of which he was editor:[13]

> I hope that Messrs. Black [publishers of the *Encyclopaedia Britannica*] understand that Totemism is a subject of growing importance, daily mentioned in magazines and papers, but of which there is no good account anywhere—precisely one of those cases where we have an opportunity of being ahead of every one and getting some reputation. There is no article in the volume for which I am more solicitous. I have taken much personal pains with it, guiding [James George] Frazer carefully in his treatment; and he has put about seven months' hard work on it to make it the standard article on the subject. We must make room for it, whatever else goes. "Torture," though a nice paper, is not at all necessary, for people can learn about torture elsewhere, and the subject is one of decaying and not of rising interest.

The State As Sacred: Rejuxtaposing the Colonial Gaze

Elsewhere—always elsewhere. Decay. But a nice paper. Such is the fate of torture, especially in the face of the rising star of Totemism. So much for the decline of the sacred. That is why the restoration of that mysterious entity as an object worthy of study by Georges Bataille's College of Sociology group in the late 1930s, and precisely its attempt to examine the place of the sacred in the modern State, strikes me as a timely task—one that I myself see as involving a somewhat larger project, yet to be worked out, namely that of rejuxtaposing the terms of the colonial inquiry, recycling and thus transforming the anthropology developed in Europe and North America through the study of colonized peoples back into and onto the societies in which it was instituted, where the terms and practices imposed upon and appropriated from the colonies, like *fetish, sorcery* (the *maleficium*), and *taboo*, are redeemed and come alive with new intensity.[14] As will become obvious from even this short attempt, such a rejuxtaposition is hardly a simple practice, certainly more than just reversing the light from the dark zones of empire. Let us being with the fetish.

The Fetish: Genealogy of Making

Bill Pietz has presented us with a genealogy of the *fetish* that grounds this eminently strange word in a western history of *making*, rooted in strategic social relationships of trade, religion, slaving, and modern science.[15] To this end he discusses certain social practices in the commerce of ancient Rome (separating natural products from *factitious*, artificially cultivated, ones), in early Roman Christianity (with God making man in His image, but man denied, therefore, similar sorts of making), in the "bad making" of the *maleficium* of the magic of the Middle Ages, in the notion of the fetish or *fetisso* in the Portuguese pidgin trading language of the West African slave routes, and, finally, in the Positivist rendering of fetishism as the sheen or mystical component of the Positivist worship of objectness itself. Quite a story.

To develop and bring to our comprehension a genealogy like this strikes me as curiously analogous to the fetish itself, in that such genealogizing assumes that the meaning of the word bears traces of epochal histories of trading with the edges of the known universe and that, although it is these traces which endow the word—as Raymond Williams in his *Keywords* might have said—with an active social history pushing into and activated by the present, these trace-meanings are nevertheless lost to present consciousness.[16] What is left, and what is active and powerful, is the word itself, enigmatically incomplete. Just the signifier, we could say, bereft of its erased significations gathered and dissipated through the mists of trade, religion, witchcraft, slavery, and what has come to be called science—and this is precisely the formal mechanism of fetishism (as we see it used by Marx and by Freud), whereby the signifier depends upon yet erases its signification.

What Pietz does for us with his genealogizing is restore certain traces and erasures and weave a spell around what is, socially speaking, at stake in *making*. This amounts to a European history of consciousness making itself though making objects, and this involves a compulsion to fuse and separate and fuse once again the maker with the making with the thing made, wrestling with poignancy and urgency with what we might call Vico's insight, which is also Marx's—God made nature, but it is man who makes history and thus can come to understand it by understanding this making. In short, the fetish takes us into the realm of praxis and to genealogize the fetish the way Pietz does is in effect to problematize praxis—the subject of making itself through making the object—and by the same token this take us into the realm of what has come to be called "agency"—the vexing problem of individual versus social determination. Now in the genealogy of fetishism as I write it, this vexing issue can be translated into a confrontation of sorcery with sociology, the sorcery of the *maleficium* that informed the fetish-word in the era of Iberian expansion into Africa and the colonization of the New World, on the other hand, and *sociology* as with Comte's successor Emile Durkheim, the sociologist's sociologist, on the other. It is to sociology as a form of inquiry enlivened by fetish powers that I now turn, and later, with Genêt, to the revelatory epistemology of the *maleficium*.

II: SOCIOLOGY

It was Durkheim and not the savage who made society into a god.
E.E. Evans-Pritchard, *Nuer Religion*[17]

How strange and multitudinous a notion "society" becomes when we thingify it, as if this very act makes it slip away from us. "Social facts are things," Durkheim grimly reiterated time and again in *The Rules of Sociological Method* (first published 1895), desperate to nail down this elusive thinghood. Things of God or things made? we might with a twinge of anxiety ask in turn, pondering the place of things-made in the abyss created between God and the sorcerer. And in keeping with that discourse, should we not allow the terminology to more fully express its sacral bent, and instead of saying social facts are *things*, say social facts are *reification*, thus entering not only into the sacrosanct language of Latin but into the holy darkness created by the Luckacsian *thing* (as in "Reification and the Consciousness of the Proletariat")? Thus Steven Lukes, in his study of Durkheim, aptly pin-points the crucial flip-flop from *res* to *deus*, the instability at the heart of the fetishization of "society"—from thing to god:

> Hence, above all, his [Durkheim's] talk of *"la société"* as a "reality" distinct from the "individual," which led him to reify, even deify "society," to treat it as a *deus ex machina*, to attribute to it "powers and qualities as mysterious and baffling as any assigned to the gods by the religions of this world."[18]

The dismay expressed by exponents of Anglo common sense at what is seen as mysticism in Durkheim's sociology is as ubiquitous as it is self-defeating. Hence the valiant attempts (as with Radcliffe-Brown for example) to extract social facticity clean of its mystical penumbra. Take this heroic attempt to sever the Durkheimian twins, the social *fact* from the social *conscience collectif* in the Introduction to the English translation of the *Rules*:

> Durkheim's method, most suggestive in itself, yet involves, it so happens, the use of the hypothesis of a collective consciousness; it results in a deplorable effort to interpret social phenomena in terms of this alleged consciousness [and thus] Durkheim is not singular among men of science in being more valuable in respect of the byproducts of his theory than in his main contention.[19]

And that erratic genius, Georges Sorel, himself no slouch when it came to both using and theorizing the powers of mystery in modern society (as in his *Reflections on Violence*, 1915), claimed that Durkheim said it was unnecessary to introduce the notion of a social mind, but reasoned as if he were introducing it.[20]

In that formidably important book, *The Structure of Social Action* (1937), Talcott Parsons represents this flip-flop from thing to god, not as the inevitable outcome of the very concept of "society," but as a movement embedded in a more familiarly acceptable form, that of narrative—an adventure of ideas in which first there was Durkheim of the Rules and of The Division of Labor, the positivist empiricist who understood social facts to be things, external and constraining *faits sociaux*, and then, years later, there emerged a new Durkheim, the idealist, beginning with his desire to identify the crucial quality of social facticity as legal and normative rules resulting, finally, with his emphasis on the weave of moral obligations as the constitutive basis to "society."[21]

We will have need to recall this adventure of ideas from *thing* to *deus* through the various types of rules—of fact, of law, of norm, and of morality—when we come to a certain sexual quality of the law and of breaking the law, the beauty and libidinality of transgression, and the place of the sacred in the profanity of modern life, particularly French versions of that life, from Georges Bataille's College of (non-Parsonian) Sociology of the late 1930s, onward into the post war period with Jean Genêt. Suffice it to reinforce the point that this noble attempt to invent for the Founding Father of Sociology a narrative of the concept "society," first thing, then God, is the consequence of the inability to appreciate that the concept *is both these simultaneously* and, in any event, the fetish character of the "social fact" as sheer thing and as moral thing is here strikingly conveyed. Which brings us to totems, their sacred power, and the rule of old men.

Intoxication

The fetish is extensively theorized—not as fetish but as totem[22]—in what is in many ways Durkheim's greatest work, *The Elementary Forms of Religious Life* (1912), the work that Parsons sees as occupying the fulcrum in the adventure of ideas where the thing becomes a god.[23] There is poignancy in Parson's representation of this travail of ideas from thing to God, for it is an inexorable journey and the stakes are high—the base of knowledge itself. Parsons writes:

> This tendency [to emphasize the idea and value factor in the constitution of society] culminated in his sociological epistemology where he identified the social factor with the a priori source of the [Kantian] categories, thus finally breaking the bond which had held it as a part of empirical reality. But having done this it was impossible for him to get back to empirical reality.[24]

It must be chilling to lock yourself out of empirical reality. But when confronted by the fact that it was this very "sociological epistemology" that allowed for the brilliance of the *Année sociologique* school, I wonder if it was such a terrible fate. My argument, of course, is that this brilliance was not the result of a narrative step-by-step development from social fact as thing to social fact as moral web and the fetishization of Society (as *deus*), but instead it was the result of a specific epistemic tension within the very notion of the Social as both thing and godly at one and the same time. In other words, far from being an unfortunate side effect, it was Durkheim's very fetishization of "society" that provided the intellectual power of his sociology. Reification-and-fetishism—*thing-and-deus*—was a powerful mode of reckoning in modern society, nowhere more so than when applied to "society" itself, and Durkheim was correct in problematizing—to the degree of fanaticism—the invisible presence, the intangibility, the literally unspeakable but begging to be spoken nature of "society." That is why I think it so half-hearted, so mindlessly self-congratulatory, to incessantly make the criticism that he (to follow Lukes)

> reified [the distinctions between society and the individual] into the abstractions of "society" and the "individual." Indeed as Morris Ginsberg justly observed, "in general 'la société' had an intoxicating effect on his mind, hindering further analysis."[25]

But as against these strictures of Messrs Ginsberg and Lukes isn't it this very intoxication that, far from hindering, facilitates further analysis? Instead of trying to cleave what is taken to be sober from intoxicated thought, why not seize upon the intoxication itself and wonder why—as so named—it is so necessary and powerful a force in this influential Sociology centrally located in the Positivist tradition? As Walter Benjamin, following the Surrealists, might have elaborated on his insight into modern society as animated by new mythic powers located in the tactility of the commodity-image, the task is neither to resist nor admonish the fetish quality of modern culture, but rather to acknowledge, even submit to its fetish-powers, and attempt to channel them in revolutionary directions. Get with it! Get in touch with the fetish!

In Touch With the Fetish: Inscription and Erasure

A picture keeps swimming in and out of focus in *The Elementary Forms*. It comes from Baldwin Spencer and Frank J. Gillen's two pioneering ethnographies (1899, 1904) of people native to central and north-central Australia, and it concerns the character of sacred objects called Churinga, the way they are touched and rubbed, the way they are emblematized with abstract designs and—according to Durkheim—stand in some ineffably complex way, involving the erasure of their meaning as signs, for the abstraction that is our old otherwise unrepresentable friend, "society," itself. It turns out that it is from the peculiar way these objects embody *and* erase that embodiment of society, that their sacred power derives.

To read Durkheim is to feel the force of these mysterious objects, standing at the center of group cults and thought by many anthropologists at one time to represent, as "totemism," a universal stage in the history of religions and serving to hold a group together. Concentrating great power, which "radiates to a distance and communicates itself to all the surroundings," having marvelous properties to heal sickness and ensure the reproduction of animal and plant life, the powers of these sacred objects can be communicated to officiants and their assistants by being "rubbed over the members and stomachs of the faithful after being covered with grease."[27] Throughout the *Elementary Forms* (as Rodney Needham and Roger Keesing have pointed out) Durkheim is disposed to reify whatever it is that is meant by sanctity, representing it as a spreading force such as might be conveyed by electricity or by fluids, unprepared contact with which can be shocking and even fatal.[28]

It is, strangely enough, the designs on the Churinga—the designs in themselves, the mark—that seem to Durkheim crucial to this force.

> Now in themselves, the churinga are objects of wood and are distinguished from profane things of the same sort by only one particularity: this is that the totemic mark is drawn or engraved upon them. *So it is the mark and this alone which gives them their sacred character.*[29]

Absolutely crucial to this argument is that the mark, which bestows sanctity, is in itself not only sanctifying but *is more sacred than what it represents*—the totem, animal species, whatever. Let us take this step by step.

Durkheim stresses that the sacred nature of the object comes not from imputations of an inner soul or from the object being an image of an ancestor's body, but that the sacred power

> comes to it, then, from some other source, and whence could it come, if not from the totemic stamp which it bears? It is to this image, therefore, that the demonstrations of the rite are really addressed; it is this which sanctifies the object upon which it is carved.[30]

The designs represent specific things, what he calls *totems*, such as trees, frogs, kangaroos. But the designs themselves are stupendously abstract, dots and circles—which fact Durkheim seizes upon with the curiously mimetic argument that this abstraction indicates the diffuse and abstract character of "society" (which, in his reading, the design stands for).[31] In the picture of a design of the frog totem (dreaming) I would have liked to have presented from Spencer and Gillen's 1899 monograph, the three large concentric circles—according to their "level" of interpretation—represent celebrated eucalyptus trees along the Hugh River at Imanda which, Spencer and Gillen

This empty space is where I would liked to have presented Spencer and Gillen's drawing of the frog totem because it seems to me next to impossible to get the points about representation across without this amazing image. But my friend Professor Annette Hamilton, of Macquarie University, Sydney, tells me that to reproduce the illustration would be considered sacrilege by Aboriginal people—which vindicates not only the power of the design but of the prohibitions against its being seen, strenuously noted but not observed by Spencer and Gillen themselves.

say, is the center of the group of the frog totem to which the owner of the totem belongs.[32]

The straight lines on one side of the Churinga represent the trees' large roots, and the little curves lines at one end stand for the smaller roots. Note that frogs are said to come out of the roots of these trees. Smaller concentric circles represent smaller roots of trees and, what to me is a radical shift in representational logic, the dotted lines alongside the edge of the Churinga are tracks of frogs hopping in the sand of the river bed. We would probably want to call this an abstract—a super-abstract—representation, but it has a decidedly mimetic concreteness to it also, as registered by those frog-tracks. This type of abstraction thus turns out to be curiously complex—like the fetish itself; spiritually material, materialistically spiritual.

Now this peculiar conflation and destabilization of (what we generally take to be) abstraction and figuration is intimately bound to the most decisive operation Durkheim carries out in order to derive the very notion of "society" as well as its sacred quality. I want you to hold these things together—the image of the old men hugging their totems; the terrific physicality of those mysterious objects; the central importance Durkheim gives to the design over and beyond what the design represents; the curious abstractness of the design—and I want you to realize that everything turns on his proposal that the representation is more important than the represented, that the totemic design itself is not only sacred and powerful, but more so than the totemic species or entity it represents, and more so than the clan it also represents, because it *in some way* represents the great and complex abstraction "society." The question then fairly becomes: what is this way—the way, we might say, of the fetish itself?

What seems crucial in this predominance of the signifier over the signified is a certain materialization; materialization by inscription. The elementary forms are not, to Durkheim's way of thinking, to be saddled with the Ur-presence of voice, nor with the hand-wringing of Lévi-Strauss's appraisal of *civilization* (as in White Man's Civilization) as a writing lesson.[33] To the contrary, writing is the elementary form, lying at the very beginnings of thought itself, in its aboriginality. For Durkheim it is the visual and tactile image which is crucial, not the spoken sign.[34] Furthermore, the representation of the totem by means of a design is, he feels, in response to the basic need to create an image, *no matter what the image is itself!* Put otherwise, the image here is an image of the need for images. In Durkheim's words, the Australian's urge to represent the totem

> is in order not to have a portrait of it before his eyes which would constantly renew the sensation of it; it is merely because he feels the need of representing the idea which he forms of it by means of material and external signs, *no matter what these signs may be.*[35]

Given that these signs are of aesthetic value as well as being, he says, "above all, a written language," it follows, he says—in one breathtaking swoop—that the origins of design and writing are one and the same and that man "commenced designing, not so much to fix upon wood or stone beautiful forms which charm the senses, as to translate his thought into matter."[36]

The Fetish is Where Thought and Object Interpenetrate in the Signification of Collective Sentiment

It is of course to this very reciprocation of thought in worked matter, and of worked matter into thought, that much of the puzzle (and all of the power) of fetishism lies. This is where I began, following Pietz' genealogy of the fetish, from ancient Roman trading through modern slaving, as a genealogy of praxis, of the maker making him/herself. And this reciprocation of thought in worked matter and of such matter in thought is crucial to Durkheim's most basic propositions concerning the nature of thought and its relation to "society." Elsewhere in the *Elementary Forms*, the Father of Sociology states that "in general a collective sentiment can become conscious of itself only by being fixed upon some material object; but by virtue of this very fact [and this is what is so, remarkably, crucial], *it participates in the nature of this object, and reciprocally, the object participates in its nature.*"[37] He also states that "the emblem is not merely a convenient process for clarifying the sentiment society has of itself; it also serves to create this sentiment; it is one of its constituent elements."

So much for the social construction of signs as arbitrary!

Sociology as the Art of Magical Correspondences

This reciprocation of collective thought in matter and of matter in collective thought, such that worked-upon matter itself acquires an animated and hence a fetish character, is crucial for what Talcott Parsons calls Durkheim's "sociological epistemology," whereby Durkheim sociologizes Kant's schematism with often wonderful results (as is also the case, for instance, in the gemlike essay of his colleague, Robert Hertz, "On the Predominance of the Right Hand").[38] What I think is exceedingly remarkable here is not only the boldness of Durkheim's sociological argument that Kant's a priori categories of space, time, cause, and so forth, stem from and express socially established classification as in settlement pattern and kinship, but that the epistemic basis of the science of sociology he was forging depends completely on an unacknowledged yet profoundly magical notion of natural correspondences.[39]

He asks whether the (Kantian) categories, because they directly translate social organization, can be applied to rest of nature only as metaphors, as "artificial symbols" with "no connection with reality." And he answers with a decisive No! The connections are real and not artificial because society is part of nature—that is why "ideas elaborated on the model of social things can aid us in thinking of another department of nature."

> It is at least true that if these ideas play the role of symbols when they are turned aside from their original signification, *they are at least well-founded symbols.* If a sort of artificiality enters into them from the mere fact that they are constructed concepts, it is an artificiality which follows nature very closely and which is constantly approaching it still more closely.[40]

In other words, it is the *social* origin of the ideas of time, space, class, cause, or personality, that leads to the theorem that "they are not without foundation in the nature of things."[41]

Where does this leave us with regard to (Durkheimian) Sociology—the modern science of man? What seemed like the most rigorous case that could ever be put for a science of society seeing society as an autonomous sphere now suddenly collapses, imploding into nature, with which it becomes subtly congruous.

This I take to be the law of the fetish itself. The most rigorously sociological sociology in the history of Western Man turns out to be bound, hand and foot to fetishism from which it is itself inseparable, and of which it becomes exemplary.

The Peeling Off of the Signifier and the Power Thereof

Durkheim provides spell-binding evocations of what I can only call imageric seduction, first of the natives, then—through them—of us. "It is the emblem that is sacred," he reiterates, and in noting that it can be painted on the body and on the rock face of caves, he attempts to invoke the attitude of the beholders toward the image drawn in human blood on the sand for the Intichiuma ("life-endowing") ritual of the emu totem.

> When the design has been made the faithful remain seated on the ground before it, in attitude of the purest devotion. If we give the word a sense

corresponding to the mentality of the primitive, we may say that they adore it.[42]

Here we are inching toward a critical dismantling of the sign in which the image lifts off from what it is meant to represent. In this peeling off of the signifier from its signified, *the representation acquires not just the power of the represented, but power over it, as well.*

The representations of the totem are therefore more actively powerful than the totem itself.[43]

It is fascinating that what we might call (with some perplexity) the *image itself* should be granted such a power—not the signified, the sacred totemic species, animal, vegetable, and so forth, but the signifier is itself prized apart from its signification so as to create a quite different architecture of the sign—an architecture in which the signified is erased. Thus can Durkheim make his final claim that what is "represented" by sacred objects is "society" itself:

Totemism is the religion, not of such and such animals or men or images, but of an anonymous and impersonal force, found in each of these beings but not to be confounded with any of them.[44]

Which force, for Jean Baudrillard, in the form of the image, would be the anonymous and impersonal one of the latest form of the commodity; the force of the capitalist market functioning at its silkiest postmodern best. Which force, for Marx, in the form of commodity fetishism, would exist and be effective *precisely on account of erasure*—of the erasure locked into the commodity in its exchange-value phase ensuring its dislocation, its being prized apart from the social and particularist context of its production. Which force, for Durkheim, is "society."[45]

This process of inscription and erasure finds an uncannily mimetic representation in Spencer and Gillen's description of the Churinga of the Arunta people of the central desert, and like all mimesis it inheres in the biological organism, in this case the aged male body, the hands and the stomach, into which the design disappears. While most Churinga have patterns incised with tooth of an opossum, they write, many are "scarcely decipherable, owing to the constant rubbing to which they have been subjected at the hands of generation after generation of natives." For "whenever the Churinga are examined by the old men they are, especially the wooden ones, very carefully rubbed over with the hands" and pressed against the stomach.[46]

III: MALEFICIUM; THE BAD-MAKING

In Pietz' genealogy of the fetish, the *maleficium*, or the sorcerer's "bad-making," enjoys a substantial place in the layering of histories that stratify the fetish-word. This seems particularly the case for the contribution of the *maleficio* in the Iberian Peninsula at the time of Portuguese slave trading along the West coast of Africa, and later on during the time of the Spanish expansion into the New World. Hence, as an instance of what I earlier proposed as the rejuxtapositioning of anthropology, I would now like not so much to *study* the sorcerer's tool of the *maleficium* as to *deploy* it as a tactic for drawing out some of the fetish power of the modern State. My deployment is unabashedly plagiaristic and comes in the name of Genêt, Saint Genêt who, because of the maleficent role in which Society cast him, and which he so manifestly made the most of, was able, to the extent that love be not blind, to illuminate the fetish force of Stately prowess. My use of Genêt as *maleficium* is not to ensorcel anyone, least of all readers or the State, but rather to do what I have seen the *maleficio* so good at doing over my years spent with healers in southwest Colombia, which is to stir the pot of discussion and scratch heads as to the perennial problems of understanding evil and misfortune in relation to social process. The *maleficio*, in other words, brings out the sacred sheen of the secular, the magical underbelly of nature, and this is especially germane to an inquiry into State fetishism in that (as I have discussed earlier, following Durkheim's view of the sacred) the pure and the impure sacred are violently at odds and passionately interlocked at one and the same time. It is to this ability to draw out the sacred quality of State power, and to out-fetishize its fetish quality, that the *maleficium*—as I use it—speaks.

Taboo; Transgression and Fantasy

Predictably, given his emphasis on the representation over the represented, Durkheim states that "contrarily to all that could be forseen," the prohibitions refering to the *representation* of the totem are "more numerous,

129

stricter, and more severely enforced than those pertaining to the totem itself." He emphasizes that uninitiated men and all women are prohibited access to the representations. Indeed, the very first thing Spencer and Gillen say in their chapter on the Churinga is that they are sacred objects "which, on penalty of death or very severe punishment, such as blinding by means of a fire-stick, are never allowed to be seen by women or uninitiated men."[47]

We are then in a situation in which "society," inscribed and erased in thereby sacred objects, can, in this peculiarly objectified and highly concentrated form, only be seen and touched by one, presumably rather small, group of persons within "society." This raises two somewhat unsettling questions. First, whether the sacred force of these objects arises only in conjunction with such seeing, touching, and absorption into the initiated male body? Second, whether it is the object's sacred force which impels such powerful taboos, as vividly expressed in the punishment of blinding with fire or, to the apparent contrary, *is it the societal prohibition itself*—the taboo—which is decisive to the sanctification of the object?

This second question tends to undermine a lot of things. It moves us into another type of world where not the solidity of substance but the diaphonous veil of negation bears the world on its back, and it makes us pose further questions: Is the sanctity of the whole that is "society" always, throughout history, in the hands of a few select men? What happens to this sacred power, expression of the whole, with the decline of the power of religion and the emergence of the modern secular State (the question posed by Bataille's "College of Sociology")? Finally, if it is restriction to a small group together with the prohibition that is decisive in sanctification, might it turn out that it is not just the sacred knowledge of myth and ritual *of the initiated* which constitutes the power of the sacred, but that instead such power derives from the *fantasies of the people prohibited* concerning the (supposed) nature of that sacred knowledge?

Secrets of State

> The real official secret, however, is the secret of the non-existence of the state.
> Philip Abrams, "Notes On The Difficulty of Studying The State."[48]

Not the anthropology of Australian aborigines but the memoir of a sheep farmer born in 1874 in Tierra Del Fuego provides me with the secret of the secret, which is to say the real, official secret. The son of British missionaries, E. Lucas Bridges grew up speaking the language of the Ona people, with whom he played as a child. Towards the end of a long life spent in the land of the Fuegians he wrote down the curious history of his now-legendary family, in which he paid a good deal of attention to the Indians, especially some Onas, into whose Lodge he had been initiated. Only men were initiated, and only initiated men were allowed close to or into the Lodge. No woman was allowed close, under penalty of death. But long ago, so the story went, things were different. For then the lodge belonged exclusively to the women. There they practised and passed on to younger women the secrets of magic and sorcery of which the men were ignorant. Frightened, the men banded together and massacred the adult women. They married the young ones and, so as to prevent them from reconstituting the link between the feminine and magical power, made their own secret society wherein they supped on supernatural nourishment brought them by a handful of monstrous and short-tempered women-hating spirits such as the two fierce sisters, the red one from red clay, the white one from cumulus clouds, and the horned man who came out of the lichen-covered rocks. When Bridges was taken into the Lodge, he was told that he would make a good impersonation of Short, a spirit who came from the grey rocks and wore a piece of parchmentlike skin over the face and head. Grey down from birds was applied to the body, and there was a good deal of variation in that the arm and the opposite leg could be painted in white or in red, with spots or stripes of the other color superimposed. Periodically, in the company of the men, Short would emerge from the Lodge, a large wigwam set a quarter of a mile or so from the village, and dart unpredictably around the village, causing the women to flee and hide their heads. On other occasions the women and uninitiated men would be summoned to appear in front of the Lodge where, to the accompaniment of an unearthly noise, the cruel sister from the clouds, dressed in heaped-up furs covered in white chalk, would slowly make her way from a clump of trees to the lodge's entrance. When the horned man appeared with his mask of red-rimmed eyes, the women fled home, threw themselves face down on the ground in groups, and covered their heads with skins.

The initiation of a man demanded ordeals and isolated journeys in which he would be shadowed by a spirit-monster, and the culminating moment arrived in the Lodge when he had to fight one of them. Bridges was present when a terrified novice was forced to engage in combat with Short, whose anger and disgust at the novice had grown to almost a frenzy. Unbeknown to the novice, the outcome was set in advance so that the novice would always win and when, in this case, he finally threw his spirit-opponent to the ground and the identity of his attacker was revealed to be a fellow-human in disguise, he attacked him with such fury, writes Bridges, "that he had to be dragged off, to the accompaniment of roars of laughter, in which Short joined heartily." Thus the novice became an inner member of the Lodge.

As this laughter finally, after many adventures of transmission through the colonial lifeline reaches through me to you, we can appreciate a certain plenitude in the hollowness—the catharsis following the vicious struggle by the firelight leading to the eventual revelation of the monster's true nature previously concealed by its appearance of parchment, paint, and down. But the catharsis is far from fulfilling. The revelation makes the novice rage. The duped then becomes the duper, obligated to support the deception. The basis of this primitive "State" is male theater organized around a female audience, and it exists as a hollow core, a meticulously shielded emptiness and magnificent deceit in whose making all members of the society, so it would seem, conspire. When Bridges suggested to the men that the women might only be acting so as to please them, the men's reaction left him in no doubt as to "their firm conviction of the women's blind credulity." To Bridges it seemed impossible that the women could be deceived, yet he noted that the male initiates, who lived constantly with their mothers for twelve years or so and would surely have heard any expression of disbelief, were undoubtedly terrified when they came face to face with Short for the first time. He leaves us with this reminder. "One thing is certain: that if any woman had been indiscreet enough to mention her doubts, even to another woman, and word of it had reached the ears of the men, the renegade would have been killed—and most likely others with her. Maybe the women suspected; if they did they kept it to themselves."[49]

Might it turn out, then, that not the basic truths, not the Being nor the ideologies of the center, but the fantasies of the marginated concerning the secret of the center are what is most politically important to the State idea and hence State fetishism? Here the secret takes on the burden of protecting not merely the deceit practised by the initiated men but of protecting a great epistemology, one that drives philosophers, scientists, social scientists, and policemen—the epistemology of appearance and reality in which appearance is thought to shroud a concealed truth—but not the truth that there is none. In so far as you can trust a thief, it is here where Jean Genêt's thief's journal can be our guide, juxtaposing to the majesty of the State the homoerotic emblem-fetishes of the criminal, Saint Genêt.

Saint Genêt and The Supreme Organ

The State is above all, supremely the organ of moral discipline.
Durkheim, *Professional Ethics & Civic Morals,* 1904[50]

It is one of Genêt's triumphs to have brought the fetish character of the modern State into a clear and sensual focus, and this could be accomplished only by one deft in the management of the ancient art of the *maleficium*, the fetish-power intrinsic to the impure sacred. By means of his remorselessly holy yet secular blend of crime and homosexuality, he does for the State what Sartre would have him do for us—he holds out the mirror in which we might see the holiness of its monstrous self. Is it necessary here, to recall Durkheim's notion, drawn from his theorizing from turn-of-the-century monographs of primitive societies, of the kinship between the pure and the impure sacreds? And Nietzsche: "It might even be possible that what constitutes the value of these good and revered things is precisely that they are insidiously related, tied to and involved with these wicked, seemingly opposite things—maybe even one with them in essence."[51]

In Genêt's case, to be deft in the management of the *maleficium* means above all to be deft with the logos. I think of him not only as the transgressor of the taboo but as the one who ably registers a vision born from its diabolic logic of mystical attraction and repulsion. This is the vision of persons who, in being prohibited access to the sacred, ensure its sanctity which, far from being a thing in itself, is what we might call a self-fulfilling fantasy of power projected into an imagined center—like that of the old men rubbing their fetishes into their bodies, their adoration of these objects, as revealed to us, but not to the tribe, by the anthropologists of long ago. But this adroit anthropology stumbles on its own taboos when it comes to gaining access, let alone reveal, the seminal centers of fetish-riddled power in its own society where male knowledge, sanctity, and age coalesce. There is no anthropology of the ruling class that rules over us, just as there is no sociology of it, either. And the time is long past for that project to have been initiated. There are institutional reasons for it not having happened. Failing that revelation, we fall back on our fantasies about the center, fantasies that in some curious back-handed and utterly effortless manner constitute that center. It is here where the great guides, the Dantes of our era, the supermarginated such as Genêt, come forth to lead us underground. For they are, thanks to their structural malposition, blessed with vision.

A Dominating Order

He loves criminals. Yet it seems to me that Genêt loves crime even more. And this is the point. For when I say "love of crime" I mean a love so strictly spiritual that it has to be carnal. For to love the abstraction "crime," there is naught else to do but make love with the infamous, the practitioners of crime, which is where another strange catch arises. As Durkheim himself made much of, there can be no spirit of Crime without its Other, no crime without Law.[52] And so we find the thief that is Saint Genêt hopelessly in love with the Dominating Order, the shimmering power that lies as mystery in the abstraction that is the State, and carnally involved with its policemen as well as with the spirit of Crime as incarnated in criminals.

Here he is, this handsome thief, caught by a Spanish coastguard on the lookout for smugglers. It is a cold night by the ocean stretching to Morocco. Who seduces whom, the criminal or the cop? Does it matter? The policeman needs the criminal and the criminal . . . "In submitting to the whims of the coastguard I was obeying a dominating order which it was impossible not to serve, namely the Police. For the moment I was no longer a hungry, ragged vagabond whom the dogs and children chased away, nor was I the bold thief flounting the cops, but rather the favorite mistress who, beneath a starry sky soothes the conqueror. When I realized that it was up to me whether or not the smugglers landed safely, I felt responsible not only for them but for all outlaws."[53]

In That Skin

Genêt, the thief, says that for him the police form a sacred power, a troublesome power that acts directly on his soul. Please note first and foremost that when he speaks of the sanctity of the police, he is speaking of them as an institution, of that "dominating order," not of individual policemen. And here's the rub. It's not a question of the particular policeman as an instantiation or symbol of the general Order. These terms are of some secondary relevance, to be sure, but there's something else, more metonymic, more carnal, tactile and sensuously material, which is central here—and this is the issue of the fetish, of the State with its big S rearing, of the Dominating Order as that which oscillates, like Durkheim's "society," between *res* and *deus*, between thing and God, with a carnal and ritualised relation to objects, as with the totems. Here the policeman and his gear are precisely that—a totem, with whom the Saint that is the thief establishes just such a carnal and ritualized relationship. Hence Bernardini, the secret policeman whom he met in Marseilles, "was to me the visible, though perhaps brief manifestation on earth of a demoniacal organization as sickening as funeral rites, as funeral ornaments, yet as awe-inspiring as royal glory. Knowing that there, in that skin and flesh, was a particle of what I would never have hoped could be mine, I looked at him with a shudder. His dark hair was flat and glossy, as Rudolph Valentino's used to be, with a straight white part on the left side. He was strong. His face looked rugged, somewhat granite-like, and I wanted his soul to be cruel and brutal."[54] Or, again, as instantiation of this the most crucial, the ultimate State fetish-move and one which we all make and succumb to: "Little by little I came to understand his beauty. I even think that I created it, deciding that it would be precisely that face and body, on the basis of the idea of the police which they were to signify."[55]

The Invisible Presence of The Object In Which The Quality of Males Is Violently Concentrated

Again, the fetish that is the other side of the reification that is the big S: Bernadino "was not aware that, beside him, at the bar, crushed by his huskiness and assurance, I was excited chiefly by the invisible presence of his inspector's badge. The metal object had for me the power of a cigarette lighter in the fingers of a workman, or the buckle of an army belt, of a switchblade, of a calliper, objects in which the quality of males is violently concentrated. Had I been alone with him in a dark corner, I might have been bold enough to graze the cloth, to slip my hand under the lapel where cops usually wear the badge, and I would have then trembled just as if I had been opening his fly."[56]

Bernadino's virility was centered on that badge just as much as in his penis. Had his penis "been roused at the touch of my fingers," continues the thief, deftly picking his pocket as well as (some of) ours, grasping at the finest nerves connecting the State with sex, reification with its fetish-creation, then that penis "would have drawn from the badge such force that it might have swelled up and taken monstrous proportions."[57]

The Body of the Nation

This circulation of forceful swellings between the State and its fetish-objectifications knows other circuits and by-ways as well. These are formed by the vital organs of the big S; its cities, its ports and railways stations of entry, its language, and its borders. In reality and in fantasy this thief's journal is a record of contested journeying through the erotic zones of the Nation-State, a sexual picaresque into the abstractions, Nation and State, including very much the reification of the nation's language itself.

The Language Mass

Reflecting on his vocation as a thief and his return to France to practice that vocation once again, the thief writes—and he is as much concerned with writing as with language—"I think that I had to hollow out, to drill through, a mass of language in which my mind would be at ease. Perhaps I wanted to accuse myself in my own language."[58] For him, crime is synonymous with treason, and it is very much as a traitor to his country that he understands his activity as attaining the status of art. But only with language, the language of the nation, can this art be practised. This language binds not only the thief to his victim, but to the thief's own victimization at the hands of the Law and the laws of Language. The reifications are as endless as they are full-bodied. "To be a thief in my own country and to justify my being a thief who used the language of the robbed—who are myself, because of the importance of language—was to give to being a thief the chance to be unique. I was becoming a foreigner."[59]

Ports

The city blurs into the male body burning with desire, and it is the city as port, entry to the nation, that establishes this incarnation.

> "What do you feel like doing?"
> "With you, everything."
> "We'll see."
> He didn't budge. No movement bore him toward me though my whole being wanted to be swallowed up within him, though I wanted to give my body the suppleness of osier so as to twine around him, though I wanted to warp, to bend over him. The city was exasperating. The smell of the port and its excitement inflamed me.[60]

This entry to the nation is immovable. "No movement bore him toward me." Yet in its very stolidity its animate quality emerges, swallowing one up into its fixed, great, and beautiful, self. This figuration of the port-city as man's body is no easy substitution. It is not a question of a code, substituting one thing for another. The thief's journal strains to establish the connection predestined in desire, the desire accompanying fetishization whereby the body is the idea of the Nation-State, here by the port where the ships of many nations lie at anchor. But how can a body be an idea? This thief is hell-bent on incarnation. He desperately wants to be in-*corporated*—em-*bodied*—and he has to work at it. It is his body that has to move and be supple so it can twine around, warp, and bend over the other. Hard labor. The city is exasperating. You smell the sweat, the inflammatory smell of the port. His semiosis is sensuous—or, rather, from his vantage point of forbidden desire, he can visualize the sets of mimetic correspondences which link the body to the Nation's ports.

Borders

Why is this thief so fascinated by borders? With his innumerable border crossings, is he not caught up in his own restless form of Statecraft, circum-navigating the body as much as the Law of the nation? "After many stays in jail the thief left France. He first went to Italy. The reasons he went there are obscure. Perhaps it was the proximity of the border. Rome. Naples. Brindisi. Albania. I stole a valise on the 'Rodi' which set me ashore in Santi Quaranta. The port authorities in Corfu refused to let me stay. Before I could leave again, they made me spend the night on the boat I had hired to bring me. Afterwards it was Serbia. Afterwards Austria. Checkoslovakia. Poland, where I tried to to circulate false zlotys. Everywhere it was the same: robbery, prison, and from every one of these countries, expulsion. I crossed borders at night, and went through hopeless autumns when the lads were all heavy and weary, and through springtimes when suddenly, at nightfall, they would emerge from God knows what retreat where they had been priming themselves to swarm in alleys, on the docks . . . ."[61]

Death and The Country

Like the Nation-State, the fetish has a deep investment in death—the death of the consciousness of the signifying function. Death endows both the fetish and the Nation-State with life, a spectral life, to be sure. The fetish absorbs into itself that which it represents, erasing all traces of the represented. A clean job. In Karl Marx's formulation of the fetishism of commodities, it is clear that the powerful phantasmagoric character of the commodity as fetish depends on the fact that the socioeconomic relations of production and distribution are erased from awareness, imploded into the made-object to become its phantom life-force. In the thief's view of the Nation-State, the policeman's badge displaces his organ which has, in turn, displaced and erased Durkheim's ("the State is the supreme organ of moral discipline"). In like fashion the State solemnly worships the tomb of the unknown soldier and (many) young men are, as Benedict Anderson reminds us, prepared not only to go to war and kill their nation's enemies, but are ready to die themselves.[62] With this erasure we are absorbed into the object's emptiness.

Less Into a Country Than to The Interior of An Image

But far from anaethetizing awareness, this involution of reference intensifies sensuousness, breaks sense into the senses, and annuls the distance between subject and object, subject and the State. The subject enters into the object as image, into the State as tomb of the unknown soldier and, with this sensuous entry, breaks radically with mere contemplation of the object. As the thief writes: "The crossing of borders and the excitement it arouses in me were to enable me to apprehend directly the essence of the nation I was entering. I would penetrate less into a country than to the interior of an image."[63]

The State as Fetish

So, we are back into the strange world of (Durkheim's) totems, where the territory was bound to the group by means of the sacred objects—by means of the images (so the arguments runs) on those objects. In that world, so the first anthropologists reported back to what was to become our patrimony, only the initiated men were allowed to see those images which, on account of their adoration, they erased over time and loving caressing into themselves. But the thief, who needs to be carefully distinguished from the anthropologist, with whom in some ways he overlaps, and from the men at the center, sees it differently. He likewise caresses the images of the State, the policeman's hidden badge, but instead of his body being penetrated by the sacred image, he says that he penetrates it. His time is modern and godless, and he is bound to the impure sacred of the margin, not the sacred center of power. He sees not the tabooed objects but imagines himself as one. "A picture is worth a thousand words," it is said. *Then what of a tabooed object? Imagine if it could talk?* Imagine this thing called Genêt as a taboo-object, epitome of the impure sacred, writing the sacred designs on himself as a Churinga of the modern Western underworld where he gathers and concentrates into himself all the fantasies of those at the center. Now he is one of Walter Benjamin's treasured devices, that infamous "dialectical image" emerging like lightning from the storm of mimetic correspondence—Genêt the petrified object being jolted awake to give voice to the modern dreamtime compacted within, opening up to the little hunchback of history that through cunning, will win every time so long as it enlists the sacred, wizened though it be. For Durkheim something called "society" spoke through—or, rather, was written into—sacred objects. That's what made them sacred, so long as this curious spirit-thing, society itself, was blocked, silenced, and the discourse bounced back into the object's design and substance. That's what made them fetishes. But as a bad fetish-object, as a *maleficium*, of what we might call Durkheim's "own society" and Nation-State, which is in many respect "ours" too, Genêt, like the little hunchback, does something wonderfully instructive to the erased presence of society animating the fetish. First of all, he disconcertingly speaks back, as fetish, and thus perturbs what was said on the fetish's behalf. In this regard he can be said to be an agent of defetishization. But in doing so, he displaces the balmy term 'society,' replacing it by the State and its sexuality, and writes with clarity and beauty the endless story of its seductive bodily prowess and the sensuous trafficking between *thing* and *spirit*, rationality and violence, as writ into the Law itself. He not only defetishizes; he reenchants. That is how he gained sainthood.

TACTILITY AND DISTRACTION

"Now, says Hegel, all discourse that remains discourse ends in *boring* man."
Alexander Kojeve, *Introduction to the Reading of Hegel*

Quite apart from its open invitation to entertain a delicious anarchy, exposing principles no less than dogma to the white heat of daily practicality and contradiction, there is surely plurality in everydayness. My everyday has a certain routine, doubtless, but it is also touched by a deal of unexpectedness, which is what many of us like to think of as essential to life, to a metaphysics of life, itself. And by no means can my everyday be held to be the same as vast numbers of other people's in this city of New York, those who were born here, those who have recently arrived from other everydays far away, those who have money, those who don't. This would be an obvious point, the founding orientation of a sociology of experience, were it not for the peculiar and unexamined ways by which "the everyday" seems, in the diffuseness of its ineffability, to erase difference in much the same way as do modern European-derived notions of the public and the masses.

This apparent erasure suggests the trace of a diffuse commonality in the commonweal so otherwise deeply divided, a commonality that is no doubt used to manipulate consensus but also promises the possibility of other sorts of nonexploitative solidarities which, in order to exist at all, will have to at some point be based on a common sense of the everyday and, what is more, the ability to sense other everydaynesses.

But what sort of sense is constitutive of this everydayness? Surely this sense includes much that is not sense so much as sensuousness, an embodied and somewhat automatic "knowledge" that functions like peripheral vision, not studied contemplation, a knowledge that is imageric and sensate rather than ideational; as such it not only challenges practically all critical practice, across the board, of academic disciplines but is a knowledge that lies as much in the objects and spaces of observation as in the body and mind of the observer. What's more, this sense has an activist, constructivist bent; not so much contemplative as it is caught in *media res* working on, making anew, amalgamating, acting and reacting. We are thus mindful of Nietzsche's notion of the senses as bound to their object as much as their organs of reception, a fluid bond to be sure in which, as he says, "seeing becomes seeing *something*."[1] For many of us, I submit, this puts the study of ideology, discourse, and popular culture in a somewhat new light. Indeed, the notion of "studying," innocent in its unwinking ocularity, may itself be in for some rough handling too.

I was reminded of this when as part of my everyday I bumped into Jim in the hallway of PS 3 (New York City Public School Number Three) where he and I were dropping off our children. In the melee of streaming kids and parents, he was carrying a bunch of small plastic tubes and a metal box, which he told me was a pump, and he was going to spend the morning making a water fountain for the class of which his daughter, age eight, was part. She, however, was more interested in the opportunity for the kids to make moulds of their cupped hands and then convert the moulds into clam shells for the fountain. I should add that Jim and his wife are sculptors, and their home is also their workplace, so Petra, their daughter, probably has an unusually developed everyday sense of sculpting.

It turned out that a few days back Jim had accompanied the class to the city's aquarium in Brooklyn which, among other remarks, triggered the absolutely everyday but continuously fresh insight, on my part as much as his, that here we are, so enmeshed in the everydayness of the city that we rarely bother to see its sights, such as the aquarium. "I've lived here all of seventeen years," he told me, "and never once been there or caught the train out that way." And he marveled at the things he'd seen at the station before the stop for the aquarium—it was a station that had played a prominent part in a Woody Allen film. He was especially struck by the strange script used for public signs. And we went on to complete the thought that when we were living in other places, far away, we would come to the city with a program of things to see and do, but now, living every day in the shadow and blur of all those particular things, we never saw them any more, imagining, fondly, perhaps, that they were in some curious way part of us, as we were part of them. But now Jim and Petra were back from the visit to the aquarium. He was going to make a fountain, and she was going to make moulds of hands that would become clam shells.

"The revealing presentations of the big city," wrote Walter Benjamin in his uncompleted *Passagenwerk*, "are the work of those who have traversed the city absently, as it were, lost in thought or worry."[2] And in his infamously popular and difficult essay, "The Work of Art in the Age of Mechanical Reproduction," written in the mid-1930s, he drew a sharp distinction between contemplation and distraction. He wants to argue that contemplation—which is what academicism is all about—is the studied, eyefull, aloneness with and absorption into the "aura" of the always aloof, always distant, object. The ideal-type for this could well be the worshipper alone with God, but it was the art-work (whether cult object or bourgeois "masterpiece") before the invention of the camera and the movies that Benjamin had in mind. On the other hand, "distraction" here refers to a very different apperceptive mode, the type of flitting and barely conscious peripheral vision perception unleashed with great vigor by modern life at the crossroads of the city, the capitalist market, and modern technology. The ideal-type here would not be God but movies and advertising, and its field of expertise is the modern everyday.

For here not only the shock-rhythm of modernity so literally expressed in the motion of the business cycle, the stock exchange, city traffic, the assemblyline and Chaplin's walk, but also a new magic, albeit secular, finds its everyday home in a certain tactility growing out of distracted vision. Benjamin took as a cue here Dadaism and architecture, for Dadaism not only stressed the uselessness of its work for contemplation, but that its work "became an instrument of ballistics. It hit the spectator like a bullet, it happened to him, thus acquiring a tactile quality." He went on to say that Dadaism thus promoted a demand for film, "the distracting element of which," and I quote here for emphasis, "is also primarily tactile, being based on changes of place and focus which periodically assault the spectator."[3] As for architecture, it is especially instructive because it has served as the prototype over millennia not for perception by the contemplative individual, but instead by the distracted collectivity. To the question 'How in our everyday lives do we know or perceive a building?' Benjamin answers through usage, meaning, to some crucial extent, through touch, or better still, we might want to say, by proprioception, and this to the degree that this tactility, constituting habit, exerts a decisive impact on optical reception.

Benjamin set no small store by such habitual, or everyday, knowledge. The tasks facing the perceptual apparatus at turning points in history, cannot, he asserted, be solved by optical, contemplative, means, but only gradually, by habit, under the guidance of tactile appropriation. It was this everyday tactility of knowing which fascinated him and which I take to be one of his singular contributions to social philosophy, on a par with Freud's concept of the unconscious.

For what came to constitute perception with the invention of the nineteenth-century technology of optical reproduction of reality was not what the unaided eye took for the real. No. What was revealed was the *optical unconscious*—a term that Benjamin willingly allied with the psychoanalytic unconscious but which, in his rather unsettling way, he so effortlessly confounded subject with object such that the unconscious at stake here would seem to reside more in the object than in the perceiver. Benjamin had in mind both camera still shots and the movies, and it was the ability to enlarge, to frame, to pick out detail and form unknown to the naked eye, as much as the capacity for montage and shocklike abutment of dissimilars, that constituted this optical unconscious which, thanks to the camera, was brought to light for the first time in history. And here again the connection with tactility is paramount, the optical dissolving, as it were, into touch and a certain thickness and density, as where he writes that photography reveals "the physiognomic aspects of visual worlds which dwell in the smallest things, meaningful yet covert enough to find a hiding place in waking dreams, but which, enlarged and capable of formulation, make the difference between technology and magic visible as a thoroughly historical variable.[4] Hence this tactile optics, this physiognomic aspect of visual worlds, was critically important because it was otherwise inconspicuous, dwelling neither in consciousness nor in sleep, but in waking dreams. It was a crucial part of a more exact relation to the objective world, and thus it could not but problematize consciousness of that world, while at the same time intermingling fantasy and hope, as in dream, with waking life. In rewiring seeing as tactility, and hence as habitual knowledge, a sort of technological or secular magic was brought into being and sustained. It displaced the earlier magic of the aura of religious and cult works in a pretechnological age and did so by a process that is well worth our attention, a process of demystification *and* reenchantment, precisely, as I understand it, Benjamin's own self-constituting and contradictorily montaged belief in radical, secular, politics *and* messianism, as well as his own mimetic form of revolutionary poetics.

For if Adorno reminds us that in Benjamin's writings "thought presses close to its object, as if through touching, smelling, tasting, it wanted to transform itself,"[5] we have also to remember that mimesis was a crucial feature for Benjamin and Adorno, and it meant both copying *and* sensuous materiality—what Frazer in his famous chapter on magic in *The Golden Bough*, coming out of a quite different and far less rigorous philosophic tradition, encompassed as imitative or homeopathic magic, on the one side, and contagious magic, on the other. Imitative magic involves ritual work on the copy (the wax figurine, the drawing or the photograph), while in contagious magic the ritualist requires material substance (such as hair, nail parings, etc.) from the person to be affected. In the multitude of cases that Frazer presented in the 160-odd pages he dedicated to the "principles of magic," these principles of copy and substance are often found to be harnessed together, as with the Malay charm made out of body exuviae of the victim sculpted into his likeness with wax and then slowly scorched for seven nights while intoning, "It is not wax that I am scorching, it is the liver, heart, and Spleen of So-and-so that I scorch,"[6] and this type of representation hitching likeness to substance is borne out by ethnographic research throughout the 20th century.

This reminder from the practice of that art form known as "magic" (second only to advertising in terms of its stupendous ability to blend aesthetics with practicality), that mimesis implies *both* copy and substantial connection, *both* visual replication and material transfer, not only neatly parallels Benjamin's insight that visual perception as enhanced by new optical copying technology has a decisively material, tactile, quality, but underscores his specific question as to what happens to the apparent withering of the mimetic faculty with the growing up of the Western child and the world historical cultural revolution we can allude to as Enlightenment, it being his clear thesis that children, anywhere, any time, and people in ancient times and so-called primitive societies are endowed by their circumstance with considerable miming prowess.[7] Part of his answer to the question as to what happens to the withering-away of the mimetic faculty is that it is precisely the function of the new technology of copying reality, meaning above all the camera, to reinstall that mimetic prowess in modernity.

Hence a powerful film criticism which, to quote Paul Virilio quoting the New York video artist, Nam June Paik, "Cinema isn't I see, it's I fly," or Dziga Vertov's camera in perpetual movement, "I fall and I fly at one with the bodies falling or rising through the air," registering not merely our sensuous blending with filmic imagery, the eye acting as a conduit for our very bodies being absorbed by the filmic image, but the resurfacing of a vision-mode at home in the pre-Oedipal economy of the crawling infant, the eye grasping, as Gertrude Koch once put it, at what the hand cannot reach.[8]

And how much more might this be the case with advertising, quintessence of America's everyday? In "This Space For Rent," a fragment amid a series of fragments entitled "One Way Street," written between 1925 and 1928, Benjamin anticipated the themes of his essay on mechanical reproduction, written a decade later, claiming it was a waste of time to lament the loss of distance necessary for criticism. For now the most real, the mercantile gaze into the heart of things, is the advertisement, and this "abolishes the space where contemplation moved and all but hits us between the eyes with things as a car, growing to gigantic proportions, careens at us out of a film screen." To this tactility of a hit between the eyes is added what he described as "the insistent, jerky, nearness" with which commodities were thus hurtled, the overall effect dispatching "matter-of-factness" by the new, magical world of the optical unconscious, as huge leathered cowboys, horses, cigarettes, toothpaste, and perfect women straddle walls of buildings, subway cars, bus stops, and our living rooms via TV, so that sentimentality, as Benjamin put it, "is restored and liberated in American style, just as people whom nothing moves or touches any longer are taught to cry again by films." It is money that moves us to these things whose power lies in the fact that they operate upon us viscerally. Their warmth stirs sentient springs. "What in the end makes advertisements so superior to criticism?" asks Benjamin. "Not what the moving red neon sign says—but the fiery pool reflecting it in the asphalt."[9]

This puts the matter of factness of the everyday on a new analytic footing, one that has for too long been obscured in the embrace of a massive tradition of cultural and sociological analysis searching in vain for grants that would give it distance and perspective. Not what the neon says, but the fiery pool reflecting it in the asphalt; not language, but image; and not just the image but its tactility and the new magic thereof with the transformation of roadway parking-lot bitumen into legendary lakes of fire-ringed prophecy so that once again we cry and, presumably, we buy, just as our ability to calculate value is honed to the razor's edge. It is not a question, therefore, of whether or not we can follow de Certeau and combat strategies with everyday tactics that fill with personal matter the empty signifiers of postmodernity, because the everyday is a question not of universal semiotics but of capitalist mimetics. Nor, as I understand it is this the Foucauldian problem of being programmed into subjecthood by discursive regimes, for it is the sentient reflection in the fiery pool, its tactility, not what the neon sign says, that matters, all of which puts reading, close or otherwise, literal or metaphoric, in another light of dubious luminosity.

This is not to indulge in the tired game of emotion versus thought, body versus mind, recycled by current academic fashion into concern with "the body" as key to wisdom. For where can such a program end but in the tightening of paradox; an intellectual containment of the body's understanding? What we aim at is a more accurate, a more mindful, understanding of the play of mind on body in the everyday and, as regards academic practice, nowhere are the notions of tactility and distraction more obviously important than in the need to critique what I take to be a dominant critical practice which could be called the "allegorizing" mode of reading ideology into events and artifacts, cockfights and carnivals, advertisements and film, private and public spaces, in which the surface phenomenon, as in allegory, stands as a cipher for uncovering horizon after horizon of otherwise obscure systems of meanings. This is not merely to argue that such a mode of analysis is simpleminded in its search for "codes" and manipulative because it superimposes meaning on "the natives' point of view." Rather, as I now understand this practice of reading, its very understanding of "meaning" is uncongenial; its weakness lies in its assuming a contemplative individual when it should, instead, assume a distracted collective reading with a tactile eye. This I take to be Benjamin's contribution, profound and simple, novel yet familiar, to the analysis of the everyday, and unlike the readings we have come to know of everyday life, his has the strange and interesting property of being cut, so to speak, from the same cloth as that which it raises to self-awareness. For his writing, which is to say the very medium of his analysis, is constituted by a certain tactility, by what we could call the objectness of the object, such that (to quote from the first paragraph of his essay on the mimetic faculty) "His gift of seeing resemblances is nothing other than a rudiment of the powerful compulsion in former times to become and behave like something else."[10] This I take to be not only the verbal form of the "optical unconscious," but a form which, in an age wherein analysis does little more than reconstitute the obvious, is capable of surprising us with the flash of a profane illumination.

And so my attention wanders away from the Museum of Natural History on Central Park, upon which so much allegorical "reading," as with other museums, has been recently expended, back to the children and Jim at the aquarium. It is of course fortuitous, overly fortuitous you will say, for my moral concerning tactility and distraction that Jim is a sculptor, but there is the fact of the matter. And I cannot but feel that in being stimulated by the "meaning" of the aquarium to reproduce with the art of mechanical reproduction its watery wonderland by means of pumps and plastic tubes, Jim's tactile eye and ocular grasp have been conditioned by the distractedness of the collective of which he was part, namely the children. Their young eyes have blended a strangely dreamy quality to the tactility afforded the adult eye by the revolution in modern means of copying reality, such that while Jim profers a fountain, Petra suggests moulds of kids' hands that will be its clam shells.

9

HOMESICKNESS & DADA

It is with homesickness that I begin and it is with homesickness that I shall surely end, hoping to make of this looping journey homeward some sense of the wondrous powers contrived from womb-sprung worlds, in particular with the power of imagined orders, systems, and other such elegant devices for explaining the magic of Others. The figure of such journeying is the figure of celestial, shamanic, flight, in many ways the obverse of terror, as I have presented it. But as obverse there nevertheless remains starkly profiled an uncanny relationship to the function of arbitrariness in terror, and that is why this journey homeward, this celestial flight, is principally a worrying about the role of order in empowering those activities deemed "explanatory." And just as the figure of celestial flight serves me as a figure for the movement of "explanation" as a curing movement deemed to transform chaos into system, then the alliance of that movement with the magic and rituals of "primitive" societies is what I want to also bring into the dialectic of Enlightenment.

Anthropology was always a homesickening enterprise. To the (not necessarily unhappy) travail of the sojourns abroad with their vivid flashes of (generally unrecorded) homely memories, one has to add the very logic of its project to connect the far away with home in ways that the folk back home could understand. Sometimes this was done in a comforting sort of way, and sometimes it was not. To that you have to add that once home, the anthropologist is likely to become homesick for that home away from home where being a stranger conferred certain powers. And so, home multiplies its temptations no less than it becomes a little sickening, and a fellow such as myself, sitting at home in Sydney, Australia, can find strange if temporary relief by journeying "home" to the cane fields and forests of southwestern Colombia by dint of the activity of writing about them— drawing them into the noose of the real by means of the snare of the text. What makes this noose of the real effective, so it seems to me, is precisely the way by which the ambivalence of this fellow's homesickness recruits, through a process of mimetic magic, the presence of that other home. That this is a rather shady business propping up, among other things, High Theory, I hope to make clearer. Let me begin with certain African teeth.

African Teeth

Seemingly at odds with the totalizing force of British Social Anthropology's reification of structure, one of Victor Turner's gifts to anthropology was to make the wandering incisor tooth of a dead hunter the container of social structure and social history. It is the healer's task to divine the presence and then magically extract the angered ancestor's tooth from where it has lodged in a sick man's body, and the healer does this to the beat of drums and the stop-start rhythm of communal singing and individual confession by the sick man's fellow villagers. Thus the healer, in Turner's account, uses ritual to create a dramatic narrative tension and catharsis to close a wounding breach in the social body and hence reproduce the traditional social structure—in a truly stunningly cathartic display of what Brecht would have called *dramatic* (Aristotelian) theater, as opposed to the *epic* form of tragedy he was developing as a revolutionary Communist artist to heal the wounding breach in 20th century capitalist social structure. Much later Turner willingly acknowledged that his conceptualization of social drama was indeed based on Aristotle's notion of tragedy as bound to narrative.[1] For Brecht, of course, a completely different view of ritual and theater was at stake. Healing of the breach in the social body of capitalism meant de-narrativizing the logosphere, not restoring the deviation to the norm, nor chaos to structure, but of estranging the normal through what Roland Barthes describes as a technique akin to but better than semiology—namely *seismology* or the production of shock.[2]

That seismology, in Brecht's words, aimed at "showing showing"— disarticulating the signifier from the signified, the reality of the illusion from the illusion of reality, the representing from the represented. Thus seismology is not only the opposite of the magic as described by Turner for the Ndembu doctor's healing of the social body, it is also a technique which invites us to question the politics of representation in that Ndembu essay itself, wherein the subject addressed and the addressing of the subject become one.

The narrative tension created by the stop-start rhythm of the ritual, as represented, pervades the very texture of the author's representation—the poetics of the essay's culminating moment—which reproduces in its argument and in its very form the catharsis described as occurring among this group of beleaguered Ndembu villagers. While the villagers, eventually, through much *Sturm und Drang*, locate their aggrieved ancestor's tooth and therewith purify the village, we piggy-back on the same magical ritual to find, not the tooth, but the purity of structure, the reality of the imaginary integrated whole.

The Magic of Mimesis

"To read what was never written." Such reading is the most ancient: reading before all languages, from the entrails, the stars, or dances. Later the mediating link of a new kind of reading, of runes and hieroglyphs, came into use. It seems fair to suppose that these were the stages by which the mimetic gift, which was once the foundation of occult practices, gained admittance to writing and language. In this way language may be seen as the highest form of mimetic behavior and the most complete archive of nonsensuous similarity. . . .
—Walter Benjamin, "On the Mimetic Faculty"[3]

The point is not whether this wonderful essay of Turner's is right or wrong according to certain Positivist criteria, but to ask how it subliminally operates on us as a ritual of truth-making, shaping our feeling and intuitive as well as highly conscious understandings concerning the security of the referent, of the character of the relationship between signs and their referents. I want to suggest that this shaping is enormously facilitated by and indeed dependent upon the text's *appropriation* of the African magic and dramatic power of the ritual it describes. There is thus an intentional or unintentional usage of Frazer's Law of Sympathy, a magical usage, not only in the actual rite itself, but in its representation by the anthropologist-writer mimetically engaging the flow of events described with the flow of his theoretical argument, to the benefit and empowerment of the latter. Not least impressive about this magical mimesis is that instead of obviously magicalizing the connectedness that holds the argument together, it naturalizes those connections.

Locating the vengeful and elusive tooth of the hunter becomes in effect a magically mimetic figure for an even more serious realization of ghostly emanations; namely, what we might call the ossification, or validation, of the construct "structure" found through the magical ministrations of the wise old healer (found and brought to the village by the anthropologist, be it noted) who bears an uncanny resemblance to the Manchester-trained anthropologist assiduously practising the craft of case-study social anthropology. Here, in the textual construction itself, ritual functions not merely to heal a breach in the (African) social body. It also serves to naturalize *structure* as the rock-hard referent of the real. In using the force of "Africa," sickness, magical ritual, and so forth, as these images detonate and denotate within the Western constellation of representations, the text moulds us into the narrative power of the Nervous System's system, not just into a particular narrative discovered in a dislocated African village, but into the power of a specifically primitivist narration to represent the real.

Durkheimian Plastic

Another way of looking at this is to consider the symbol (or sign). In Turner's rituals the self is seen as Durkheimian plastic zombied-out in the liminal period, to have, as wax impressed by a seal, the society's dominant symbols imposed upon its inner being. This, of course, takes us into the heartland of German Romantic theory of the Symbol, a tradition which Walter Benjamin, in his study of allegory, drew upon and worked against. In that tradition allegory was contrasted invidiously with symbol: e.g. Goethe, as cited in Benjamin.

> There is a great difference between a poet's seeking the particular from the general and his seeing the general in the particular. The former gives rise to allegory, where the particular serves only as an instance or example of the general; the latter, however, is the true nature of poetry; the expression of the particular without any thought of, or reference to, the general. Whoever grasps the particular in all its vitality also grasps the general, without being aware of it, or only becoming aware of it at a later stage.[4]

Benjamin cites F. Creuzer, for whom the symbol could be defined (against the allegorical) in terms of the momentary, the total, the inscrutability of its origin, and the necessary. With regard to the first property, that of being momentary, he made (what Benjamin finds to be an excellent point) the observation that "that stirring and occasionally startling quality is connected to another, that of brevity. It is like the sudden appearance of a ghost, or a flash of lightning which suddenly illuminates the dark night. It is a force which seizes hold of our entire being."[5]

As against this totalizing force of the mystical instant in "which the symbol assumes the meaning into its hidden and, if one might say so, wooded interior," in allegory the signifier is held apart from "its" signified by "a jagged line of demarcation" which is both death and history.[6] Allegory disrupts the mystical fusion that constitutes the Symbol, and just as it can be used to rail against the Saussarian fusion constitutive of the Sign (signifier/signified), so it maintains that strategic gap of meaning in which, unlike the Symbol, there can be no redemption with nature passing transcendentally into (a higher) meaning.

Arbitrariness

It is a sign of all reification that the things can be named arbitrarilly. . . .
—T.W. Adorno[7]

Whereas Benjamin modernized the *allegorical* mode of the Baroque (coming, in the late 1920s, to refashion allegory in the notion of the *dialectical image*, via Marx's celebrated notion of commodity fetishism), Saussure, the father of modern semiotics, can be seen as modernizing the *Symbol*, taking it from the Romantics, cleansing it of its dubious humanist effulgences, locating it in a tradition of linguistic analysis attuned to the notion of the arbitrariness of linguistic conventions, a tradition that stretched back through the eighteenth century, to Hobbes as well as Plato.[8] What is perhaps the novelty of the Saussurian emphasis, and the reason for its popularity in the 20th century, is precisely its shock effect combining a resolute attachment to arbitrariness, with a resolute adherence to an overarching system. Of course the Sign was Arbitrary—but that served only to further enforce the system, ensuring just that final solution of totalizing closure with which the mystical fusion of the

Symbol had been entrusted. Saussure's operation here reminds me of Kafka, but in a back-handed sort of way, because of the way it so politically intertwines arbitrariness with meaning to the benefit of power. It is Kafka but without the estrangement and without the slightest sense of critique. It is the voice of the modern state apparatus, the voice of the modern corporation, the quintessence of that everyday but nevertheless still disturbing phrase "The Arbitrariness of Power"—both systemic and arbitrary, in short the NS in one of its many guises.

The Swiss Connection

> The dadaist puts more trust in the honesty of events than in the wit of people. He can get people cheaply, himself included. He no longer believes in the comprehension of things from *one* point of view, and yet he is still so convinced of the unity of all beings, of the totality of all things, that he suffers from the dissonances to the point of self-disintegration.
>
> —Hugo Ball, *Flight Out of Time*[9]

Halfway into the Great War, in 1916, the year in which Saussure's lectures were posthumously published in Geneva, a radically different approach to the famous "Arbitrariness of the Sign" was undertaken—at Zürich, with what came to be called dada.[10] Here it was the very arbitrariness of the sign which provided the terrain on which politics and history were acted—not acted out, as in Nedembu ritual, but acted on, by means of what we have come to understand as modern Performance in a zone we can now, looking back, define roughly by the coordinates of Artaud and Brecht.

Arbitrariness was used to contest the arbitrariness of the sign that went into the systematizing of system.

Reality was seen as Swiss cheese.

The nervousness of the Nervous System was used against itself. Signifiers were dismantled, language became sound, and all around lay the petrified primordial landscape of the Great War.

Birds in Cages

"We were like birds in cages surrounded by lions," wrote Hugo Ball who, together with his lifelong companion Emmy Hennings, began the dada show at the Cabaret Voltaire. The cannons could be heard not far from Zürich as the war thundered on. Lenin lived a few blocks away at the time, but is not recorded as having attended dada evenings.

Emmy Hennings

John Elderfield writes that when Ball met her she was an itinerant actress and a night-club performer with "a highly unorthodox background."[11] What is meant by this I do not know, although next he says she had traveled in Russia and Hungary, had a broken marriage, suffered a time in prison, and was a suspected murderer. She was the one who got the job, singing, at what came to be called the Cabaret Voltaire, and persuaded the owner to take Ball along too, as the piano player. She is not accorded much importance in the origin or development of dada, which is basically an all-male movement. But she was certainly one of the few women involved with dada. There is an entry in Ball's memoir, for 1916, of what appears to be a notice from a Zürich newspaper, the *Züricher Post*:

> The start of the cabaret, however, is Mrs. Emmy Hennings. Star of many nights of cabarets and poems. Years ago she stood by the rustling yellow curtain of a Berlin cabaret, hands on hips, as exuberant as a flowering shrub; today too she presents the same bold front and performs the same songs with a body that has since then been only slightly ravaged by grief.[12]

Hans Arp has left us with a memorable description of dada nights at the cabaret. Only five performers are mentioned. Emmy Hennings is one of them.

> Total Pandemonium. The people around us are shouting, laughing, and gesticulating. Our replies are sighs of love, volleys of hiccups, poems, moos, and meowing of medieval *Bruitists*. Tzara is wiggling his behind like the belly of an Oriental dancer. Janco is playing an invisible violin and bowing and scraping. Madame Hennings, with a Madonna face, is doing the splits. Huelsenbeck is banging away nonstop on the great drum, with Ball accompanying him on the piano, pale as a chalky ghost.[13]

We will come back to this image of the Madonna doing the splits, especially in relation to the dada man as ghost. She is a particularly interesting image in that as Emmy Hennings she is to be later accused of straightening out Ball's image after his death in 1927, characterizing dada as little more than a youthful excess on his path to righteousness and Catholic conversion, that fine old story of the inevitable movement from chaos to order.[14] And in her own memoir, as we shall see much later, Hennings herself invoked the Madonna as Ball's origin, and destiny.

According to a letter written by Hans Richter, Emmy Hennings died in a small room above a grocery store in Magliaso (Tesson) in 1949. She must have been at least in her late fifties, and to survive she was working day shifts in a factory.[15]

Flight Out of Time

In the memoir *Flight Out of Time*, drawn from his diaries for the years 1910–21 and published in 1927, the year of his death from stomach cancer at the age of forty-one, Ball conveys the sense that dada for him is not simply the mere negative of the established order, but the attempt to make a mobile position that is resonant with the mobility of the Nervous System itself. On Huelsenbeck's poetry, for instance, he writes (in 1916) that it is

> an attempt to capture in a clear melody the totality of this unutterable age, with all its cracks and fissures, with all its wicked and lunatic genialities, with all its noise and hollow din. The Gorgon's head of a boundless terror smiles out of the fantastic destruction[16]

Not merely a formal problem of totality and fragmentation, but the destructive terror of this literally unutterable age. In this problematic is indicated the response. "What we are celebrating," he writes, "is both buffoonery and a requiem mass." Deceit is met with masks; social conventions are met with enthusiasm for illusions, and primitivism holds out powerful tools, especially that of magic. "The dadaist loves the extraordinary and the absurd," he writes:

> He knows that life asserts itself in contradiction, and that his age aims at the destruction of generosity as no other age has ever done before. He therefore welcomes any kind of mask. Any game of hide-and-seek, with its inherent power to deceive. In the midst of the enormous unnaturalness, the direct and the primitive seem incredible to him.[17]

Preoccupied with poetry and the voice, Ball experimented with sound along the lines of Wasilly Kandinsky's abstract expressionist painting. "The image of the human form," he wrote, "is gradually disappearing from the painting of these times, and all objects appear only as fragments. This is one more proof of how ugly and worn the human countenance has become. . . . The next step is for poetry to decide to do away with language for similar reasons. These are things that have probably never happened before."[18]

The Magical Bishop, Into the Abyss: From Theater to Ritual

Three months later (according to how he presents himself in his memoir), Ball is writing that "we have now driven the plasticity of the word to the point where it can scarcely be equaled. We achieved this at the expense of the rational, logically constructed sentence. . . ."[19] And five days later he attempted his great experiment with language, performing his sound poem *Karawane* with his legs and waist immobilized in a blue cardboard cylinder (an obelisk is how he referred to it), his arms and upper body sustaining a cape of wings, and on his head a large conical "witch doctor's" hat. He had to be carried onto the stage, where he had set three music stands for his manuscript. As he progressed with his recitation,

> gadji beri bimba
> glandridi lauli lonni cadori
> gadjama bim beri glassala

he found himself in trouble, unable to go on. Then came the moment when the performance was taken over, his voice being transformed into what he later described as "the ancient cadence of priestly lamentation, that style of liturgical singing that wails in all the Catholic churches of East and West."[20]

He had wanted to break open words and meaning, analogous to what had been done to the human figure by the artist and by the world around us. He had begun his recitation by renouncing the corruption of the word and of writing by modern society. He had begun saying that to do this we had to "return to the innermost alchemy of the word," and he had ended in the order of Catholic liturgy. He writes that he does not know what gave him the idea of this liturgical singing but that

> for a moment it seemed as if there were a pale, bewildered face in my cubist mask, that half-frightened, half-curious face of a ten year old boy, trembling and hanging avidly on the priest's words in the requiems and

high masses in his home parish. Then the lights went out, as I had ordered, and I was carried down off the stage like a magical bishop."[21]

The translation in Motherwell's edition reads, "I was carried, moist with perspiration, like a magical bishop, into the abyss."[22] John Elderfield claims that the recitation was privately planned by Ball as his final performance, but despite the planning, it "not only alarmed the audience but also so unnerved Ball himself that he had to be carried off the stage when the performance ended."[23] Dadaism was at once the climax of Ball's commitment to an activist aesthetic, notes Elderfield, "and the point beyond which he dared not move." This event is commonly portrayed not only as the climax of Ball's dadaism, but his rejection of it as well.

The steps subsequent to Ball's fall into the abyss, however, were not without significant ambiguity. For while he spent the next three years severing himself from the Zürich dadaists, partly in exile in the countryside, he was also striking out into the world of politics as a radical journalist on *Die Freie Zeitung*, in Bern, as well as becoming absorbed into a mysticism of saints and angels which was, after 1920 and his and Emmy Henning's disappointment with German revolutionary movements, to claim him so firmly.

It is hard to resist a particular mythification of Hugo Ball's Magical Bishop, in part because it has become a legend of dada, and in part because of the drama so easily read into that truer-than-life performance of the hero struggling to transcend the disordered order of his time, taking disorder to its limit in a new type of dramatic art, only to break under the strain and, at the mercy of forces beyond his control, find himself sutured into the rhythmic order of the Church. In destroying the word, he was brought back to the Word. What began as art and anti-art, became a derailed sacred act. Was Ball perhaps too serious, too religious, and too political to transformatively enact the political implications of the arbitrariness of the sign? But might not it have been the case that just this degree of seriousness was what was required for dada's playfulness and purposeful lack of purpose?

Because he provokes these questions, Ball is for me the most interesting of all the dadaists. He establishes an agenda for our postdada and postmodern age with which to reconsider the social and indeed political history of the sign and its relation to primitivism where the word and the Word stand in such marvelous tension as in his sound poem performances. To appreciate the stakes involved, we need now to turn from his flight out of time to the pervasive aura in our time of shamanic flight and its implications for narrative order.

Shamanic Flight: The Magic of Narrative

The celestial ascent [appears] to be a primordial phenomenon, that is, it belongs to man as such, not to man as a historical being; witness the dreams, hallucinations, and images of ascent to be found everywhere in the world, apart from any historical or other "conditions." All these dreams, myths, and nostalgias with a central theme of ascent or flight cannot be exhausted by a psychological explanation; there is always a kernel that remains refractory to explanation, and this indefinable, irreducible element perhaps reveals the real situation of man in the cosmos, a situation that, we shall never tire of repeating, is not solely "historical."
—Mircea Eliade, *Shamanism: Archaic Technique of Ecstasy*[24]

If later, in regard to the traditional philosophical texts, I not so much let myself be impressed by their unity and systematic coherence as I concerned myself with the play of opposing and conflicting forces which goes on under the surface of every self-contained theoretical position, [it was certainly Siegfried Kracaeur who showed me] how the most eloquent parts of the work are the wounds which the conflict in the theory leave behind.
—T. W. Adorno, "Der wunderliche Realist: Uber Siegfried Kracauer"[25]

Mircea Eliade's classic *Shamanism: Archaic Techniques of Ecstasy* epitomises the way anthropology and the comparative history of religion established the "shaman" as an Object of Study—first a real "type" to be found in the wilderness of Siberia (among the Tungus), now everywhere from New York City to Ethnopoetics. Crucial to what I take here to be a potentially fascistic portrayal of third world healing is the trope of magical flight to the Other World, from life to death to transcendent rebirth, across the treacherously narrow bridge or through the perilous way by means of "archaic techniques of ecstasy," generally and mightily mysteriously male. Here we encounter, in one of its more potent manifestations, not only the mystifying of Otherness as a transcendent force, but the reciprocating dependence on narrative which that mysterious stress on the mysterious entails.

But if we try to scrutinize the evidence—taking into account how extraordinarily slippery such evidence must be—concerning the narrative character of these magnificent and perilous flights, several cautions emerge, suggesting that the narrative form (one step bound to the following, beginning, middle, cathartic end) is the exception, not the rule, and that it is a certain sort of anthropology and social science, geared to particular notions of the primitive, of story-telling, of boundaries, coherence, and heroism, that has thus recruited "shamanism" for the heady task of ur-narrativity.

I want to argue that the evidence, such as it is, suggests a type of modernism in which parts are only loosely connected one to the other, there is no centralizing cathartic force, and there exists an array of distancing techniques involving and disinvolving the reader or spectator and thus, potentially at least, dismantling all fixed and fixing notions of identity. If we search for a reference point in western history, Benjamin's commentary on Brecht's epic theater springs to mind (certainly with regard to my own experiences with "shamanism" in Latin America) because it suggests ways by which this "modernism" has a long, if underground and repressed genealogy:

> Often in conflict with its theoreticians, such drama has deviated time and again, always in new ways, from the authentic form of tragedy—that is from Greek [Aristotelian] tragedy. This important but badly marked road (which may serve here as the image of a tradition) ran, in the Middle Ages, via Hroswitha and the Mysteries; in the age of the baroque, via Gryphius and Calderon. Later we find it Lenz and Grabbe, and finally in Strindberg. Shakespearian scenes stand as monuments at its edge, and Goethe crossed it in the second part of *Faust*. It is a European road, but it is a German one too. If, that is, one can speak of a road rather than a stalking path along which the legacy of medieval and baroque drama has crept down to us.[26]

Also at issue here is the degree of certainty attached to the "shamanic" experience, a point poignantly made by Roger Dunsmore in his extraordinary commentary on the famous visions of the Oglala Sioux, Black Elk, but which never seems to be made by professional anthropologists or folklorists. In Black Elk's "words" (as we know them after being translated verbally by his son Ben into English, then edited with a pretty strong hand by John Neihardt from the transcription made by his daughter, Enid Neihardt):

> As I lay thinking of my vision, I could see it all again and feel the meaning with a part of me like a strange power floating over in my body: but when the part of me that talks would try to make words for the meaning, it would be like a fog and get away from me . . . It was as I grew older that the meanings came clearer and clearer out of the pictures and the words; and even now I know that more was shown me than I can tell.[27]

"If we take him as a sort of paradigm," writes Dunsmore,

> of what it means to be a man of vision, he *overturns our expectation* that the holy man arrives somewhere at the Truth, which is recognizable to him and to us. Instead Black Elk is deeply involved in *not knowing*, and in the *risk* that when he gives his vision away it will be ignored, misunderstood, or misused.[28]

It is to that *not knowing*, and to that *risk*, that we must, I feel, refer shamanic discourse—very much including the great trope of flight out of body, out of time. And if we but pause a moment, to let sink in the significance of the depth of the physical violence that the U.S. colonial relationship, together with the appropriation by White mysticisms, has by and large entailed, then the risk involved in giving the vision away looms very high indeed, and we then begin to realise what is incumbent upon us who receive the vision as members of a colonial institution—Anthropology, Comparative Religion, or whatever names and ciphers are here relevant. "What becomes clear through his life story," notes Dunsmore, "is that a great vision is only a beginning, a starting place or point of departure, not an end, not final." What we do with that radical uncertainty is the measure not only of our ability to resist the appeal for closure, but also of our ability to prise open history's closure with the lever of its utterly terrible incompleteness. After the battle at Wounded Knee, Black Elk (through a chain ending with John Niehardt) recalls:

> And so it was all over.
> I did not know then how much was ended. When I look back now from this high hill of my old age, I can still see the butchered women and children lying heaped and scattered all along the crooked gulch as plain as when I saw them with eyes still young. And I can.see that something else died there in the bloody mud, and was buried in the blizzard. A people's dream died there. It was a beautiful dream.[29]

Retracing the History of the World: The Magic of Origins

No matter how often the critique of the search for origins is made, no matter how sophisticated the person, origin is the goal. Its promises are as tenacious as they are vague, lost in a melee of yearning energizing the discipline of history itself. The Euro-American fascination with shamanism is a specially revealing strand in this allure of origin in which the shaman becomes a figure combining Primitivism with Woman—with the womb of time itself. For catharsis lies not only with narrative closure, but with the return to origin, for which there is no better western model than Dante's *Divine Comedy*, wherein the preeminently Christian Poet recruits the pagan Virgil as his shamanic guide from the dark woods of confusion down to the pit of hell in which the awesome confrontation with the spirit of evil takes place. This confrontation sets the preconditions for the finding of the self, but the definitive act occurs in the encounter with woman in the transcendent figure of Beatrice as guarantor of the mystical illumination, thus fetishizing one of the great "codings" of Western culture. In his essay on Surrealism, Benjamin singles out the importance of this encounter for (man's) *profane* as well as *mystical* illumination. Breton's Nadja becomes the Modern, profane, equivalent to Dante's Beatrice, and the profane illumination Benjamin directs us to consider is no less intriguing than its mystical counterpart in that it renders the everyday mysterious, the mysterious as everyday. This formula condenses the heart of the importance the Surrealists would claim for the "marvelous," no less than Benjamin, in all his own writing, struggles not simply for a mode of critical analysis which demystifies, but instead one which demystifies and reenchants. It is also a formula which in startling fashion conveys the sense of the uncanny—the everyday as mysterious, the mysterious as everyday—and it is the uncanny which Freud himself so movingly illuminated as connected to both homesickness and a man's desire to approach his place of birth, his mother's womb.

It is to the conflation as magical force of Woman with Primitivism, that I now wish to turn, to examine the post-medieval yet "magically real" landscape of the first's world's third world, where time and space become united in a geography through which, as through the sacred flightpath, the Westerner undertakes the great odyssey of Self-Making, again and again. Nowhere is this clearer for me than in Alejo Carpentier's novel, *Los Pasos Perdidos (The Lost Steps)*, written in the mid-twentieth century. This work is all the more fascinating in that Carpentier, a Cuban and his own sort of Marxist, had by his own account self-consciously broken with the avant garde of the first world to give voice to what he took to be a more authentic and richer expression, in the popular culture of his third world, of what that first world's avant garde, in Surrealism, was trying to achieve. With the advantage of hindsight, it is now all too easy to claim that despite all his claims to the contrary he was in fact carrying out a western European avant garde project and perceiving the popular culture of the poverty-stricken third world with exactly the same primitivistic optic that Surrealism itself stimulated. (I say all too easy because it is difficult, if not impossible, to elude this defining power of the Center). It was to what he called *lo real maravilloso* (cf. Breton's "marvelous") that Carpentier was drawn, the everyday magical quality of lived experience he detected as powerful in times past as present in islands such as Cuba and Haiti, and in Venezuela in whose wooded interior the Lost Steps are traced.

Alienated from modern civilization, the protagonist undertakes a type of magical flight from Europe to the interior of Latin America. Traveling from city to town, from town to hamlet, from hamlet to the forest, he is also passing back through time, into (what is, in effect, a European coding of) history. At the end of his journey, deep in the forest with a peasant woman, fecund and compliant, he finds the beginning of human history in the figure of an Indian shaman trying to sing a dead hunter back to life. As he approaches the Originary which shamanism establishes with the same power as does Woman, he notes:

> We were intruders, ignorant outlanders—late arrivals—in a city born in the dawn of History. If the fire the women were now fanning was suddenly to go out, we would be unable to rekindle it if we had to depend on our own unskilled hand.[30]

There is this fear that life, for which we can also read Self, will disappear if woman is unable to fan the fire at the dawn of history. As for his newly found companion, Rosario:

> It did not matter to her where we went, nor whether the lands we visited were near or remote. For Rosario the idea of being far away from some famous place where life could be lived to the full did not exist. The center of the universe for her, who had crossed frontiers without a change of language, who had never dreamed of the ocean, was where the sun shone at midday overhead. She was a woman of the earth, and as long as she walked the earth, and ate, and was well, and there was a man to serve as mold and measure, with the compensation of what she called "the body's pleasure," she was fulfilling a destiny that it was better not to analyse too

much, for it was governed by "big things" whose workings were obscure and, besides, were beyond man's understanding.[31]

Deep in the forest he encounters Indians whom he sees as "human larvae, from whose loins hung virile members, like my own," ensuring the narrative's questing thrust in a spate of dizzy regression to origins. Yet there is further to penetrate. The striving for completeness finally locates its most othered Other, the pre-Oedipal phallic mother. Amid the reed hammocks

> where they lay and fornicated and procreated, there was a clay object baked in the sun, a kind of jar without handles, with two holes opposite each other in the upper part, and a navel outlined in the convex surface by the pressure of a finger when the clay was still soft.
> This was God. More than God it was the Mother of God. It was the Mother, primordial in all religions. The female principal, genesial, womb, to be found in the secret prologue of all theogenies. The Mother, with swollen belly, which was at one and the same time breasts, womb, and sex, the first figure modeled by man, when under his hands the possibility of the object came into being. . . . The Mother, "lonely, beyond space and even time, whose sole name, *Mother* Faust twice uttered with terror."[32]

Where the Indians lie fornicating, this sun-baked belly-dimpled earthen pot empties out the heavy atmospherics of Eliade's "celestial ascent" that "belongs to man as such." His "archaic techniques of ecstasy" and Rothenberg's "technicians of the sacred" (a figure taken from Eliade), are indeed revelatory (as Eliade claims) of "the real situation of man in the cosmos"— in which the flight to the shaman, no less than the flight of the shaman is, for us, a home run to mom (not to mention that dimple in her tum). It is here, also, that language itself is born. For following the Mother, what the hero now sees is a shaman trying to snatch a still-warm corpse from the jaws of death. He is shaking his pebble-filled gourd rattle over the body and as he does so, he sings—or, rather, voices emerge from his mouth, spirit-voices haggling over death. It is here, then, that the Mother of God gives birth to the shaman's song in the primal enactment of the phallologocentric order—and, lest we forget, of the ever-present, imminence of its dissolution as well.

"And in the vast jungle filling with night terrors," continues the narrator of *lo real maravilloso*, "there arose the Word. A word that was more than word." A word that imitates both the voice of the speaker and that of the spirit of the dead man. They alternate. They harangue each other; one from the throat of the shaman, the other from his belly. Trills, panting, guttural *portamenti* ending in howls, the hint of a rhythm every now and again, the vibration of the tongue, "the panting contrapuntal to the rattle of the gourd. This was something far beyond language, and yet still far from song. Something that had not yet discovered vocalization, but was more than word."[33] We pay homage to Hugo Ball.

The shamanic flight rests at this point, poised permanently between word and the inarticulable where narrativity begins. The dead man stays dead. The Word grows faint, but the melody lingers on. And if through daring or necessity we go back farther in time we encounter the loneliness of the Creator "when the earth was without order and empty and darkness was upon the face of the deep."[34]

Soul-Loss: Vaginal Odyssey

Westward along the Caribbean coast from Carpentier's Venezuelan en-counter in the forest with the origin of the word that is more than word, a woman lies heaving in obstructed labor in the San Blas islands off Panama and Colombia. She falls unconscious. She has lost her *purba*, "essence" or "soul."[35] The midwife rushes for the shaman. Cocoa beans are burnt under the sick woman's hammock, strengthening the clothes of the shaman (who is wearing European trousers, clean white shirt, tie, and felt hat) in the presence of his wooden spirit-helpers carved in the form of Europeans (p. 167), giving them the courage to begin the voyage that will bring them face to face with Muu who is not only the spirit creator of the fetus, but is responsible for abducting the laboring woman's soul as well.[36]

Thus, for what continues for some twenty-four printed pages (first published in 1947 by the Swedish ethnographers Nils Holmer and Henry Wassén), begins the shaman's two to three hours' long song aimed at recapturing the woman's soul from Muu—who is also, (according to Holmer and Wassén's mentor, Baron Erland Nordenskiold) "in some measure" the same person as "the original mother" from whose womb all being becomes.[37] Together with seven other women, she rules over a city of the dead, recycling the dead into fetuses.[38] Once again the Great Mother beckons as the telos of shamanic flight. Only here, with regard to the shaman singing for the woman in labor, the flight is not only explicitly male, but is tracked by Holmer and Wassén and, following them, in a justly celebrated essay, by Claude Lévi-Strauss, "The Effectiveness of Symbols," as identical to the movement of the penis along her vagina.

It is this phallic penetration, according to Lévi-Strauss (who, like me, never did fieldwork amongst the Cuna), which gives to this text its "exceptional interest." Indeed, he regards it as "the first important South-American magico-religious text to be known," and this on account of its "striking contribution" to the solution of the problem of how "specific psychological representatives are invoked to combat equally specific physiological disturbances."[39] To the native mind, he writes, Muu's way and the abode of Muu "are not simply a mythical itinerary and dwelling place. They represent literally the vagina and uterus of the pregnant woman, which are explored by the shaman and *nuchu* [meaning wooden figurine/spirit-helper] and in whose depths they wage their victorious combat."[40] He refers to this as "the myth being enacted in the internal body [which] must retain throughout the vividness and the character of lived experience." He emphasises how the spirit-helpers, "in order to enter Muu's way, take on the appearance and the motion of the erect penis," and he advises us that "the technique of the narrative aims at recreating a real experience in which the myth merely shifts the protagonists. The *nelegan* [spirit-helpers] enter the natural orifice, and we can imagine that after all this psychological preparation the sick woman actually feels them entering."[41]

This is indeed extraordinary, and for all the talk here of *merely* shifting the protagonists and of "recreating a *real* experience [for the woman]," it surely stretches credulity to claim that the shamans and/or their spirit-helpers assume phallic form such that they actually enter the actual vagina and the sick woman "actually feels them entering." I cannot but feel that the rhetorical device here wherein Lévi-Strauss writes, "We can imagine that after all this psychological preparation the sick woman actually feels them entering," is indicative of a strategic move for his own technique of narrative whereby through "the first important South American magico-religious text to be known," he is mimetically evoking a wildly improbable yet stunningly dramatic *mis en scène* for the staging of his own magical performance. "We can imagine. . . ."

And what do we imagine? Where will our imaginings through this body

Guillermo Hayan's drawing of wooden figures used in song for obstructed labor.[42]

of (Indian) Woman take us? Why! Into the rhapsody of ordering chaos, creating meaning and therewith a physiological cure. Lévi-Strauss's aim is nothing less than to provide an explanation of how symbols work, of how this song can have a beneficial physiological effect on the laboring woman and, beyond that, to use this song as a vehicle for illustrating how Structuralism, derived from the linguistics of Saussure, serves to explain the effect of mind on body. All this in a handful of pages hanging from the thread of a healer's chant.

His principal claim is that the song provides the woman with a "structure," which, like a language, makes her condition meaningful—"meaningful" in such a way that the form developed by the song becomes the form to be developed by the laboring body on its way to cure. Obviously a great deal, indeed a world, depends on the power of the meaning here of "form," an innocuous word, not like "magic" or "spirit." He fortifies his argument by characterizing the woman's initial state of soul-loss as one in which the plug has been pulled from structural cohesion. In other words, we are back in the familiar terrain not of Indian but of Western mythology in which, as with Dante, lost in the woods of confusion, ritual's aim and the source of its transcendent power is to establish order (through the encounter with evil and then with woman), and order is at one with the Godhead itself. And just as the woman's body is designated chaotic, so likewise the spirit Muu, having abducted the woman's soul, is described by Lévi-Strauss as a "force gone awry." Hence his (ethnographically unsupported) assertion that "In a

167

difficult delivery the 'soul' of the uterus has led astray all the 'souls' belonging to other parts of the body. Once these souls are liberated, the soul of the uterus can and must resume cooperation."[43]

Can and must!

This metaphysic of order is pursued with relentless vigor. Where he introduces the argument that the laboring woman becomes incorporated into what he calls the myth of the shaman's song, for instance, Lévi-Strauss characterises the Cuna world as one in which the spirits and the monsters and the magic "are all part of a coherent system on which the native conception of the universe is founded."[44] Given the ethnography available this is pure supposition, dogma, with immense consequences, allowing Lévi-Strauss to come down pretty hard on what he calls incoherence identified no less than as alien, the enemy of meaning, and the sign of pain. It's as if some Natural Law has been transgressed, bringing into natural reaction the soothing harmonies of the (Holy) Whole. He assures us that whereas the sick woman accepts (or at least has never questioned) the existence of the mythical beings that make up this "coherent system," what she does not accept "are the incoherent and arbitrary pains, which are an alien element in her system but which the shaman, calling upon the myth will re-integrate within a whole where everything is meaningful."[45] Structure itself becomes a magical operator, not for the Indians but for their analyst restructuring the disordered body of Woman, as where he writes:

> The shaman provides the sick woman with a *language* by means of which unexpressed, and otherwise inexpressible, psychic states can be immediately expressed. And it is the transition to this verbal expression—at the same time making it possible to undergo in an ordered and intelligible form a real experience that would otherwise be chaotic and inexpressible—which induces the release of the physiological process, that is, the reorganization, in a favorable direction, of the process to which the sick woman is subjected.[46]

Everything hinges on this question of order. And what's really crucial is that the *order of meaning* has to hook up with *the wisdom of the body*, its spontaneous and unconscious physical order. "Here too it is a matter of provoking an experience," writes Lévi-Strauss. "As this experience becomes structured, regulatory mechanisms beyond the subject's control are set into motion and lead to an orderly functioning."[47]

This naturalizing of "structure" pin-points the target of the analysis; the demonstration that it is this ordering of order by Saussurian Structure which transmutes myth into physiologic health. This not only explains the (alleged) efficacy of the song, but effectively universalizes Structuralism and the metaphysics of Order. Comparing the Cuna shaman's chant with psychoanalysis, Lévi-Strauss writes:

> It would be a matter, either way, of stimulating an organic transformation which would consist essentially in a structural reorganization, by inducing the patient intensively to live out a myth—either received or created by him—whose structure would be, at the unconscious level, analogous to the structure whose genesis is sought on the organic level. The effectiveness of symbols would consist in this "inductive property," by which formally homologous structures, built out of different materials at different levels of life—organic processes, unconscious mind, rational thought—are related to one another."[48]

Here, then, is the transcendant claim for the supremacy of a metaphysic of Order. By a process surely no less mysterious than the magic it purports to explain, all of life is encompassed by "inductive properties" cascading through "homologous structures" in the body as much as in mind and culture.

What makes this Cuna analysis so important is not that it successfully demonstrates the role of a purported "structuralism" in the cure of a bodily problem, but that the demonstration itself reveals a lust for order as the movement of the phallus in its shamanic flightpath along the vagina to the womb as telos. Akin to Turner's mimetic recruitment of the dead hunter's incisor's tooth to prove the underlying existence of British *social structure* in Africa, so here Lévi-Strauss piggy-backs on Indian magic to prove the underlying existence of French *structuralism* in the New World.

The Representational Bleed

What I am concerned to argue here is not only the important point of rhetoric, that the vaginal staging grants dramatic power to Lévi-Strauss's demonstration, and that this demonstration becomes in turn an almost wilfully iconic performance of Western phallologocentrism, but that we have to radically rethink what it means to *take an example* or use some *concrete* event as *illustration* of an abstract idea. For I am arguing that in this Cuna essay, there is a strategic slippage; something essential to what is to be explained enters into the power-apparatus used to explain. More than an ends-means reversal, this is a fascinating, unnoticed, and probably very common representational bleed in which the referent referred to, in this case the laboring woman's body and the curing *mis en scène*, creates the *sensuous* correspondence—not *formal* or *structural* ones—necessary for the conceptual thought and abstract theory brought by the anthropological theorist to bear on it. Moreover, I am not so sure that this mimetic piggybacking procedure does not significantly parallel the mimetic magic, specifically the Cuna magic, it purports to explain yet rests upon. In any event it is also crucial to point out that on closer perusal this representational bleed infusing western structuralist science founders grievously, for the reason that far from sustaining order, this infusion subverts it in a thoroughgoing manner. That which is deemed chaos, the woman's body and the spirit of the womb, turns out not to be so easily recruited for the higher cause of structure; the famous arbitrariness of the sign turns out not to be so easily systematized; and the mimetic principle, on which this representational bleed as much as Cuna magic is based, turns out to be the Nervous System par excellence in that magically potent copies are faithful and faithless representations at one and the same time. On this massive dilemma, in my opinion, both magic and shamanism are founded, and the lust for Order proves to be yet another feint in the Nervous System's phantom objectivity. This can be seen by some further consideration of the famous structuralist incantation.

The Gang of Four

In good part this phallic narrative of redemption is deemed by Lévi-Strauss to work around a simple structural device whereby the spirit-helpers fight their way through the vagina in single file, followed by their successful return four abreast with the woman's soul. The chant owes its (alleged) effectiveness therefore to the fact that it thus widens the birth canal by providing the laboring woman with a structure by means of which the disorder of her body can be made intelligible (to her, of course), hence orderly and capable of giving birth. "No doubt," writes Lévi-Strauss (in his analysis which ignores the performative, social, colonial and micro-historical contexts of the song-text), "the purpose of such an alteration in the details of the myth is to elicit the corresponding organic reaction, but the sick woman could not integrate it as experience if it were not associated with a true increase in dilation [of the birth canal]." In point of fact the shaman's song-text barely mentions single file/rows of four; the former once, the latter twice, in a text that spans twenty-four pages. Nor does the song indicate in ways direct or metaphoric that this transition is a key feature in the dilation of the birth canal. Rather, rows of four is first mentioned when the forcible entry into Muu's abode occurs (line 388), and the second and final mention is made (line 428, but merely as "march in a row," not quite the same as "rows of four") at the same anatomical juncture, namely Muu's gate, now juxtaposed with the woman's "gate" when her soul is restored into her from *outside* her body and not, as Lévi-Strauss writes, simply when the spirit-helpers emerge from Muu's abode in some allegedly cathartic release cascading through "homologous structures." That line reads in a far more complex fashion: "The spirit helpers go out, the spirit helpers march in a row, they are going to enter by the woman's gate." Exit is conflated with entry, inside with outside, and leaving with restoration. What must be grasped here is that the mimetic evocation becomes an elusive and complicated action, no less so than the representation of the body in question and its relation to its simulacrum in the soul upon which the magical mimesis so utterly depends. Moreover, one cannot ignore that "rows of four" is here to do with forcible entry into the body, and not with "downwards" movement out of it, "isomorphic" with the expulsion of the fetus.

What needs emphasis, therefore, is that this body of primitive woman, as represented, does not so easily provide the raw material for the staging of a structuralist psychodrama empowering Theory. Indeed Holmer and Wassén, the authors of the song-text used by Lévi-Strauss, had already struggled manfully with contradictions within the text. There was a deeply puzzling feature about this body of woman being traversed internally by a spirit-helpers who, when they gained possession of the lost soul, addressed it: "Your body lies in front of you in the hammock" (line 430). Previously all the action appears to have been inside the woman's body. Now, suddenly, it's outside, just when the laboring woman's soul is being restored. Holmer and Wassén say here that "The Indian trend of thought is neither always strictly logical nor consistent in a text of this kind."[49] Yet they seem concerned by this apparent inconsistency. In the song lines immediately following, in which the shaman, likened to the penis, that is, to the action of the penis, wipes the inner place dry, they rather anxiously reaffirm the interior—the vaginal—location of the action in language that is a study in indeterminacy, combining the interrogative with the subjunctive moods. "The dessication . . . again indicates that the place in question is supposed to be located inside the woman."[50]

Penis or Hummingbird?

There is, furthermore, every reason to be skeptical of the major *frisson* of the work, where erotics and exotics were conflated into their alteric best, namely the identification of the narrative movement as one of the penis moving vaginaward to *telos*. For it is confidently stated by an anthropologist comfortable with the Cuna languages (everyday and spiritual), Norman Macpherson Chapin, that the word *nuspane*, translated by Holmer and Wassén as penis, is woefully mistranslated and in fact means 'hummingbird'! This puts a rather different complexion on things, most important of which, to my mind, is the sacrifice we are now facing—the sacrifice of clarity, the inability to salvage meaning from the third world for the sake of Theory. It's not simply the penis that has gone up in smoke. Chapin's rendering of this problem in a truly baffling footnote serves as one of the great illustrations of Nervous System poetics. It reads:

> The word 'penis' is a mistranslation of *nuspane*, which means 'humming-bird.' This error was made because both *nusu* ('worm') and *pane* ('frigate bird') are common euphemisms for 'penis' in colloquial Kuna [which is different to the spirit-language sung by the curer]. The correct correspondence, however, is *nusu* ('worm') + *aipane* ('to move back and forth'). Thus: 'the worm that moves back and forth,' or 'hummingbird.'[51]

And he goes on to say that he questioned his informants repeatedly as to the possibility that *nusupane* meant penis. At first they were amused; later they were impatient.

Mimetic Worlds: Invisible Counterparts

So much for the (mis)representation of the male organ as it slips from colloquial Cuna to the language of the spirit, the spirit world being, according to Cuna ethnography, the invisible *replication* of the material world. It is this massively important quality of the Cuna world, its replication in spiritual realms, that allows for magical power—the power of mimesis. For by acting on spiritual copies, as in the song, the shaman can affect material reality. "In this way one evidently can say," wrote Baron Nordenskiold in the 1930s, after lengthy discussion with the Cuna Rubén Pérez in the Ethnological Museum in Gothenburg, "that everything, people, animals, plants, stone, things made by man etc., have invisible counterparts which we sometimes see in dreams and which leave the body or at least for the most part leave it when it dies."[52] "Even when we awake," he added, "we can sometimes feel manifestations of this invisible world, in the warmth of the sun, the noise of thunder, in music, etc." More self-assuredly, Chapin explains from his fieldwork in the San Blas islands fifty years later:

> The world as it exists today has a dual nature: it is composed of what is termed 'the world of spirit' and 'the world of substance.' The world of spirit is invisible to a person's waking senses, yet surrounds that person on all sides and resides inside every material object. Human beings, plants, animals, rocks, rivers, villages, and so forth, all have invisible 'souls' which are spiritual copies of the physical body.[53]

And he points out that the *purba* or "soul" of a human being is, "in its general form and appearance, a representation of the body in which it lives. The *purba* of a man with one leg, for example, also has only one leg."[54]

The healing chants are themselves mimetic with this mimetic world of invisible counterparts. They create word-copies of the spirit-world, itself a replica of the material world, and thus, as Joel Sherzer so neatly puts it, "The subsequent narration of actions and events, addressed to the spirit world, *causes their simultaneous occurrence* in the mirror image physical world" (emphasis added).[55]

Yet there is deep-seated mischief afoot here. For while every material thing has its spirit double visible to the specialists, and it is this doubling which provides the basis for both misfortune and curing practice, the fact of the matter is that the spirit world is characterized by its tremendous capacity for trickery, transformation, and fantasy. Chapin notes, for instance, that "while all the inhabitants of the spirit world are able to change their shapes at will, and are therefore sometimes seen as animals, plants, or grotesque distorted monsters, they are frequently pictured in human form. They are also dealt with as if they were human."[56]

In other words, the spirits can be considered the mimetic principle unleashed; not just passive copies but copiers, not just prototypes, but chameleons. It is this quality which makes them not only material for the shaman to work with, but a power for confusion and evil. You see this particularly, but by no means solely, with the *nia* or evil spirits who often, to quote Chapin, "disguise themselves as alluring men or women and try to seduce Kunas of the opposite sex."[57] Indeed we could say that it is this capacity of spirits to serve not only as copies but as copiers that makes shamans necessary, for it is the shamans who have to figure out the real spiritual copy from the "fake," and it is they who can work on the copy, through song, so as to affect its material "original." Rubén Peréz told Baron Nordenskiold about a girl in the Narganá community who used to dream a lot about people who had died. Peréz took a curing figurine that she had held in her hands for a few minutes to a shaman who was then able to diagnose her visions as those of evil spirits and not of deceased persons. He declared that unless she bathed in certain medicines she would go mad.[58]

As I read the evidence, the crucial point is that this is not so much a system as a Nervous System. As such it resists structuralist machinery via the penis *or* the hummingbird if only because the system is composed of and requires copies that are not copies. There is this fateful power for deceit and confusion at the heart of the mimesis, and yet mimesis lies at the heart of the world, its manifestations, its misfortunes, its curings. While spiritual access to mimetic copies—to the alter world of spiritual reality—is both necessary and magically empowering, and while that other world is deemed mimetic of this world of substance, and modeled on it (or is it vice versa?), there is also this curiously noncopied and fake-copied aspect to this mimetic doubling which creates acute and life-threatening representational dilemmas as well as strange fantasy worlds such as the Kalus or spirit-fortresses. A glance at a Cuna drawing of such a spirit fortress suggests not merely the degree of contradiction involved in claiming that the spirit world is modeled on the physical or "real" world, but the strange beauty of that contradiction. The arbitrariness of the sign is here construed in terms drastically different to the totalizing closure claimed for it by Saussure and Lévi-Strauss. We are

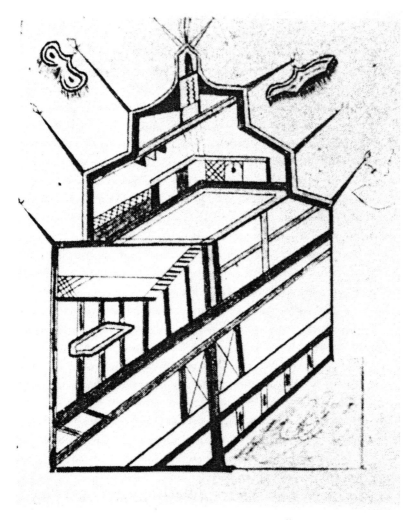

A Spirit-Fortress as Drawn by Alfonso Díaz Granados in 1973.[59]

in a mobile world in which meaning, or at least reference, is both fixed and slipping—and what this Cuna song and Cuna woman, now so famous in the world ethnological industry which has so enthusiastically recruited them, show us, is that the womb, the telos of the shamanic flight, is precisely where reproduction creates, as Derrida might have it, *Being under erasure*, copies that are both copies and not copies.

Mimetic Vertigo

A dramatic illustration of representational dizziness is provided by the nature of the body traversed by the shaman's helpers. We have already had occasion to note the perplexity it created for Homer and Wassén, when being inside suddenly became being outside. An apparent solution to this disorientation is provided by Chapin, who claims that Holmer and Wassén's rendering (and therefore that of Lévi-Strauss too) is grievously in error because, in this world of spirit replicas, these interpreters have *too literal* an understanding of the woman's body. Instead of it being an actual woman's body that is penetrated, says Chapin, the song depicts (and therefore, on my argument, gains mimetic magical force from) a *spiritual journey* through a *spiritual copy* of the woman in question. For those with supernatural vision, he writes, the soul of the woman "is in every detail, identical in appearance and behavior to the body in which it is housed."[60] What is more, this copied body of the laboring woman becomes in some inexplicable manner the body of the Great Mother, Muu, from whose womb came all things (including the magically powerful wood, such as balsa, from which the shaman's curing figurines are made). During pregnancy a woman's soul becomes "one with the cosmos itself. The two spiritual realms are fused together in the never-ending process of creating offspring and replenishing the Earth's stock of living beings."[61] Thus the song enacts a vaginal journey in two spirit-streams at one and the same time; into the cosmic body of the Great Mother, and into the soul or spiritual copy of the actual women's material body. This puts Lévi-Strauss, "We can imagine . . ." on a new footing.

So far, so good. At least everything seems matched up, copies of copies, plus a little magical fusion between the soul and the cosmos. Then comes the decisive play of scene-changing. To quote Chapin once again. "When the spirit helpers arrive at Muu's house [cosmic level], they come to the [real woman's] spiritual womb. *At this point in their journey, however, the landscape alters (as often happens in the exotic world of spirit)* and Muu's house becomes the woman's spiritual body."[62] The walls of Muu's house are now her ribs, the door is her vulva, the door frame is her thighs, and the door chain is her pubic hair—all this, I might add (emphasizing the terms of my own interpretation), in a song designed to alter reality by acting on faithful copies of it.

A dizzying passage indeed—"as often happens in the exotic world of spirit"—just when they reach telos, the cosmic womb, no less, the arche-organ of reproduction of simulacra with which the magician and healer set to work. Far from ensuring the fidelity of his master's voice, to evoke this telos for the celestial harmonies of order is to merely give the Nervous System another fix.

Understanding Understanding and the Chaos of Woman

But maybe all this concern with the true and real meaning of the text is irrelevant, anyway. For not only does it appear to crumble at our analytic touch, resisting interpretation that would reduce it to another sphere of reference, such as the chaotic body or the straightened-out-body, but one has to bear with a considerable weight of hermeneutic doom because—and one can hardly over-emphasize this—we have to seriously question how much of the song the laboring woman actually understands. (And of course once one raises this doubt, it takes root. What, after all, is meant by "actually understands"?) All this on account of an observation in the Holmer and Wassén text that Lévi-Strauss overlooked:

> Like so many other species of literary composition of a magical or mystical nature, the song of *Mu-Igala* cannot be rightly understood except by the Indian medicine man himself or by those initiated by him.[63]

The point, in Cuna theory, is that the chant is addressed not to the patient but to the spirits and therefore has to be sung in their language, not that of colloquial Cuna. Yet for Lévi-Strauss it is crucial that the woman herself understands. Everything depends upon this. "The shaman provides the sick woman with a *language*," he writes with emphasis, "by means of which unexpressed and otherwise inexpressible psychic states can be immediately expressed." This language makes it possible for her

> to undergo in an ordered and intelligible form a real experience that would otherwise be chaotic and inexpressible—which induces the release

of physiological process, that is, the reorganization, in a favorable direction, of the process to which the sick woman is subjected.[64]

In short, "Once the sick woman understands," she gets well.

But not only are we now saddled with ineradicable doubts about what it is that the woman "understands," this woman for whom so many men are speaking, but we have also to question whether in fact she does "get well." The aim of the essay is in its title, "The Effectiveness of Symbols" (L'Efficacité symbolique). Yet what if the symbols are not effective? Surely their efficacy cannot be assumed but has to be demonstrated. More to the point, what is it that is being made efficacious? Is it the birthing of a child by what Lévi-Strauss calls organ-manipulation through symbols, or is it the recruitment of the magic of Indians and the body of soulless woman so give birth to something else? And in the latter eventuality, are we not, in reading Lévi-Strauss' explanation as the great drama of birthing from chaos to order, being sutured into yet another system of signs in which the arbitrariness of power is channeled into one of the truly great systems of power—that of "explanation" as man amidst magically empowering smoke singing unintelligible text into the birth canal of the world, forever chaotic and female, so as to reproduce "structure"?

Homesickness

Given their neglect of questions of affect, it is impossible to tell from ethnographic sources whether magic creates a sense of the uncanny amongst the Cuna. But it certainly can have that effect in Euro-American societies for whose men, at least, in what is by now a homely quotation, Freud wrote:

> This unheimlich [unanny] place, however, is the entrance to the former Heim [home] of all human beings, to the place where each one of us lived once upon a time and in the beginning. There is a joking saying that "Love is home-sickness"; and whenever a man dreams of a place or a country and says to himself, while he is still dreaming: "this place is familiar to me, I've been here before," we may interpret the place as being his mother's genitals or her body.[65]

And he adds, "In this case too, then, the unheimlich [the uncanny] is what was once heimisch, familiar; the prefix un is the token of repression."

In keeping with this little dance of repression and desire, it should be noted that discussion and witnessing of sex and birth are severely taboo amongst the Cuna, while at the same time no medicine will work unless it has sung to it the history of its origin. Guillermo Hayans, one of Holmer and Wassén's Cuna informants, supplied them with a such an Origin History, that of the balsa wood—it being from balsa that the most powerful curing figurines are carved. He supplied a drawing of this history as well, in an unmistakably homely framework (p. 180), and Baron Nordenskiold was clearly impressed by the frequent accounts in which "these Indians imagine that everything has, in a natural manner, sprung from her [the great mother's] womb without there being any mention of fatherhood."[66] This notion of a womb-sprung world is also to be found amongst the Kogi in northern Colombia (eastward along the Caribbean coast from the Cuna) as related by Gerardo Reichel-Dolmatoff, whose work in this respect is referred to in several places in the Holmer and Wassén analysis of the Cuna birthing song.

From Holmer and Wassén we learn that when a Kogi woman is having a complicated labor, the shaman sings a song directed to the "primordial mother."[67] From Reichel-Dolmatoff's ethnography itself, we also learn that the Kogi world is conceived of as so many different manifestations of the womb—the men's ceremonial house being one such manifestation—and that in a beguiling inflection of the Oedipal complex, boys are frequently seduced at puberty by their mothers, continuing to have sexual intercourse with their mothers even after they have achieved adulthood and are married. Indeed many Kogi men assured the ethnographer that only with one's mother could a man have a satisfying copulation. In the men's (there is no women's) ceremonial house, however, the young men are, before all else, warned of the great danger their mothers represent. Thus, after describing still more entailments of the Kogi world as a uterine universe, Reichel-Dolmatoff is able to conclude, "Therefore it becomes comprehensible that the mother becomes the central figure in a religion whose great promise is the return of the individual to the womb."[68] Indeed, his own discursive process of self-comprehension provides confirmation of how seductive this call of the womb can be and its decisive influence for the clear-sighted, scientific, systematizing, study of the Other. "At the beginning," he writes of his work, "when I slowly penetrated the Kogi world, I felt attracted by the exuberance of its images; it was a world made impressive by its coherence and organization."[69] The resemblance to Lévi-Strauss's machine are obvious. It promises a totaliz-

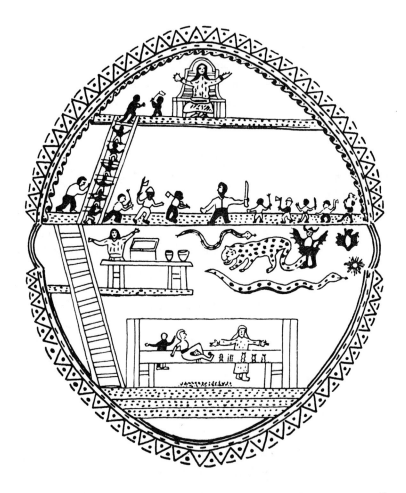

Drawing of Guillermo Hayans to illustrate the *secreto* of the curing song, the *Nia-Ikala*.[70]

ing (albeit "humanist") worldview, a philosophy created out of Anthropology. "In reality what I found amongst the Kogi," continues Reichel-Dolmatoff, "was not a dried out *corpus* of data that could be made into an academic essay, but the coherent knowledge of a reality profoundly relevant for my own cultural tradition. The years I spent with the Kogi taught me that the detailed study of the last remaining societies, ineptly called 'primitive,' constitutes the last opportunity to know our own cultural roots."[71] There, the womb of the Great Mother. With us, "our cultural roots." The flight to the former takes us back to the latter. This is the flight path of that activity known as Anthropology. Origin is the goal, and the exuberance of images initially encountered shall serve as mere prelude to the discovery of an orchestrating system. In the beginning.

We can imagine. . . .

Homesickness and Dada

When a man dies, nostalgia may set in, and an image is sought to capture if not revivify his soul. This requires finding meaning in his life, and that means tracing some sort of connecting thread. This is even more the case with our mother's death, whose role it is (as with the Virgin) to hold that man's soul in a certain image of truth, if not truth-seeking. Take the case of Hugo Ball and the Madonna. We try to read Ball one way, but the nervousness of his system throws us into an-other way, the opposite way on which the first way depended. It is entirely plausible to see him as tripping up power in its own disorderliness. That is what I would call a post-modernist strategy. But it is also entirely plausible to see him—at the very same time of the Cabaret Voltaire creating sound poems and destroying language—as engaged in an "essentialist" recuperation of an Adamic language of naming. What we find here is the deeply perplexing question of realism, which could be summed up by asking: So what if the sign is arbitrary, given that despite their *fictive* character, social conventions are nevertheless *real*? This is why it is simply not enough to belabor the point that gender, race, capital, shamanism, Africa . . . are "merely" social constructions. Their mere "mereness" is enough. This is where our criticism has stopped, as against a brick wall, for the past few years, not knowing what to do with this strange and often violent power once it has been thus identified (and, be it noted, identified long before our present, post-structuralist, generation, as with Durkheim's concept of the "social fact" and as with Marx's conceptualization of value and hence capital itself). The "arbitrariness of the sign" is constantly poised between and dependent upon the alternatives of essentialism and anarchy, and that is why we can read a dadaist like Ball in both these ways. His ritual performance of the Magical Bishop, now a dada-legend, aimed at a return to origins with, amongst other things, his wearing of a shaman's hat and an angel's wings, and he relates (in his memoir, note the title, *Flight Out of Time*) the dramatic climax to his attempt to break the logically constructed sentence. He collapsed back into the rhythm of the Church and subsequently broke with dada to renew his childhood infatuation with the mysteries of the Church of Rome. In pondering why this dada-failure has become such a powerful myth (for there is every reason to contest its veracity, except as a myth),[72] we might note not only the attraction of tragic despair, but also the way the divine mother is recruited to hold the dead man's image in flight not out of time but back to the beginning of time. Sure we can read (Ball) in two opposed ways, fixing and slipping, but either way we have to remember Emmy Henning's remembrance—Emmy Hennings whom Jean Arp described on the stage of the Cabaret Voltaire as a Madonna doing the splits; Emmy Hennings who is criticized by Elderfield for trying to clean up Ball's dada act after his untimely death; Emmy Hennings who lived with Ball before, during and after dada (and serendipitiously started it). Ball wrote that at the moment of (supposed) crisis, when his sound poem was "saved" for rhythmic order, it seemed to him as if there was in his cubist mask (as he now calls it), the pale bewildered face of a ten-year-old boy, half-frightened, half-curious, hanging on the priest's words in the requiems and high masses in his home parish—and it is a slightly earlier version (for we are moving, still, back through time) of this boy whom Emmy Hennings portrays in her introduction to my edition of *Flight Out of Time*, the child who, because he could not sleep at night without all his family around his bed, made friends with the angels. For above his bed, she writes, there was a picture of the Sistine Madonna with two little angels at her feet, leaning on cushions of clouds. The boy's lips formed an outline over their wings, and in the morning there they were, having kept faithful watch. In this way he kept track of his growth; when he was seven, she says, he had been able to reach the cloak, the skirt of the Queen of Heaven, with his lips, without having to stand up or stretch his toes.

NOTES

1. WHY THE NERVOUS SYSTEM?

1. Edmund Burke, *A Philosophical Enquiry into the Origin of Our Ideas of the Sublime and the Beautiful*, ed. Adam Phillips (Oxford: Oxford University Press, 1990), pp. 53–56.

2. Bertolt Brecht, *The Exception and the Rule*, in *The Jewish Wife and Other Short Plays*, trans. Eric Bentley (New York: Grove Press, 1965), p. 111.

3. "The Anxieties of the Regime," in *Bertolt Brecht Poems, 1913–1945*, ed. Ralph Manheim and John Willet (London: Methuen, 1976), pp. 296–97.

4. *The Devil and Commodity Fetishism in South America* (Chapel Hill: University of North Carolina Press, 1980), and *Shamanism, Colonialism, and the Wild Man: A Study in Terror and Healing* (Chicago: University of Chicago Press, 1987).

5. For a derivation of the social history of the European usage of "fetishism," see William Pietz, "The Problem of the Fetish," *RES* 9 (Spring, 1985), 5–17.

6. Karl Marx, *Capital*, vol. 1, p. 72, translation of the 3rd German edition by S. Moore and E. Aveling (New York: International Publishers, 1967; 3rd printing, 1970).

7. Jean Genêt, *The Thief's Journal*, trans. Bernard Frechtman (Harmondsworth: Penguin Books, 1967), p. 39.

8. T. W. Adorno, *Aesthetic Theory* (unfinished work, ed. Gretel Adorno and Rolf Tiedermann), trans. C. Lenhardt (London & New York: Routledge and Kegan Paul, 1984), p. 457.

3. VIOLENCE AND RESISTANCE IN THE AMERICAS

I would like to thank Rachel Moore and Adam Ashforth for their comments on an earlier draft of this paper. I want also to thank Santiago Mutumbajoy for his perceptions on Machu Picchuism, and the late Walter Benjamin, to whose theories on the philosophy of history I am deeply indebted.

References

Benjamin, Walter 1969 'Theses on the Philosophy of History,' in *Illuminations*, ed. Hannah Arendt, pp. 253–64. Schocken: New York.

Bingham, Hiram 1948 *Lost City of the Incas: The Story of Machu Picchu and its Builders*. New York: Duell, Sloan and Pearce.

Franco, Jean 1986 'Death Camp Confessions and Resistance to Violence in Latin America', in *Socialism and Democracy*, 2.

Hertz, Robert 1960 'A Contribution to the Study of the Collective Representation of Death', in *Death and the Right Hand*, Aberdeen: Cohen and West [first published in 1907].

Mitchell, Stanley 1973 'Introduction,' in *Walter Benjamin: Understanding Brecht*. London: New Left Books.

Neruda, Pablo 1966 *The Heights of Macchu Picchu*, translated by Nathaniel Tarn. New York: Farrar, Strauss, & Giroux.

—— 1976 *Memoirs*. New York: Farrar, Strauss, & Giroux.

O'Gorman, Edmundo 1961 *The Invention of America*. Bloomington: Indiana University Press.

Vidal, Hernán 1982 *Dar la vida por la vida: La Agrupacíon Chilena de Familiares de Detenidos y Desaparecidos (Ensayo de Antropología Simbólica)*. Minneapolis: Institute for the Study of Ideologies and Literature.

4. THE AUSTRALIAN HERO

In addition to Sid, this essay owes much to the inspiration and advice of Professor Bernard Cohn of the Departments of Anthropology & History of the University of Chicago. Neither he nor Sid can be blamed for my oversights and interpretations. Without the research by Joanna Penglaze in Sydney into the history of the Holden, this essay could not have been written.

1. Walter Benjamin, "The Storyteller," in *Illuminations*, ed. Hannah Arendt (New York: Schocken, 1969), pp. 83–110. Also see his "What is Epic Theater?" Ibid., pp. 147–55.

2. Susan Buck-Morss, "Benjamin's *Passagen-Werk*: Redeeming Mass Culture for the Revolution," *New German Critique* 29, (Spring/Summer, 1983), 225.

3. Ibid., 218. Also see Benjamin's "Konvolut N," translated as "Theoretics of Knowledge: Theory of Progress," in *The Philosophical Forum*, (Fall/Winter, 1983–84), 6–7.

4. Laurence Hartnett, *Big Wheels and Little Wheels* (Australia: Gold Star Publications, 1983), p. 66.

5. Ibid.

6. Ibid., pp. 183–93. Also see Shane Birney, *A Nation on Wheels: Australia and the Motor Car* (Sydney: Dreamweaver Books, 1984), pp. 101–02.

7. Norm Darwin, *The History of Holden Since 1917* (Newstead, Victoria, Australia: E. L. Ford Publications, 1983), p. 135.

8. Hartnett, op. cit., 178.

9. Russell Braddock Ward, *The Australian Legend* (Melbourne: Oxford Univesity Press, 1978, New Illustrated Edition), pp. 16–17.

10. Walter Benjamin, "Theses on the Philosophy of History," in *Illuminations*, ed. Hannah Arendt (New York: Schocken, 1969), pp. 253–64.

11. Alan Moorehead, *Gallipoli* (London: Hamish Hamilton, 1956), p. 236.

12. Ward, op. cit., 11.

13. Walter Benjamin, *Charles Baudelaire: A Lyric Poet in the Era of High Capitalism* (London: New Left Books, 1973), pp. 103–104.

14. Ward, op. cit., pp. 202–03.

15. It is striking how relevant—or even more relevant—the imagery of the bush and the bushman is in Australia and in Australian politics today. For example in November, 1986, Sir Joh Bjelke-Petersen, the right-wing populist and since many years Premier of the State of Queensland, is reported as saying on the occasion of yet another successful (and largely gerrymandered) election that "If you come from the bush you understand the people from the bush, and you should know why we won. . . . We people from the bush, we have had to work hard, battle hard, learn to develop our own initiative by sheer circumstances. . . . my whole make-up is fight because I have had to struggle. And all of this puts something into you that no Liberal can buy" (*The Australian*, Monday, Nov. 3, 1986, pp. 1–2). Sir Joh announced that he now intends to set the political agenda to destroy the Hawke (Federal) Government. On perhaps a lesser note I was struck on reading in *The Daily Journal* (Caracas, Venezuela, Jan., 8, 1987) how the Executive Director of the sailing vessel, Australia IV, described the crew of Kookaburra III, the other Australian contender for the America's Cup. 'They're like dingoes,' he said, angered by their rash of protests. "They can't cop it when they get beaten."

16. Ward, op. cit., p. 281.

17. Moorehead, op. cit., pp. 131–32.

18. Ibid.

19. Ibid., p. 234.

20. Peter H. Liddle, *Gallipoli 1915: Pens, Pencils, and Cameras at War* (London: Pergamon, 1985), p. 12.

21. Patsy Adam-Smith, *The Anzacs* (London: Hamish Hamilton, 1978), p. 47.

22. Compton Mackenzie, *Gallipoli Memories* (Garden City, N.Y.: Doubleday, 1930), p. 78.

23. *Official History of Australia in the War of 1914–1918.* Volume One: *The Story of Anzac; The First Phase*, by C. E. W. Bean (Sydney: Angus and Robertson, 1935), p. 6.

24. Bill Gammage, *The Broken Years: Australia's Soldiers in the Great War* (Canberra: Australian National University Press, 1974), p. 231.

25. Bean, op. cit., p. 48.

26. Ibid., p. 15.

27. Gammage, op. cit., pp. 1–2.

28. Stanley Diamond, "The Rule of Law vs. the Law of Custom," *Social Research*, Vol. 38, 47–72.

29. Bean, op. cit., p. 6.

30. Ibid.

31. Gammage, op. cit., p. 247.

32. Ibid., p. 245.

33. Ibid., p. 247.

34. *The Kiaora Cooee: The Magazine for the Anzacs in the Middle East, 1918*, 1 (March, 1918), 9.

35. Moorehead, op. cit.

36. Bean, op. cit., p. 3.

6. REIFICATION AND THE CONSCIOUSNESS OF THE PATIENT

I wish to thank Drs Tom O'Brien and Steven Vincent for helping me begin this project, and the members of the 1977 Marxist Anthropology seminar at the University of Michigan, Ann Arbor, for their comments on an early draft of this paper.

1. Georg Lukács, "Reification and the Class Consciousness of the Proletariat," in *History and Class Consciousness* (London: Merlin Press, 1971), pp. 83–222.

2. E. E. Evans-Pritchard, *Witchcraft, Oracles and Magic among the Azande* (Oxford: Clarendon Press, 1937).

3. Jean-Paul Sartre, *Being and Nothingness* (Secaucus N.J.: Citadel Press, 1956), abridged ed., pp. 279–80.

4. P. Radin, *Primitive Man as a Philosopher* (New York: Dover, 1957), p. 274.

5. Susan Sontag, *Illness as Metaphor* (New York: Farrer, Strauss & Giroux, 1978).

6. R. Linder, "Diagnosis: Description or Prescription?" *Perc. Mot. Skills* 20(1965), 1081; cited in M. Blaxter, "Diagnosis as Category and Process: The Case of Alcoholism," *Social Science and Medicine* 12(1978), 12.

7. Michel Foucault, *Madness and Civilization* (New York: Mentor Books, 1967).

8. Ivan Illich, *Medical Nemesis* (London: Caldar & Boyars, 1975).

9. J. Horn, *Away with All Pests* (New York: Monthly Review Press, 1969).

10. L. Goodman and A. Gilman, eds., *The Pharmacological Basis of Therapeutics*, 5th ed. (New York: Macmillan, 1975), pp. 166–67.

11. Steckel, S. Boehm and M. Swain, "Contracting with Patients to Improve Compliance," *Journal of the American Hospital Association* 51(1977), 82.

12. Ibid., p. 81.

13. Steckel S. Boehm, "The Use of Positive Reinforcement in Order to Increase Patient Compliance," *Journal of the American Association of Nephrology Nursing Technique* I(1974), 40.

14. Ibid.

15. A. Kleinman, L. Eisenberg, and B. Good, "Culture, Illness and Care: Clinical Lessons from Anthropologic and Cross-cultural Research," *Annals of Internal Medicine* 88(1978).

16. Kleinman et al., *ibid.*, 256.

17. Ibid., 257.

18. Ibid.

19. V. Turner, "A Ndembu Doctor in Practice." *The Forest of Symbols* (Ithaca: Cornell Univ. Press, 1967), p. 392.

20. Claude Lévi-Strauss, "The Sorcerer and His Magic." *Structural Anthropology* (New York: Anchor Books, 1967), pp. 161–80.

7. MALEFICIUM: STATE FETISHISM

1. My own introduction to the cultural study of the modern State and to see this as a problem worth thinking about comes from *The Great Arch: English State Formation As Cultural Revolution* by Philip Corrigan and Derek Sayer (Oxford: Basil Blackwell, 1985), by way of the insights and encouragement of Professor Bernard Cohn of the University of Chicago.

2. Edmund Burke, *A Philosophical Enquiry Into The Origin of Our Ideas of the Sublime and Beautiful,*

edited and with introduction by Adam Phillips (Oxford, New York: Oxford University Press, 1990), p. 59.

3. Thomas Hobbes, *Leviathan: Or The Matter, Forme and Power of a Commonwealth Ecclesiasticall and Civil* (New York: Collier MacMillan, 1962), p. 132.

4. Shlomo Avineri, *Hegel's Theory of the Modern State* (Cambridge, Cambridge University Press, 1972), p. ix. A.R. Radcliffe-Brown, preface, in *African Political Systems*, ed. M. Fortes and E. E. Evans-Pritchard (Oxford: Oxford University Press, 1970), pp. xi–xxiii.

5. Radcliffe-Brown, p. xxiii, emphasis added.

6. Philp Abrams, "Notes on The Difficulty of Studying the State," *Journal of Historical Sociology*, 1:1 (1988), 58.

7. Ibid., p. 77.

8. Ibid.

9. Ibid.

10. Quoted in *The New York Times*, May 3, 1990 (p. B 1), in the coverage of the violent dispute over gambling on the Mohawk reservation upstate New York.

11. Max Weber, "Politics As a Vocation," in *From Max Weber: Essays in Sociology*, trans. and edited by Hans Gerth and C. Wright Mills (London: Routledge and Kegan Paul, 1948), p. 79.

12. I am indebted to Adam Ashforth for bringing this observation of Benjamin's to my attention.

13. Quoted in Robert Ackerman, *J. G. Frazer: His Life and Work* (Cambridge: Cambridge University Press, 1987), p. 63.

14. In his foreword to an exhaustive collection of essays and talks prepared by the College of Sociology group around Bataille, Caillois, and to some extent, Leiris (to name the best-known), Denis Hollier indicates the College's vexed dependence on Durkheim and his school, especially in relation to the place of the "primitive" and "the sacred" in modern West European society; see Denis Hollier, ed., *The College of Sociology, 1937–39* (Minneapolis: University of Minnesota Press, 1988). While many of the key concepts of Durkheim, almost by default, would be theirs too, there were also profound differences, beginning with the question that formed the basis to their project—namely, the place of the sacred in modernity. Another outstanding difference is the College's notion of the sacred as not only a force for Durkheimian social solidarity, but also the opposite, the sacred as an excess, as "the outburst," as Caillois put it in 1938, "of violations of the rules of life," which is, of course, thoroughly consistent with Bataille's fascination with taboo and transgression—a "post-Durkheimian" rewriting of the Liberal problematic of reason and violence; Roger Caillois, in *The College of Sociology, 1937–39*, p. 152.

15. William Pietz, "The Problem of the Fetish: I," *RES*, 9 (Spring 1985), 5–17, and unpublished 227-page manuscript on the history of the fetish.

16. Raymond Williams, *Keywords: A Vocabulary of Culture and Society* (New York: Oxford University Press, 1976).

17. Quoted in a footnote in Steven Lukes, *Emile Durkheim: His Life and Work* (Harmondsworth: Penguin Books, 1973), p. 35.

18. Ibid., pp. 34–35.

19. George Catlin, "Introduction To The Translation," in Emile Durkheim, *The Rules of Sociological Method* (New York: The Free Press, 1964), p. xiv.

20. Lukes, op. cit. pp. 11–12.

21. Talcott Parsons, *The Structure of Social Action: A Study in Social Theory With Special Reference to a Group of Recent European Writers* (New York: The Free Press, 1937).

22. As far as I can determine, Durkheim uses the term "fetish" but once in *The Elementary Forms of Religious Life* (New York: The Free Press, 1965), p. 144, and does so in order to

dissociate the totem from it. But this dissociation is implausible and probably reflects his need to distance himself from the theory of animism and fetishism put forward by the British anthropologist E. B. Tylor. Durkheim's sociological analysis of "totemism" (guided by extant ethnography), in particular his tying sacred designs to a specific and bounded social grouping (hence "society"), is now considered wrong in important ways, ways that reflect profoundly on the present-day politics of land-claims by Aboriginal people against the Australian State. For important revisions of the sociology of the Australian "totemism" see W. E. H. Stanner, "Religion, Totemism and Symbolism," in *White Man Got No Dreaming* (Canberra: Australian National University Press, 1979), pp. 106–43, and also his "Reflections on Durkheim and Aboriginal Religion," in Maurice Freedman, *Social Organization: Essays Presented to Raymond Firth* (Chicago: Aldine, 1967), pp. 217–40. For a debunking of the social philosophical basis of the anthropology of totemism, see Claude Lévi-Strauss, *Totemism* (Boston: Beacon Press, 1963).

23. Parsons, op. cit., p. 469, footnotes that Durkheim failed to admit that there was any such transformation.

24. Ibid.

25. Lukes, op. cit., p. 21.

26. Walter Benjamin, "Surrealism: The Last Snapshot of the European Intelligentsia," in *Reflections* (New York: Harcourt Brace Jovanovich, 1978), pp. 177–92, Of course I have taken great liberties here with Benjamin's suggestion.

27. Durkheim, *The Elementary Forms*, pp. 142–43.

28. Roger Keesing, "Rethinking Mana," *Journal of Anthropological Research*, 40 (1984), 137–56. Also R. Needham, "Skulls and Causality," *Man* (n.s.), 11(1977): 71–78. This image of magical force as miasma is also crucial to Freud's analysis of imitation and contagion in *Totem and Taboo*.

29. Durkheim, *The Elementary Forms*, p. 144, emphasis added. It is obvious from Spencer and Gillen that the designs and the churingas are far from being all that goes into invoking sacred power. These elements are inserted into performative routines in which singing the dreamtime and dance are essential. Durkheim himself cites many passages indicating this too. Nevertheless it is to the designs on the objects that he attributes central importance.

30. Durkheim, *The Elementary Forms*, p. 145.

31. He employs this argument vigorously with regard to what he identifies as sacred force in the principles *mana*, in Oceania, and *wakan*, in North America, and so forth.

32. Baldwin Spencer and F. J. Gillen, *The Native Tribes of Central Australia* (New York: Dover, 1968), pp. 145–47; first published in 1899.

33. Claude Lévi-Strauss, "A Writing Lesson," in *Tristes Tropiques: An Anthropological Study of Primitive Societies in Brazil*, trans. John Russell, p. 286–97 (New York: Atheneum, 1968).

34. Durkheim, *The Elementary Forms*, p. 266.

35. Ibid., p. 149, emphasis added.

36. Ibid.

37. Ibid., p. 269, emphasis added.

38. Parsons, op. cit., p. 268.

39. See also the 1903 work *Primitive Classification*, by Durkheim and Marcel Mauss.

40. Durkheim, *The Elementary Forms*, p. 31 emphasis added.

41. Ibid., p. 32.

42. Ibid., p. 148. See Spencer and Gillen's version of this, *The Native Tribes of Central Australia*, p. 181.

43. Durkheim, *The Elementary Forms*, p. 156.

44. Ibid., p. 217.

45. Many are the ironies created by such a comparison. Chief of them is that for Marx, the primitive world is one in which the social character of the (economic) object is transparent

to all involved—quite opposite to the situation he describes for people in the capitalist economy of nineteenth-century western Europe. But in Durkheim's argument this is not the case; in primitive society the social character of the (sacred) object is erased, hence fetishized!

46. Ibid., pp. 144, 288.

47. Spencer and Gillen, op. cit., p. 129.

48. Abrams, op. cit., p. 77.

49. E. Lucas Bridges, *Uttermost Part of the Earth* (London: Hodder & Stoughton, 1951), pp. 424–25.

50. Emile Durkheim, *Professional Ethics and Civic Morals* (London: Routledge and Kegan Paul, 1957), p. 72, first published, in French in 1904.

51. Friederich Nietzsche, *Beyond Good and Evil*, trans. W. Kauffman (New York: Vintage, 1966), p. 10.

52. Emile Durkheim, *The Rules of Sociological Method* (New York: Free Press, 1938), p. 70. Thus, since there cannot be a society in which the individuals do not differ more or less from the collective type, it is also inevitable that, among these divergences there are some with a criminal character. What confers this character upon them is not the intrinsic quality of a given act but that definition which the collective conscience lends them. If the collective conscience is stronger, if it has enough authority practically to suppress these divergences, it will also be more sensitive, more exacting; and, reacting against the slightest deviations with the energy it otherwise displays only against more considerable infractions, it will attribute to them the same gravity as formerly to crimes. In other words, it will designate them as criminal.

Crime is, then, necessary; it is bound up with the fundamental conditions of all social life, and by that very fact it is useful, because these conditions of which it is a part are themselves indispensable to the normal evolution of morality and law.

53. Jean Genêt, *The Thief's Journal* (Harmondsworth: Penguin Books, 1967), p. 141.

54. Genêt, p. 157.

55. Ibid.

56. Ibid, p. 159.

57. Ibid.

58. Ibid., p. 94.

59. Ibid., p. 95.

60. Ibid., pp. 101–102.

61. Ibid., p. 75.

62. Benedict Anderson, *Imagined Communities* (London: Verso, 1983), p. 16.

63. Genet, op. cit., p. 39.

8. TACTILITY & DISTRACTION

This essay was written for the conference "Problematics of Daily Life," organized by Marc Blanchard, Director, Critical Theory, University of California, Davis, November, 1990.

1. F. Nietzsche, *On The Genealogy of Morals*, Walter Kauffman ed. (New York: Vintage, 1989), p. 119.

2. Walter Benjamin, "Paris of the Second Empire in Baudelaire," in *Charles Baudelaire: Lyric Poet of High Capitalism* (New Left Books: London, 1973), p. 69.

3. Benjamin, "The Work of Art in the Age of Mechanical Reproduction," in *Illuminations*

(Schocken Books: New York, 1969), p. 238. In emphasizing the tactile in the reorganization of the human sensorium in the early twentieth century, Benjamin was echoing not only Dada but even earlier statements, such as that of the Russian, Tatlin, in 1913: ". . . the eye should be put under control of touch." Benjamin Buchloh, from whose article on "From Faktura to Factography," in *October: The First Decade; 1976–1986*, ed. Annette Michelson (Cambridge: MIT Press, 1987), p. 81, I take this quotation, adds to it Marcel Duchamp's "famous statement" that he wanted to "abolish the supremacy of the retinal principle in art."

4. Benjamin, "A Short History of Photography," in *One Way Street*, (London: New Left Books, 1979), p. 44.

5. T. W. Adorno, "A Portrait of Walter Benjamin," p. 240, in *Prisms* (Cambridge: MIT Press, 1981). I have used Susan Buck-Morss' translation of this passage from her *Origin of Negative Dialectics* (New York: The Free Press, 1977), p. 83.

6. J. G. Frazer, *The Golden Bough, Part 1: "The Magic Art and the Evolution of Kings*, vol. 1, 3rd edition, (London: Macmillan, 1911), 57.

7. Take the opening paragraph of Benjamin's 1934 essay, "On the Mimetic Faculty," in *Reflections* (New York: Harcourt, Brace, Jovanovitch, 1978), p. 333, which reads:

> Nature creates similarities. One need only think of mimicry. The highest capacity for producing similarities, however, is man's. His gift of seeing resemblances is nothing other than a rudiment of the powerful compulsion in former times to become and behave like something else. Perhaps there is none of his higher functions in which his mimetic faculty does not play a decisive role.

Adorno had much to say about the relation between alleged origins of mankind, mimesis, and magic, in his posthumously edited *Aesthetic Theory* (London and New York: Routledge and Kegan Paul, 1984; first published in German in 1970). A good place to begin is with Appendix II, "Thoughts on the Origins of Art—An Excursus," pp. 447–55.

8. Gertrude Koch, "Mimesis and the Ban on Graven Images," paper distributed in Dept. of Cinema Studies, New York University, 1990, forthcoming in *October*. See also Sergei Eisenstein's 1935 lecture, "Film Form; New Problems," in his *Film Form*, trans. Jay Leyda (New York: Harcourt, Brace, Jovanovich, 1977), pp. 133–45.

9. Benjamin, "One Way Street," in *Reflections*, 86.

10. Benjamin, "On the Mimetic Faculty," op. cit., 333.

9. HOMESICKNESS & DADA

This is a modified version of my essay, "The Nervous System: Dada and Homesickness," which appeared in the *Stanford Humanities Review* 1:1 (Spring 1989), 44–81.

1. Victor Turner, *From Ritual to Drama: The Human Seriousness of Play* (New York, Performing Arts Journal Publications, 1982), p. 72.

2. Roland Barthes, "Brecht and Discourse: A Contribution to the Study of Discursivity," *The Rustle of Language*, trans. Richard Howard (Oxford: Basil Blackwell, 1986), 212–22.

3. Walter Benjamin, "On the Mimetic Faculty," in *Reflections*, trans. Edmund Jephcott, ed. Peter Demetz (New York & London: Harcourt Brace Jovanovitch, 1978), p. 336.

4. W. Benjamin, *The Origin of German Tragic Drama*, trans. John Osborne (London: New Left Books, 1977), p. 161.

5. Ibid., p. 163.

6. Ibid., p. 165.

7. Theodore W. Adorno, *Gessammelte Schriften, 1, Philosophische Fruhscritten*, ed. Rolf Tiedemann (Frankfurt am Main: Suhrkamp Verlag, 1973), p. 367.

8. This discussion needs to be supplemented by a history of Saussure's forbears. See J. G. Merquior, *From Prague to Paris* (London: Verso, 1986), pp. 10–12, and Hans Aarslef, *From Locke to Saussure: Essays on the Study of Language and Intellectual History* (Minneapolis: University of Minnesota Press, 1982).

9. Hugo Ball, *Flight Out of Time*, ed. and introduction by John Elderfield, trans. Ann Raimes, with foreword to 1946 edition to Emmy Ball Hennings (New York: Viking Press, 1974), p. 66.

10. The pertinence of this connection was pointed out to me in a lecture at Columbia University in 1984 by Professor Sylvère Lotringer of the Dept of French of that university.

11. Elderfield, in Ball, op. cit., p. xxiii

12. Ball, op. cit., p. 63

13. Elderfield, in Ball, op. cit., p. xxiii.

14. Ibid., pp. xliii–xliv

15. Robert Motherwell, *The Dada Painters and Poets* (Boston: G.K. Hall, 1981), p. xxvi.

16. Ball, op. cit., p. 56.

17. Ibid., p. 65.

18. Ibid., p. 55.

19. Ibid., p. 67.

20. Ibid., p. 71.

21. Ibid.

22. Motherwell, op. cit., pp. xxv–xxvi.

23. Elderfield, in Ball, op. cit., p. xxv.

24. Mircea Eliade, *Shamanism: Archaic Techniques of Ecstasy*, trans. W. R. Trask, Bollingen Series LXXVI (Princeton: Princeton University Press, 1964), p. xv.

25. T. W. Adorno, "Der Wunderliche Realist: Uber Siegfried Kracauer," cited in Susan Buck-Morss, *The Origin of Negative Dialectics: Theodore W Adorno, Walter Benjamin, and the Frankfurt Institute* (New York: Free Press, 1977), p. 80.

26. Benjamin, *Understanding Brecht*, trans. Anna Bostock (London: Verso, 1983), pp. 17–18.

27. Roger Dunsmore, "Nickolaus Black Elk; Holy Man in History," *Kuksu: Journal of Back Country Writing* 6 (1979), 9.

28. Ibid., p. 8.

29. Black Elk through John Nierhardt in *Black Elk Speaks* (Lincoln, Nebraska: University of Nebraska Press, 1979), p. 270.

30. Alejo Carpentier, *The Lost Steps*, trans. Harriet du Onis (New York: Knopf, 1974), p. 179.

31. Ibid., p. 180.

32. Ibid., p. 183.

33. Ibid., p. 184.

34. Ibid., p. 187.

35. I am unhappy using this word "soul" as a translation for the Cuna *purba*. So was Erland Nordenskiold, who wrote that *"Purba* is the only word which the Cuna Indians who know some foreign language, translate as soul . . . but I still prefer not to translate it at all. It means so much." Erland Nordenskiold, *An Historical and Ethnographic Survey of the Cuna Indians, in Collaboration with the Cuna Indian Rubén Pérez Kantule*, ed. Henry Wassén, *Comparative Ethnographical Studies*, No. 10 (Goteburg, 1983), p. 334.

36. The wooden figurines are said by Nordenskiold to be carved in the form of Europeans, and as "Non-Indians," by Norman Macphesron Chapin, "Curing Among the San Blas Kuna of Panama (unpublished Ph.D. dissertation, University of Arizona, 1983), pp. 94–95. Yet the spirit-power is said by native informants to derive from the wood itself, and not the outer

form. Why, then, bother carving the outer form and carving it with a deliberately Other referent?

37. Nils Holmer and Henry Wassén, "The Complete Mu-Igala in Picture Writing," *Etnologisker Studier* No. 21, (Goteburg: Etnografiska Museum, 1953), and "Mu-Igala, or the Way of Muu, a Medicine Song from the Cunas of Panama," Etnografiska Museum, 1947. Unless otherwise specified I will be referring to the 1953 publication, which is the same as the 1947 one except for the addition of the picture-language text.

38. Nordenskiold, op. cit., pp. 442, 372–73.

39. Claude Lévi-Strauss, "The Effectiveness of Symbols," in his *Structural Anthropology* (New York: Doubleday, 1967), p. 186.

40. Ibid., p. 183.

41. Ibid., p. 189.

42. Drawing by Guillermo Hayans in Holmer and Wassén, op. cit., p. 86.

43. Lévi-Strauss, p. 185.

44. Ibid., p. 192.

45. Ibid., pp. 192–93.

46. Ibid., p. 193.

47. Ibid., p. 195.

48. Ibid., p. 197.

49. Holmer and Wassén, op. cit., p. 107.

50. Ibid., p. 108.

51. Chapin, op. cit., p. 425.

52. Nordenskiold, op. cit., p. 355.

53. Chapin, op. cit., p. 75, (Cuna words deleted).

54. Ibid., pp. 75–76. I have maintained Nordenskiold's orthography for the sake of consistency.

55. Joel Sherzer, *Kuna Ways of Speaking: An Ethnographic Perspective* (Austin: University of Texas Press, 1983), p. 215.

56. Chapin, op. cit., pp. 88–89.

57. Ibid., p. 93.

58. Nordenskiold, op. cit., p. 427.

59. "Mitología Cuna: los Kalu según Alfonso Díaz Granados," arranged and with commentary by Leonor Herrera and Marianne Cardale de Schrimpff, in *La revista colombiana de antropología* 17 (1974), 201–47.

60. Chapin, op. cit., p. 431.

61. As Chapin puts it, ibid., p. 433.

62. Ibid., emphasis added.

63. Holmer and Wassén, op. cit., p. 14.

64. Lévi-Strauss, "The Effectiveness of Symbols," p. 193.

65. Sigmund Freud, "The Uncanny," first published 1919, *Standard Edition of the Complete Psychological Works*, trans. James Stratchey (London: The Hogarth Press, 1955), vol. XVII, p. 245.

66. Nordenskiold, op. cit., p. 438.

67. Holmer and Wassén, "The Complete Mu-Igala,"

68. Gerardo Reichel-Dolmatoff, *Los Kogi: Una tribu de la Sierra Nevada de Santa Marta de Colombia* (Bogotá: Procultura, 1985), vol. II, p. 255.

69. Reichel-Dolmatoff, op. cit., vol. I, p. 15.

70. Drawing by Guillermo Hayans in Nils Holmer and Henry Wassén, "Nia-Ikala: Canto mágico para curar la locura," *Etnologisker Studier*, No. 27 (Goteburg: Etnografiska Museum, 1958), p. 35.

71. Ibid., p. 16, and dust-jacket.

72. The presentations of Ball's Magical Bishop act are many and varied. In addition to what I have described from Ball and Motherwell, there is Mel Gordon describing Ball as going into a state of possession and flapping his wings at that inspired instant when he began reciting in the style of the Catholic liturgy. Gordon typically renders this as the climactic end to Ball's dada and radical political interests as well. Mel Gordon, *Dada Performance* (New York: PAJ Publications, 1987), p. 15. On discrepancies in the representations of the Magical Bishop act, and its meaning and aftermath, see P.H. Mann, "Hugo Ball and the 'Magic Bishop' Episode: A Reconsideration," *New German Studies* 4:1 (1976), 43–52.

BIBLIOGRAPHY

Aarslef, Hans. *From Locke to Saussure: Essays on the Study of Language and Intellectual History.* Minneapolis: University of Minnesota Press, 1982.

Abrams, Phillip. "Notes on the Difficulty of Studying the State." In *The Journal of Historical Sociology*, 1:1 (1988), 58–89.

Ackerman, Robert. *J. G. Frazer: His Life and Work.* Cambridge: Cambridge University Press, 1987.

Adam-Smith, Patsy. *The Anzacs.* London: Hamish Hamilton, 1978.

Adorno, Theodor W. *Aesthetic Theory.* Unfinished work, edited by Gretel Adorno and Rolf Tiedemann. [First published in German in 1970.] Translated by C. Lenhardt, London and New York: Routledge, and Kegan Paul, 1984.

Adorno, Theodor W. "A Portrait of Walter Benjamin," In *Prisms.* Cambridge; MIT Press, 1981, 227–242.

Adorno, Theodor W. *Gesammelte Schriften 1, Philosophische Fruhschritten.* Edited by Rolf Tiedemann. Frankfurt-am-Main: Suhrkamp Verlag, Vol. I, 1973.

Anderson, Benedict. *Imagined Communities.* London: Verso, 1983.

Avineri, Shlomo. *Hegel's Theory of the Modern State.* Cambridge: Cambridge University Press, 1972.

Ball, Hugo. *Flight Out of Time.* Edited with an Introduction by John Elderfield, with foreword to the 1946 edition by Emmy Ball Hemmings. Translated by Ann Raimes. New York: Viking Press, 1974.

Barthes, Roland. "Brecht and Discourse: A Contribution to the Study of Discursivity." In *The Rustle of Language.* Translated by Richard Howard, pp. 212–22. Oxford: Basil Blackwell, 1986.

Bean, C. E. W. *Official History of Australia in the War of 1914–1918.* Volume 1: *The Story of the Anzacs; The First Phase.* Sydney: Angus and Robertson, 1935.

Benjamin, Walter. "The Storyteller." In *Illuminations.* Edited by Hannah Arendt. Translated by Harry Zohn, pp. 83–109. New York: Schocken, 1969.

Benjamin, Walter. "Theses on the Philosophy of History." In *Illuminations.* Edited by Hannah Arendt. Translated by Harry Zohn, pp. 253–64. New York: Schocken, 1969.

Benjamin, Walter. "The Work of Art in the Age of Mechanical Reproduction." In *Illuminations.* Edited by Hannah Arendt. Translated by Harry Zohn, pp. 217–251. New York: Schocken, 1969.

Benjamin, Walter. *Charles Baudelaire: A Lyric Poet in the Era of High Capitalism.* London: New Left Books, 1973.

Benjamin, Walter. *The Origin of German Tragic Drama.* Translated by John Osborne. London: New Left Books, 1977.

Benjamin, Walter. "On the Mimetic Faculty." In *Reflections.* Edited by Peter Demetz. Translated by Edmund Jephcott, pp. 333–36. New York and London: Harcourt Brace Jovanovich, 1978.

Benjamin, Walter. "Surrealism: The Last Snapshot of the European Intelligentsia." In *Reflections,* pp. 177–92. New York: Harcourt Brace Jovanovich, 1978.

Benjamin, Walter. "One-Way Street." In *One Way Street and Other Writings.* Translated by Edward Jephcott and K. Shorter, pp. 45–106. London: New Left Books, 1979.

Benjamin, Walter. "A Short History of Photography." In *One Way Street and Other Writings.* Translated by Edmund Jephcott and K. Shorter. London: New Left Books, 1979.

Benjamin, Walter. "N [Theoretics of Knowledge: Theory of Progress]." In *The Philosophical Forum,* 15:1–2 (Fall/Winter, 1983–84). Translated from "Konvolut N" of *Das Passagen-Werk.* Vol. 2, pp. 570–611. Frankfurt-am-Main: Suhrkamp Verlag, 1982.

Benjamin, Walter. *Understanding Brecht.* Introduction by Stanley Mitchell. Translated by Anna Bostock. London: Verso, 1983.

Bingham, Hiram. *Lost City of the Incas: The Story of Machu Picchu and its Builders.* New York: Duell, Sloan and Pearce, 1948.

Birney, Shane. *A Nation on Wheels: Australia and the Motor Car.* Sydney: Dreamweaver Books, 1984.

Boehm, Steckel S. "The use of positive reinforcement in order to increase patient compliance." *Journal of the American Association of Nephrology Nursing Technique,* 1:40, 1974.

Boehm, Steckel S. and Swain M. "Contracting with patients to improve complaince." *Journal of the American Hospital Association* 51:82, 1977.

Brecht, Bertolt. *Brecht On Theatre.* Edited by John Willett. London: Methuen, 1964.

Brecht, Bertolt. *The Exception and the Rule.* In *The Jewish Wife and Other Short Plays.* Translated by Eric Bentley. New York: Grove Press, 1965.

Brecht, Bertolt. "The Anxieties of the Regime." In *Bertolt Brecht Poems, 1913–1956.* Edited by Ralph Mannheim and John Willet, pp. 296–97. London: Methuen, 1976.

Bridges, E. Lucas. *Uttermost Part of the Earth.* London: Hodder and Stoughton, 1951.

Buchloh, Benjamin, H. D. "From Faktura to Factography." In *October: The First Decade, 1976–86.* Edited by Annette Michelson, pp. 76–113. Cambridge: MIT Press, 1987.

Buck-Morss, Susan. "Benjamin's *Passagen-Werk*: Redeeming Mass Culture for the Revolution." *New German Critique* 29 (Spring/Summer, 1983), 211–241.

Buck-Morss, Susan. *The Origin of Negative Dialectics: Theodore W. Adorno, Walter Benjamin, and the Frankfurt Institute.* New York: Free Press, 1977.

Burke, Edmund. *A Philosophical Inquiry into the Origin of our Ideas of the Sublime and the Beautiful.* Edited by Adam Phillips. Oxford: Oxford University Press, 1990.

Carpentier, Alejo. *The Lost Steps.* Translated by Harriet de Onis. New York: Knopf, 1974.

Catlin, George. "Introduction to the Translation." In *The Rules of Sociological Method,* by Emile Durkheim. New York: The Free Press, 1937.

Certeau, Michel de. *The Practice of Everyday Life.* Translated by Steven Rendell. Berkeley: University of California Press, 1984.

Chapin, Norman Macpherson. "Curing Among the San Blas Cuna of Panama." Unpublished Ph.D. dissertation. University of Arizona, 1983.

Corrigan, Philip and Derek Sayer. *The Great Arch: English State Formation As Cultural Revolution.* Oxford: Basil Blackwell, 1985.

Darwin, Norm. *The History of Holden Since 1917.* Newstead, Victoria, Australia: E. L. Ford Publications, 1983.

Diamond, Stanley. "The Rule of Law Versus the Law of Custom." In *Social Research*, 38, 47–72.

Dunsmore, Roger. "Nickolaus Black Elk: Holy Man in History." *Kuksu: Journal of Back Country Writing*, 6 (1974), 4–29.

Durkheim, Emile. *Professional Ethics and Civic Morals.* London: Routledge and Kegan Paul, 1957.

Durkheim, Emile. *The Elementary Forms of Religious Life.* [First published in Paris: Alcan Publishers, 1912; in English, London: George Allen & Unwin, 1915.] New York: The Free Press, 1965.

Durkheim, Emile. *The Rules of Sociological Method.* Glencoe: Free Press, 1938.

Durkheim, Emile and Marcel Mauss. *Primitive Classification.* Chicago: University of Chicago Press, 1963.

Elderfield, John. "Introduction." In *Flight Out of Time*, by Hugo Ball, pp. xiii–xlvi. New York: Viking Press, 1974.

Eliade, Mircea. *Shamanism: Archaic Techniques of Ecstasy.* Translated by W. R. Trask. Bollingen Series LXXVI. Princeton: Princeton University Press, 1964.

Evans-Pritchard, E. E. *Witchcraft, Oracles and Magic Among the Azande.* Oxford: Clarendon Press, 1937.

Foucault, Michel. *Madness and Civilization.* New York: Mentor Books, 1967.

Franco, Jean. "Death Camp Confessions and Resistance to Violence in Latin America." In *Socialism and Democracy.* 2, 1986.

Frazer, J. G. *The Golden Bough, Part 1: The Magic and the Evolution of Kings*, vol. 1, 3rd. ed. London: Macmillan, 1911.

Freedman, Maurice. *Social Organization: Essays Presented to Raymond Firth.* Chicago: Aldine, 1967.

Freud, Sigmund. "The Uncanny." First published 1919. *Standard Edition of Complete Psychological Works.* Translated by James Strachey. Volume 17, pp. 217–52. London: The Hogarth Press, 1955.

Gammage, Bill. *The Broken Years: Australia's Soldiers in the Great War.* Canberra: Australian National University Press, 1984.

Genêt, Jean. *The Thief's Journal.* Translated by Bernard Frechtman. Harmondsworth: Penguin Books, 1967.

Goodman, L. and A. Gilman (eds.) *The Pharmacological Basis of Therapeutics*, 5th edition, pp. 166–67. New York: Macmillan, 1975.

Gordon, Mel. *Dada Performance.* New York: Performing Arts Journal Publications, 1987.

Hartnett, Lawrence. *Big Wheels and Little Wheels.* Australia: Gold Star Publications, 1983.

Herrera, Leonor, and Marianne Cardale de Schrimpff, "Mitología Cuna: los Kalu según Alfonso Díaz Granados." In *La revista colombiana de antropología*, 17 (1974), 201–47.

Hertz, Robert. "A Contribution to the Study of the Collective Representation of Death." In *Death and the Right Hand*, first published 1907. Aberdeen: Cohen and West, 1960.

Hobbes, Thomas. *Leviathan: Or The Matter, Forme and Power of a Commenwealth Ecclesiasticall and Civil.* New York: Collier MacMillan, 1962.

Hollier, Denis, ed. *The College of Sociology, 1937–39.* Minneapolis: University of Minnesota Press, 1988.

Holmer, Nils and Henry Wassén. "Mu-Igala, Or The Way of Muu: A Medicine Song from the Cuna of Panama." *Etnologiska Studier.* Gotesburg: Etnografiska Museum, 1947.

Holmer, Nils and Henry Wassén. "The Complete Mu-Igala in Picture Writing: A Native Record of a Cuna Medicine Song." *Etnologiska Studier 21.* Gotesburg: Etnografiska Museum, 1953.

Holmer, Nils and Henry Wassén. "Nia-Ikala: Canto mágico para curar la locura." *Etnologiska Studier* 23. Gotesburg: Etnografiska Museum, 1958.

Horkheimer, Max and Adorno, Theodor W., *Dialectic of Enlightenment*. Translated by John Cumming. New York: Continuum, 1987.

Horn, J. *Away With All Pests*. New York: Monthly Review Press, 1969.

Illich, I. *Medical Nemesis*. London: Caldar & Boyars, 1975.

Keesing, Roger. "Rethinking Mana." *Journal of Anthropological Research* 40 (1984), 137–56.

Keesing, Roger. "Conventional Metaphors and Anthropological Metaphysica: The Problematic of Cultural Translation." *Journal of Anthropological Research* 41 (1985), 201–217.

Kleinman, A., Eisenberg, L. and Good B. "Culture, Illness and Care: Clinical Lessons from Anthropologic and Cross-Cultural Research." *Annals of Internal Medicine* 88 (1978), 251–258.

Koch, Gertrude. "Mimesis and the Ban on Graven Images," paper distributed in the Department of Cinema Studies, New York University, 1990, and forthcoming in *October*.

Lévi-Strauss, Claude. *Totemism*. Boston: Beacon Press, 1963.

Lévi-Strauss, Claude. "The Effectiveness of Symbols." In *Structural Anthropology*, pp. 181–201. New York: Doubleday, 1967.

Lévi-Strauss, Claude. "The Sorcerer and His Magic." In *Structural Anthropology*, pp. 161–80. New York: Doubleday, 1967.

Lévi-Strauss, Claude. "A Writing Lesson." In *Tristes Tropiques: An Anthropological Study of Primitive Societies in Brazil*. Trans. John Russell. New York: Atheneum, 1968.

Liddle, Peter H. *Gallipoli, 1915: Pens, Pencils and Cameras at War*. London: Pergamon, 1985.

Linder, R. "Diagnosis: description or prescription?" *Perceptual and Motor Skills* 20 (1965), 1081. Cited in Blaxter, M. "Diagnosis as Category and Process: the Case of Alcoholism." *Social Science and Medicine* 12(1978), 12.

Lukács, Georg. "Reification and the Class Consciousness of the Proletariat." In *History and Class Consciousness: Studies in Marxist Dialectics*. Translated by Rodney Livingstone, pp. 83–222. London: Merlin Press, 1971.

Lukes, Steven. *Emile Durkheim, His Life and Work: A Critical Study*. Harmondsworth: Penguin, 1973.

Mackenzie, Compton. *Gallipoli Memories*. Garden City, N.Y.: Doubleday, 1930.

Mann, P. H., "Hugo Ball and the Magical Bishop Episode: A Reconsideration." *New German Studies* 4:1(1976), 43–52.

Marx, Karl. *Capital*. Volume 1. Translation of the 3rd German edition by S. Moore and E. Aveling. New York: International Publishers, 1967.

Merquior, J. G. *From Prague to Paris*. London: Verso, 1986.

Mitchell, Stanley. Introduction to *Understanding Brecht*, by Walter Benjamin. London: New Left Books, 1973, vii–xix.

Moorehead, Alan. *Gallipoli*. London: Hamish Hamilton, 1956.

Motherwell, Robert. *The Dada Painters and Poets*. Boston: G. K. Hall, 1981.

Needham, R. "Skulls and Causality." *Man* (n.s.), 11 (1978): 71–73.

Negt, Oscar and Alexander Kluge. "The Public Sphere and Experience: Selections." In *October*. 46 (1986), 60–82.

Neihardt, John. *Black Elk Speaks*. Lincoln, Nebraska: University of Nebraska Press, 1979.

Nietzsche, Friederich. *Beyond Good and Evil*. Translated by W. Kauffman. New York: Vintage, 1966.

Nietzsche, Friederich. *On the Genealogy of Morals*. Ed. Walter Kauffman. New York: Vintage, 1989.

Neruda, Pablo. *The Heights of Macchu Picchu*. Translated by Nathaniel Tarn. New York: Farrar, Straus & Giroux, 1966.

Neruda, Pablo. *Memoirs*. New York: Farrar, Straus & Giroux, 1976.

Nordenskiold, Erland. *An Historical and Ethnographic Survey of the Cuna Indians, in Collaboration with the Cuna Indian Rubén Peréz Kantule*. Edited by Henry Wassén. *Comparative Ethnographical Studies*, No. 10, Goteburg, 1938.

O'Gorman, Edmundo. *The Invention of America*. Bloomington: Indiana University Press, 1961.

Parsons, Talcott. *The Structure of Social Action: A Study in Social Theory With Spécial Reference to a Group of Recent European Writers*. New York: The Free Press, 1937.

Pietz, William. "The Problem of the Fetish, I." *RES* 9 (Spring, 1985): 5–17.

Pietz, William. Unpublished MS on Fetishism, nd.

Radcliffe-Brown, A. R. "Preface." In *African Political Systems*, edited by M. Fortes and E. E. Evans-Pritchard, pp. xi–xxiii. Oxford: Oxford University Press, 1970.

Radin, Paul. *Primitive Man as a Philosopher*. New York: Dover, 1957.

Reichel-Dolmatoff, Gerardo. *Los Kogi: un tribu de la Sierra Nevada de Santa Marta, Columbia*. 2 Vols. Bogota: Procultura, 1985.

Sartre, Jean-Paul. *Being and Nothingness* (abridged edition), pp. 279–80. Secaucus, New Jersey: Citadel Press, 1956.

Sartre, Jean-Paul. *Saint Genêt: Actor and Martyr*. New York: Pantheon, 1963.

Sherzer, Joel. *Kuna Ways of Speaking: An Ethnographic Perspective*. Austin: University of Texas Press, 1983.

Sontag, Susan. *Illness as Metaphor*. New York: Farrar, Straus, & Giroux, 1978.

Spencer, Baldwin and F. J. Gillen. *The Native Tribes of Central Australia* [first published 1899]. New York: Dover, 1968.

Stanner, W. E. H. "Religion, Totemism and Symbolism." In *White Man Got No Dreaming*, pp. 106–43. Canberra: Australian University Press, 1979.

Stanner, W. E. H. "Reflections on Durkheim and Aboriginal Religion." In Maurice Freedman, *Social Organization: Essays Presented to Raymond Firth*, pp. 217–40. Chicago: Aldine, 1967.

Taussig, Michael. *The Devil and Commodity Fetishism in South America*. Chapel Hill: University of North Carolina Press, 1980.

Taussig, Michael. "The Rise and Fall of Marxist Anthropology." *Social Analysis*. 21 (1987), 101–113.

Taussig, Michael. *Shamanism, Colonialism and the Wild Man: A Study in Terror and Healing*. Chicago: University of Chicago Press, 1987.

The Kiaora Cooee: The Magazine for the Anzacs in the Middle East, 1918. 1:9 (March, 1918).

Turner, Victor. "A Ndembu Doctor in Practice." In *The Forest of Symbols*. Ithaca and London: Cornell University Press, 1967.

Turner, Victor. *From Ritual to Theater: The Human Seriousness of Play*. New York: Performing Arts Journal Publications, 1982.

Vidal, Hernán. *Dar la vida por la vida: La Agrupacíon Chilena de Familiares de Detenidos y Desaparecidos (Ensayo de Antropología Simbólica)*. Minneapolis: Institute for the Study of Ideologies and Literature, 1982.

Ward, Russel Braddock. *The Australian Legend*. Melbourne: Oxford University Press, New Illustrated Edition, 1978.

Weber, Max. "Politics As a Vocation." In *From Max Weber: Essays in Sociology*. Translated and edited by Hans Gerth and C. Wright Mills. London: Routledge and Kegan Paul, 1948.

Williams, Raymond. *Key words: A Vocabulary of Culture and Society*. New York: Oxford University Press, 1973.

INDEX

CPSIA information can be obtained at www.ICGtesting.com
Printed in the USA
LVOW10s1050040314

375889LV00012B/314/P